· DEATH ON THE BEACH ·

Just past Edgecliff, the spaniel stopped at the head of one of the pebbly channels that had been carved out of the cliff by water runoff. He began barking again. Charlotte followed him down the channel, which was overgrown with underbrush. As she rounded the promontory, Charlotte saw what the dog had been barking about.

At the far end of the cove, a body lay on the shingle beach at the foot of the temple. From this distance, it looked like an elegant porcelain Japanese doll. But, she realized with alarm, it wasn't a doll, it was a geisha. . . .

Praise for
MURDER AT TEATIME . . .

"A gripping mystery, with a splendidly authentic background of magical Maine coast."
—Janwillem van de Wetering,
author of *Inspector Saito's Small Satori*

. . . and praise
for Charlotte Graham:

"An off-beat heroine who is . . . the sophisticated, American woman sleuth that the mystery world has been lacking."
—*Murder ad lib*

Charlotte Graham Mysteries by Stefanie Matteson

MURDER
ON THE
CLIFF

STEFANIE MATTESON

DIAMOND BOOKS, NEW YORK

MURDER ON THE CLIFF

A Diamond Book / published by arrangement with
the author

PRINTING HISTORY
Diamond edition / November 1991

ISBN: 1-55773-596-4

Diamond Books are published by The Berkley Publishing
Group, 200 Madison Avenue, New York, New York 10016.
The name "DIAMOND" and its logo are trademarks
belonging to Charter Communications, Inc.

PRINTED IN THE UNITED STATES OF AMERICA

10 9 8 7 6 5 4 3 2 1

Through a black night of cloud and rain
The Black Ships ply their way—
Alien things of evil mien—
Across the waters gray.

—Old Japanese song

AUTHOR'S NOTE

This novel is based on the story of Townsend Harris, the first American consul to Japan, and the geisha Okichi. Although Harris and Okichi are historical figures, their descendants are products of the author's imagination, as are the places and incidents associated with them. Any resemblance to actual events or persons, living or dead, is entirely coincidental.

The author is indebted to Oliver Statler, author of *Shimoda Story,* and to Liza Crihfield, author of *Ko-uta: "Little Songs" of the Geisha World.*

· I ·

CHARLOTTE GRAHAM STOOD on the lawn of the Newport Art
Association waiting for one of the handsome young officers
from the U.S. Naval War College to escort her to her seat.
As an official representative to the Black Ships Festival, she
couldn't just sit down, she had to be escorted. She was glad the
art museum was located on one of Newport's highest points:
a breeze off the ocean relieved the heat, which at ten in the
morning was already intense. The traffic heading down Memorial Boulevard toward the beach was already heavy. Much of
it was motorcycle traffic. Newcomers quickly learned that in
order to get around Newport during the season, you had to
give up the idea of driving a car. She had driven up last night
from New York and was staying with her old friends, Connie
and Spalding Smith. Spalding, a retired foreign service officer
who had been posted for many years in Tokyo, was president
of the Black Ships Festival. Connie and Spalding had invited
her to join the United States delegation, and she had readily
accepted. "The city by the sea" was one of her favorite places.
She loved its smell—the pungent odor of old boxwood and
privet, the cool, salty smell of the sea, the sweet honey scent
of lindens in bloom. She loved the shimmering sea light that
made you feel as if you were in Deauville or Honfleur, and
the soft, sweet air, swept clean by the sea mist and fog. Even
in the off season, there was an easy sense of leisure about the
town, as if it were always a lazy summer afternoon. She also
loved the variety of the architecture: the colonial mansions
of Newport's golden age, the sprawling cottages of the high
Victorian era, and the imposing palaces of the robber barons,

which attracted millions of tourists each summer. Newport
even had an example of Viking architecture, or so it claimed.
The mysterious stone tower in the park across the street was
said to be the remains of an old Norse church built by Viking
explorers.

Against the backdrop of the mystery tower, a large tent
had been set up for the opening ceremonies. The tent faced
a statue of Commodore Matthew Calbraith Perry which was
encircled by red-and-white striped banners of the kind used
by the Japanese on festive occasions. Old Bruin surveyed the
scene majestically from his lofty perch, looking more like a
vainglorious Roman emperor than a distinguished naval hero.
He clutched a cape, toga-like, in one hand, and a dress sword
in the other. He was facing East, of course. Before Perry sailed
into the Bay of Tokyo (then called Edo) in 1853 with his black-
hulled fleet, the forbidden empire had been closed to the world
for two hundred and fifty years. No one allowed in; no one
allowed out, except for a few Dutch traders. The shogunate
had even banned the construction of oceangoing vessels. Only
frail little junks were permitted. But Perry had changed all that.
Although the history books claimed he won over the Japanese
with his negotiating skills, the cannon assembled on the decks
of his "floating volcanoes" probably had a lot more to do with
his success than diplomacy. In any case, Perry was revered
as a hero by the Japanese for reasons Charlotte didn't quite
understand (although he came as an enemy, he did so with
great style; and the Japanese always held style over substance,
Spalding explained), which is how the Black Ships Festival
came to be held every year in his home town. It combined
the celebration of Japanese-American friendship with the celebration of Japanese culture: sumo wrestling, kite flying, the
tea ceremony, flower arranging, paper folding, puppet thea-
ter . . . And this year, for the first time, geishas.

Which was how Charlotte came to be there. That, and
her friend Connie, or rather Constance Harris Montgomery
Brandolini Smith. For Connie had been married almost as
many times as Charlotte.

In the park a Marine Corps color guard was presenting the
Stars and Stripes, and the white flag with the red ball in the

center which represented the Empire of the Rising Sun. A Navy band in dress whites played the "The Battle Hymn of the Republic," and then the Japanese national anthem.

"I hope they come for us soon," said Connie, fanning her face with her program. "This heat is getting to me."

Her makeup had started to cake and damp marks had appeared under the arms of her green silk suit. Looking at Connie now, it was hard to believe she had once been one of Hollywood's most beautiful stars. She had the kind of delicate complexion that didn't stand up well to time and she had gained a lot of weight, but the passage of the years couldn't erase her lovely pale blue eyes and the charm that had endeared her to millions of fans.

It was said that Perry unlocked the door to Japan but Townsend Harris opened it. A distant relative of Connie's, Townsend Harris was the first American consul to Japan and the first foreign diplomat of any stripe. He arrived in the small fishing village of Shimoda in 1856 (the Japanese had barred foreigners from the capital) and spent two lonely years hammering out Japan's first foreign trade treaty. Or maybe not-so-lonely years. Harris was famous in Japan, not as a diplomat, but for his love affair with a beautiful young geisha named Okichi. After Harris's return to America, Okichi was scorned by the townspeople because of her association with the foreign barbarian. For years she waited in vain for his return. Despised by her countrymen and despondent over her abandonment, she sought solace in Japanese rice wine. Over the years she sank deeper and deeper into poverty. Finally she took her life by plunging off a cliff. Or so the story went. Historians dismissed much of it as the fabrication of romantic minds, but it was nevertheless the most famous love story in Japan and the subject of countless books, plays, and movies. The most famous of the movies was *Soiled Dove*, the extravagant Hollywood production in which Charlotte had played Okichi opposite Lincoln Crawford as Townsend Harris (a miscasting if there ever was one). It had been her biggest box-office success, thanks in part to the sizzling love scenes. Charlotte's on-the-set affair with her leading man had been one of her most notorious, though she was thankful she had had the good sense—on that occasion, at any rate—not to ruin it by marrying him. He had died shortly afterward in a car accident.

Though much of the Okichi story may have been a myth, Okichi's union with Harris had produced a child. Now, a descendant of Okichi's child was coming to Newport with a group of geishas from a famous geisha house in Kyoto. Known as Okichi-*mago*, or "grandchild of Okichi" (though she was really a great-great-etc.-grandchild), the descendant of Okichi's love child had traded on the famous story to become one of Japan's most famous geishas. She would be the mistress of ceremonies for the Afternoon of Japanese Culture to be held on Okichi Day, the third day of the Black Ships Festival and the hundredth anniversary of Okichi's suicide.

As she waited for her escort, Charlotte cursed herself for being there. Although she loved Newport, she hated these kinds of functions. But she almost always gave in. Out of sense of obligation, she supposed. She felt that she owed it to her fans, who had been loyal to her for fifty years: half a century! More than that, if you counted the ones who'd been around when she'd made her first movie in the late thirties. God, she was getting old! Just how old always caught her by surprise when she thought about it, which wasn't often. It also surprised her fans, who still expected her to look just as she had then. She sometimes understood why Garbo had closed the door on her public when she was still a young woman. But despite her age, Charlotte wasn't doing too badly. Although they sometimes expressed surprise that she was still alive, her fans still recognized her. Indeed, she still looked much as she had in her youth: the strong jaw-line; the alabaster white skin; the glossy black hair, once worn in a famous pageboy, but now pulled back into a tight chignon; the thick, winged eyebrows that had become a *cause célèbre* when she refused to let the studio makeup men pluck them to pencil-line thinness. Most of all, her elegant carriage and her long, leggy stride still identified her as someone special, even to those who had no idea that she was one of the century's foremost stars of stage and screen.

The young naval officers were seating the delegates according to status: first American, then Japanese. First to be seated were the governor of Rhode Island and the Japanese consul general for New England and their wives. Next came the mayor of Newport and the mayor of Shimoda, Newport's sister city. As they awaited their escorts, an American couple broke away from a knot of Japanese delegates on the lawn and headed toward Connie and Charlotte.

"My cousin," Connie explained.

An ardent Japanophile, Connie's cousin, Paul Harris, was responsible for the addition of Okichi Day to the Black Ships Festival program. It was he who had arranged to import the geishas and had put Connie and Spalding up to asking Charlotte to participate. Charlotte had talked with him several times on the phone in the course of making arrangements, but she'd never met him. He was a short, homely man with warm brown eyes and a neatly clipped beard.

"Miss Graham," he said, bowing slightly from the waist, Japanese style. "We're delighted that you could be here."

"I'm pleased to meet you. I've heard a lot about you from Connie," she replied, and immediately regretted her words.

He and Connie's daughter, Marianne Montgomery, had been involved in a bitter and protracted legal battle over a house they had both inherited: the house that Townsend Harris had built on the Cliff Walk after his return from Japan.

"If you've heard about me from Connie, it probably wasn't favorable," he replied good-naturedly.

"Not at all," objected Connie. "You know I have only good things to say about other members of the family. The Harrises have to stick together."

Though Connie had come to the rescue, it was nevertheless an awkward moment, which Charlotte did her best to smooth over by introducing herself to Paul's companion, whose name was Nadine Ogilvie.

"Paul is very happy that you could be here," said Nadine. She had a low, melodic voice and a heavy French accent. She was a beautiful woman with strong features and glossy black hair. She was impeccably dressed in a stunning red suit, and wore a small fortune in diamonds and pearls. She was also Paul's mistress, and had been for many years.

"At last," said Connie as a young naval officer came to seat her and Spalding and their Japanese counterparts, the president of the annual Black Ships Festival in Shimoda, and his wife.

Charlotte detected a note of relief in Connie's voice. She would be glad to get out of the sun, but also glad to get away from her cousin and Nadine. She didn't want the family squabble to interfere with the festival.

Connie and Spalding and their Japanese counterparts were fifth on the list, after the president of the Naval War College and a lieutenant in the Japanese Maritime Self-Defense Forces.

Once they had gone, Charlotte checked the program to see where she was listed. Which was at the bottom, just after Paul, who was listed as chairman of the Okichi Day Committee. It was obviously difficult to fit a movie star into the official protocol. The program identified her as "Miss Charlotte Graham: Okichi Day Delegate from the United States." Had it identified her further, it might have said "first American to play a Japanese geisha." Or "movie star who shocked the public by portraying an interracial romance." Not only an interracial romance, but an extramarital one as well. On top of that, *Soiled Dove* had been one of the first films to deal with the theme of suicide, which had always been considered box-office poison.

Charlotte considered *Soiled Dove* her best picture. It was the one she should have won the Oscar for—not that she hadn't deserved her other four—but Okichi had been one of her best roles. Awarding her the Oscar, however, would have been endorsing the daring sexual content of the film.

How times had changed.

Finally a young naval officer arrived to escort Paul and Nadine to their seats, leaving Charlotte with the public relations people. Like the other U.S. delegates, she had a Japanese counterpart, Okichi-*mago*. But she was recovering from jet lag at Paul's home, or rather Paul and Marianne's home.

Charlotte's escort finally arrived. "Miss Graham?" he said, offering her his arm. As he escorted her to her seat, they chatted about *Soiled Dove*. It was one of his favorite movies. He had seen it four times, and planned to see it again that night; it was being shown throughout the festival at a local movie house.

It was interesting that despite its dated subject matter—a relationship between a Japanese geisha and an American diplomat was hardly likely to raise eyebrows anymore—*Soiled Dove* had retained its popularity, and was among the most popular "classic" movies at the video stores.

The ceremonies began shortly after Charlotte was seated. Spalding was master of ceremonies. After welcoming the Japanese delegates, he introduced the first speaker, a Shimoda official who spoke about the long friendship between the United States and Japan. Glossing over the "difficulties" of the past (What difficulties was he referring to? Charlotte wondered. Pearl Harbor? The Bataan Death March? Hiroshima?), he called for strengthening the relationship between the two countries. "As in a marriage, we need to work tirelessly to improve our efforts at understanding." He was followed by four other Japanese speakers, none of whom spoke English. An elderly Japanese man translated their speeches, each of which then became twice as long. The fifth speech seemed interminable. Charlotte could feel her eyelids getting heavy, and fanned the sultry air with her program to keep herself awake. Platitudinous phrases drifted in and out of her consciousness: "The relationship between our two peoples has never been as important as it is today." . . . "Our relationship is important not only to our two countries, but to the entire world." . . . "We are poised to usher in a new era of peaceful competition and mutual understanding."

She was jerked back to consciousness by Spalding's fidgeting. Tall, portly, and patrician, Spalding was usually a genial sort—he was known around town as Mr. Newport for his leadership in local charitable affairs—but at this moment he didn't look genial at all. He was staring at the speaker, his bushy, gray-white eyebrows knitted together in a frown.

Charlotte had lost track of what the speakers were saying, but she now pricked up her ears.

The speaker was a slightly built Japanese man with wire-rimmed glasses. His snow-white hair was parted in the middle and combed straight back from his forehead. Unlike the earlier speakers, he spoke perfect English. But instead of platitudes about mutual understanding, he was talking about the end of the American century: "A century in which the typical American executive drives a Japanese automobile, cooks his food in a Japanese microwave, watches a Japanese television set, records his family vacations with a Japanese video recorder, and works in a high-rise office building owned by a Japanese company."

He was talking about an American economy "that has no substance."

Even American defense, he pointed out, depended on the Japanese: without Japanese semiconductors, American missiles couldn't hit their targets. If the Japanese were to stop selling semiconductors to the United States, it could upset the military balance of the world.

Charlotte could see a red flush rising like a tide from the stiff white collar of the vice admiral who was president of the Naval War College, and who sat directly in front of her.

And to what did the speaker attribute the end of the American century? "A family in decline, an educational system that doesn't work, a corporate culture in which long-term refers only to the next quarter, and a failure to save."

Connie patted her husband's arm; his face by now matched the color of the brick-red trousers he wore with a navy blue blazer. Several members of the audience got up and marched out.

It was time, the speaker continued, for Japan to stand on its own two feet, for Japan to take the leadership in world affairs, in defense, in foreign aid. It was time for Japan to stop thinking of itself as a colony of the United States. As for the United States: if it didn't mend its ways, it might find itself being considered a colony of Japan.

There was a charged silence as the speaker returned to his seat. A few polite members of the audience clapped. Looking up at the statue of Old Bruin, Charlotte half expected it to topple over in astonishment.

Then Spalding took the podium. After conspicuously failing to thank the previous speaker for his remarks, he delivered his closing comments with something less than his usual aplomb, and announced the laying of the wreaths. In pairs—one Japanese, one American—the official representatives placed the red and white chrysanthemum wreaths with black ribbons in front of the black wrought-iron fence at the foot of Perry's statue. As each set of wreaths was laid, the Newport Artillery Company, wearing the uniforms of Revolutionary War soldiers, fired a smoky salute from an antique Paul Revere cannon.

After the cannon salutes, the color guard retired as the Navy band played "The Stars and Stripes Forever" (with more than the usual fervor, Charlotte thought) and the ceremonies were over.

· 2 ·

AFTER THE OPENING ceremonies, the delegates drifted back across the street to the art museum for a reception. Charlotte stood on the porch of the grand old house, which had once been one of the summer cottages for which Newport was famous, sipping a lemonade and savoring the cool ocean breeze.

Spalding stood nearby, Connie at his side. He was giving a mild dressing down to a young Japanese man named Kenzako (Just-call-me-Ken) Mori, who was on the staff of the Japanese consul general's office in Boston and was a member of the Black Ships Festival Committee as well. He had been responsible for extending an invitation to the last speaker.

"What could I do?" he was saying to Spalding in self-defense.

Charlotte had met him earlier at Connie and Spalding's. He was an energetic man with a bouncy step and a taste for American living. He wore a sleek gray double-breasted suit and sporty aviator glasses. He also drove a baby blue Cadillac, which Charlotte found amusing, especially in light of the last speaker's remarks. "American cars have the best design," Mori had told her.

Connie explained to Charlotte what was going on. The last speaker, whose name was Hiroshi Tanaka, was president of a privately held Japanese electronics company and one of the richest men in the world. He was also the head of a Japanese trade organization which had recently purchased one of Newport's mansions.

"They plan to use it as a corporate retreat and for entertaining American clients," Connie said. "Newport was up in arms about it for a while, but as far as I'm concerned, the Japanese are no more foreign to Newport than the Texans."

Tanaka had volunteered the mansion, a huge Gothic pile of red sandstone called Edgecliff, for the Black Ships Festival Mikado Ball. Which was why Just-call-me-Ken had invited him to speak. That, and pressure from the governor. Tanaka's company owned a factory which employed close to a thousand Rhode Islanders.

Little had Mori known that Tanaka would use the opportunity to vent his spleen about what was wrong with the good old U.S. of A.

"It really wasn't his fault, poor man," said Connie as she looked over at Mori, who was about half her husband's size. "I hope Spalding isn't too hard on him. He's worked so hard on the festival."

As Charlotte headed over to the refreshment table to refill her glass of lemonade, she could hear Spalding ordering Mori to keep a muzzle on Tanaka for the remainder of the festival.

Meanwhile, Tanaka stood at the center of a knot of adulatory Japanese, smiling broadly and bobbing his snow-white head in acknowledgment of their compliments. Apparently he had said what they all had been wanting to say for a long time: which was "Go to hell, America."

As Charlotte stood talking with Connie, her daughter, Marianne, came drifting over, or rather, clacking over. On her feet she wore the four-inch platform sandals the Japanese called *geta*. They were made of black lacquer.

"You remember Marianne," said Connie.

"Of course," said Charlotte as Marianne pecked the air on either side of her face. How could she forget. Marianne Montgomery was a well-known fashion designer. Well-known for her sex life as well as her fashions. Charlotte and Connie might have tallied up four and three marriages respectively, but they had nothing on Marianne, who at fifty or so—she looked at least fifteen years younger—had been married half a dozen times, the last time, which was seven or eight years ago, to a twenty-year-old Italian prince.

"I like your outfit," said Charlotte.

She was wearing a voluminous kimono-like orange silk robe over a long, heavily textured silk skirt. The robe was tied with an obi-like sash of a metallic gold fabric. Against her white face, which was framed by shiny black hair cut in a Cleopatra style, the effect of the brightly colored masses of fabric was highly dramatic.

"Thank you," she replied. "It's from my new collection—'Geisha.' We're having a charity show at the casino on Saturday in honor of Okichi Day. I hope you'll be able to come. It's only fitting that the most famous geisha of the American screen should be there."

Charlotte smiled. "Of course I'll be there," she replied. "I read the reviews last week. You've made quite a splash."

"Thank God," she said with a grin.

"I never thought about it before, but I guess a good review is as important to a fashion collection as it is to a Broadway show," said Charlotte.

"With one big difference. In the theatre, a hit show usually means a long run, the sale of movie rights, sweatshirts, posters; in fashion, a hit collection means that you're expected to repeat the same success again next season." She shook her head. "It's a bitch of a business."

"But she loves it," said Connie.

"I'm hooked," Marianne agreed.

Marianne's story was a familiar one in the fashion world. She had started out in a basement with two sewing machines, and twenty years later, she was a millionaire. Of course, her family connections had helped—Connie's Hollywood friends and Spalding's society friends had lots of money to spend on clothes. But connections were no good if you didn't have talent too. Her new collection was eliciting raves from the fashion magazines. She had taken the kimono-inspired shapes popularized by the Japanese designers and done them one better, replacing their dark, somber tones (one fashion magazine had dubbed it "the Hiroshima bag lady look") with bright, vibrant ones.

"Even the Japanese are raving about it," said Connie. "Spalding says that Marianne is going to single-handedly rectify the balance of trade."

Several times a year Marianne unveiled a new collection, each more stunning than the last. Each collection had a theme—

Egypt, the Old West, Russia. Many of the themes were tied in to her romances: the Egyptian statesman, the rodeo star, the Russian ballet dancer. Not in recent years, however. For the last five or six years she had confounded all expectations by remaining with the same man, with only an occasional lapse from the straight and narrow path of monogamy. Nor had her collections suffered as a result. If anything, they had become more complex and sophisticated.

Her boyfriend was a freewheeling Texas tycoon named Lester Frame who loved her for her keen business acumen and her offbeat personality. She in turn loved him for his buccaneering spirit. Most of the time, she was faithful to him, but there was the occasional slip. If an analogy could be drawn between Marianne's addiction to sex and a drunkard's to alcohol, Marianne belonged in the periodic binge category. After months of sobriety, she was off on a bender.

Lester was not a favorite of Connie and Spalding's—it was probably Lester to whom Connie was referring when she had made her cutting remark about Texans. He was vulgar and rude, especially when he was drunk, which wasn't infrequently. He was also a convicted felon, who had DONE TIME: eighteen months in a Federal minimum security prison for white-collar criminals. His crime was insider trading. Although it had been a big scandal at the time, it was small potatoes by comparison with the insider trading scandals that were to follow. He had passed along to a golfing buddy a tip about the takeover plans of a company whose board he sat on. The golfing buddy in turn had passed the tip along to his girlfriend and a dozen others. The golfing buddy and his girlfriend and the others had all made a pile of money as a result, but Lester himself hadn't made a cent. Many felt he'd been betrayed by his friends and unfairly penalized by a judge who was out to prove that bigwigs weren't outside the law. Dozens of influential friends had testified as to his patriotism, integrity, honesty, and so on. But whether or not he deserved his punishment was immaterial to Connie and Spalding. In their eyes, he was a criminal, period. Especially to Spalding, who came from a family with impeccable social credentials. But even a criminal was preferable to the parade of dark-skinned foreigners whom Marianne had been dragging through their living room for years. At one point, Spalding was convinced that she was taking her cues for her choice of lovers from the covers of *National Geographic*: in March, it had been the Spanish bullfighter; in April, the Nicaraguan freedom fighter; in May, the Indian filmmaker. Lester may have been a criminal, but at least he was a) an American criminal; b) a white Anglo-Saxon criminal; c) a rich, successful, and politically conservative criminal; d) a criminal who could be charming when he wanted to be; e) a criminal of a suitable age for Marianne; and f) a criminal who genuinely loved her. None of which meant they had to *like* him.

Charlotte could see him chatting with Tanaka on the other side of the porch—one tycoon to another. No one would ever doubt he was a Texan. He wore a wide-brimmed felt hat and cowboy boots with two-inch heels made of some kind of exotic reptile skin. Not known for mincing words himself, he'd probably enjoyed Tanaka's provocative speech.

As Charlotte looked on, Marianne surveyed the gathering, her gaze sweeping the porch like a klieg light. She had the practiced eye of the entrepreneur who depends on self-promotion to bring in business: she was always on the lookout for someone to have her picture taken with, someone to buy her fashions, someone to give her a good write-up.

Finally her sharp brown eyes fixed on Nadine, who was talking animatedly with one of Spalding's cronies in Newport's old guard.

"I see the gold digger of the year is here," she said to her mother. Resting her chin on her hand, she carefully took in every detail of Nadine's appearance, from her elegant spectator pumps to the expensive scarf around her long, white neck to her neat French twist. "She's wearing a new Chanel," she observed. "Paul must have handed over his charge card again. Chanel— how boring. I would have expected the mistress of a rich man to have more imagination, wouldn't you, Mother? A jacket with four pockets, a straight skirt, and a bunch of pearls. She might as well be wearing a uniform."

Charlotte thought Nadine looked terrific.

The rivalry between Marianne and Paul's mistress was of long standing. They hated one another, and for good reason:

each was what the other was not but wanted to be. Marianne had sometimes been called the ugly daughter of a beautiful mother. She had oodles of style, but at the price of hours of slavish attention to her appearance. Nadine came effortlessly by the glamor that Marianne labored so hard to achieve, but she had no worldly status. She was the widow of a wealthy man from a prominent family who had given most of his fortune away to noble causes and then died suddenly, leaving her with two little boys, a sprawling old Victorian cottage on Bellevue Avenue, and no money to speak of.

"You should be nice to her, dear," said Connie with a mischievous little smile. "Maybe she'll give you a good write-up in the *Newport Daily News*."

Marianne snorted in contempt. Her face had a hint of innocent malice about it that Charlotte found intriguing. Her eyes were a little too close together, the corners of her mouth given to devilish little quivers.

Nadine made a living of sorts as the society reporter for the local paper, which allowed her to attend the right parties and mingle with the social set, but it was sorry compensation for someone whose aspiration was to marry Paul Harris and become the doyenne of Newport society. As Connie put it: "First she had the name and no money; now she has the money [Paul's] and no name. She wants the name *and* the money." But Paul wasn't cooperating. After five years, he'd still made no move toward marriage. To the contrary, he seemed to delight in his role as wealthy bachelor. Having a beautiful French mistress enhanced his man-about-town image; having her as a wife would only detract from it. It was getting to be a desperate situation for Nadine, who was faced with the choice of sticking with Paul in hopes that he would eventually marry her, or seeking her fortune elsewhere before time took too great a toll on her looks. A man who wanted a woman as an ornament generally wanted a bright and shiny one.

Marianne was surveying the gathering again. This time, her sharp brown eyes alighted on a tall, muscular, and very handsome man in a navy blue kimono, on the other side of the porch. His dark brown hair was slicked back and fastened in a topknot, the traditional hair style of the sumo wrestler.

Connie followed her daughter's gaze and then looked over at Charlotte with dismay. They had both seen that look before. It was not unlike that of a bird dog in pursuit. Marianne's jaw stuck out, her nose pointed at her quarry, and her nostrils quivered with anticipation. Had she possessed a tail, it would have stuck straight out in excited agitation. It was a look that was reserved for something that she had to possess, usually a man. The last time Charlotte had seen it was when Marianne had spotted the handsome young Italian prince at a party at her stepfather's *palazzo* in Venice.

"Following in Mother's footsteps," Marianne had said of the Italian prince. But there was a difference. When Connie had married Cornelio, a. k. a. Count Brandolini, she had been forty-five, the count fifty-one. When Marianne had married her Italian prince, she had been forty-five, the prince twenty. It had provoked quite a scandal. Though she denied it had been a motive, the marriage had also been good publicity for her "Palazzo" collection. She had no regrets, Marianne had told the gossip columnists when she split up with her young prince six months later. She claimed to have been in love with all the men she had relations with. Each of the men in her life was a point of light on her path to artistic enlightenment.

Now another point of light was beaming its signal across the room, and Marianne was responding like a moth to a flame.

"Mother, who *is* that gorgeous man?"

"Shawn Hendrickson," Connie replied. "He's a sumo wrestler. He's wrestling in the Black Ships exhibition tournament. One of the first Americans to reach the top division. A graduate of Yale, I think. An Ivy League wrestling champion who took up sumo. An Asian studies major; speaks fluent Japanese. Spalding's followed his career pretty closely. He can tell you all about him."

"A sumo wrestler." Marianne resumed her fixed stare.

Charlotte could see the wheels spinning. An American sumo champion. What good publicity for her "Geisha" collection!

"What did you say his name was, Mother?"

"Shawn Hendrickson."

Hendrickson looked over in their direction and caught Marianne's eye.

"Excuse me." Lowering her chin like a predator that's spotted its prey, Marianne clattered off across the porch. *Geta* weren't supposed to be worn indoors, but *geta* etiquette was a nicety that was lost on Marianne. Actually she didn't do too badly for someone who wasn't accustomed to walking in them. It had taken Charlotte a lot of practice to get it right for *Soiled Dove*.

"I shouldn't have said anything about him," said Connie, berating herself. "She always goes on the prowl like this after a successful show; it's as if success fires up her sex hormones. She can't calm down until she's seduced someone. At least it's a *man* this time—if you can call twenty-five a man—and not a boy." She rolled her pale blue eyes to the heavens and shook her head. "Oh Lordy, where did I go wrong."

Charlotte smiled. She was was familiar with the syndrome; it was common enough in Hollywood. But in her experience, it was usually the man who craved sex after nailing down the big deal or delivering the unforgettable performance. She remembered reading a study somewhere which reported that men's testosterone levels surged after being awarded their M.D. degrees.

The same was probably true of women; it was just that they'd never had the arena in which to assert their social dominance. It was certainly true of Marianne. She was simply exercising the sexual prerogatives of power, like the studio chief who has sex with the starlet on the casting couch.

"Lester is not going to like this," Connie predicted.

Lester had also spotted Marianne and was watching her as intently as her mother was. Like her, his look of perturbation revealed that he was anticipating another slip.

"Besides," Connie added, "she's not going to get anywhere with him."

"Why's that?"

"I should have told her." Connie giggled guiltily. "But she ran off so fast, I didn't have a chance. She'll find out soon enough. Oh, it's a big scandal in Japan. It's been on the front pages of the newspapers for a week. Are you familiar with the geishas' patron system?"

Charlotte nodded. She had learned a lot about geisha life

in researching the role of Okichi. Although many prostitutes called themselves geishas, the true geisha was a skilled artist, talented in such traditional arts as singing, dancing, and flower arranging. A businessman hired a geisha to entertain himself and his friends for the evening. "Pillow service" was not part of the deal. Except for the patron, or *hanna*. The patron was a rich businessman who offered the geisha financial support—often setting her up as proprietress of her own teahouse—in exchange for her becoming his mistress. She was free to carry on with her geisha activities, but she was expected to have sexual relations only with him. Being a patron was a status symbol among wealthy businessmen. It was a very cut and dried arrangement: often a business contact was drawn up.

Connie nodded at Tanaka. "Tanaka is Okichi-*mago*'s patron. He set her up in her own teahouse six years ago. With his backing, she's become the most well-known hostess in Kyoto, and her teahouse has become the most fashionable. It's called the 'American Tea House.' People seek it out the way they might a restaurant owned by a movie star here."

"And?" prompted Charlotte.

"Last week, she threw him over. Announced that she was breaking her contract. The Japanese are outraged. They're calling her every name in the book. There are even editorials bemoaning the national decline of honor. Humiliating one of their leading citizens for . . ." Connie's gaze shifted to the other side of the porch, where Marianne was flirting outrageously with Shawn.

Charlotte completed the sentence: "An American sumo wrestler."

If body language could be X-rated, Marianne's was. From across the room, Lester stared at her, his forehead creased in a frown. He had seen her through several of these flirtations—most recently with a college sophomore—and would probably see her through several more, but he clearly wasn't happy about it.

"If you ask me, that's why Tanaka was so nasty. Getting back at the Americans for Shawn's stealing his geisha. He's probably mad at him for his success in sumo too. Spalding says the Japanese have really given Shawn a hard time. A lot of Japanese hate to see a foreigner succeed at their national sport, and to succeed so quickly."

"I'm surprised he's gotten as far as he has," said Charlotte, knowing how xenophobic the Japanese could be. "Did you say there have been other American sumo wrestlers?"

"Two," Connie replied.

"Did they run into trouble too?"

"Not as much. They're both Hawaiians. One's retired now; he's the one Spalding wrote the book about. He's going to be here too. The Japanese felt some kind of racial kinship, I guess. Actually, it's more than just race. Shawn is a Japanophile: he studies Zen, he does ink-wash paintings, he speaks perfect Japanese. He's more Japanese than most Japanese, and that rankles them."

Charlotte looked over at Shawn. He was big and handsome with heavy, dark eyebrows and deep green eyes, but it wasn't only his size and looks that made him attractive. He had grace and style, and conveyed the sense of power in repose that was typical of top athletes at the peak of their form. In short, a young god—a lot younger than Marianne.

"Nice-looking, isn't he?" said Connie, who wasn't immune to the blandishments of male charm herself.

Had Connie been about twenty years younger, Charlotte suspected it would have been she who was making the play for Shawn instead of her daughter. Though she had settled down in her later years, it was no mystery from whom Marianne had inherited her inability to control her reckless impulses.

As they watched, a photographer approached the couple. As he aimed his camera, Marianne grinned and draped herself over Shawn. They made a striking picture, and she knew it.

Leaving Connie to Spalding, who had worked out the Tanaka problem with Mori, Charlotte headed inside to the gallery, where there was an exhibition of the famous Black Ships Scrolls. The long scrolls were arrayed around the room with translations of the Japanese inscriptions underneath. Charlotte started at the right of the longest one and worked her way to the left. Backwards by Western standards, but from beginning to end by Japanese. The depictions of Perry's expedition had been executed by Japanese painters on the spot. The first boats to greet Perry's expedition had been filled with artists who had recognized the market for paintings of the foreign barbarians and their awesome ships. The scrolls were far from fine art, but they had a primitive charm. Charlotte was amused by the depictions of Perry as a comical swaggerer with slanted eyes and a huge nose, of the dragonlike black ships belching clouds of steam and smoke, and of drunken crewmen with copious body hair consorting with courtesans, perhaps Okichi—pre-Townsend Harris—among them.

A voice interrupted her thoughts. "I like this one, don't you?" it said.

Charlotte looked down into the deep blue eyes of a very old woman. She had a marvelous face: fine and old and lovely, as if it had been carved from ivory. It was framed by a white kerchief, which was tied behind her neck. She gave the impression of being not of this century.

The drawing she referred to depicted the telegraph and the miniature steam locomotive that Perry had bestowed on the Japanese commissioners as a gift. Unlike the human figures, which were whimsically portrayed as strange and comical, the mechanical objects were rendered in painstaking detail.

"Prophetic, isn't it?" she went on. "From their first contact with Western technology, they were fascinated." She pointed to the translations on the wall next to the scrolls. "I did the translations. My name's Lillian Harvey," she said, extending her hand, "but you can call me Aunt Lillian—everybody else does."

"Charlotte Graham," said Charlotte, returning her handshake. "Very nice to meet you. Do you speak Japanese, then?"

"Oh yes. I lived in Japan for many years. I used to teach English at a Quaker girls' school in Tokyo. I first went there in 1914—it seems such a long time ago now. I went back again in the late thirties, just before the war."

Charlotte did a quick mental calculation. If she'd been a teacher when she first went to Japan, she must have been at least eighteen, which meant that she was now well into her nineties.

She looked up at Charlotte intently, with her clear, sparkling eyes, which were like sunlight on a deep blue sea. "You're the actress who played Okichi in *Soiled Dove*, aren't you?"

Charlotte nodded.

"You did a beautiful job. Of course, you never could have played her on stage." Leaning back, she eyed Charlotte's height. "I never realized how tall you were. Much too tall for a Japanese. The man who played Uncle Townsend was a *fright*. He should have stuck to Westerns."

She was absolutely right. Linc Crawford had been all wrong for the part—he had all the diplomatic subtlety of a cattle rustler. She could still hear his Texas drawl ringing in her ears.

"Are you related to Townsend Harris?" asked Charlotte.

"Oh yes," Aunt Lillian said. "The Harris descendants are legion. He was my great-uncle. He had no children, of course. Or rather," she continued, "no *legitimate* children. But he had four brothers and a sister, all of whom had children."

"Aunt Lillian's the matriarch of the family now," said a voice from behind.

Charlotte turned around. The voice belonged to Paul Harris.

"She'll be joining us for the geisha party this evening as the eldest representative of the Harris family." He gave her a peck on the cheek. "How old are you now, Lillian dear?"

"As old as the earth, and you know it," she replied with a twinkle.

Along with her host and hostess, Charlotte had been invited to a geisha party at Paul's house that evening. Actually, Paul and Marianne's house.

The house on the Cliff Walk, which had been built by Townsend Harris upon his return from Japan, had been left in trust to Connie and Paul by a great-aunt. Connie had wanted nothing to do with it. She had her own house in Newport, or rather Spalding had. For years, she and Paul had let Townsend Harris's house out. Then Paul started taking an interest in it. His mother, with whom he had lived for years, had died, and he was looking for a summer place of his own. He began pouring money into the place. Under the guidance of a team of architectural historians, he spent hundreds of thousands restoring it to its original pre-Civil War condition. It was no wonder that he was resentful when Marianne decided to assert her claim, or technically, her mother's claim, to it.

Paul now occupied the place for half the summer. Half, because he shared the house with Marianne—by court decree. Under a court order of occupancy and use, each had use of the house for alternating two-weeks periods: Wednesday to Wednesday, all neatly spelled out in court documents. Each party had the right to decorate certain rooms, with the dining room divided between them: Marianne could decorate the north and east walls, Paul the south and west walls. Certain rooms were to be left as they were; certain rooms were reserved exclusively for one party or the other. The expenses were shared; any failure to pay meant a forfeiture of that party's right to occupy.

Charlotte wondered how much money the state had spent over the years adjudicating the case. As a taxpayer in New York, where the aunt's will was filed, she was appalled that her tax money was being used to mediate such an infantile dispute.

"It's been a long time since you've gotten the family together, Paul," observed Aunt Lillian. "Fifteen years or more."

Her comment reflected Charlotte's own thoughts. It was a mystery why Paul had proposed this little party. Especially since there was no end in sight to the bickering. According to the will, when Connie and Paul died the trust ceased and the house passed to their descendants. But since Paul had no heir, the house would eventually go to Marianne's daughter, Dede. To prevent Dede from inheriting the house, Paul was trying a new tactic. Arguing that his great-aunt had intended to leave the house to him and Connie and not to their descendants, he had offered to buy it from the trust and turn it over to the Preservation Society of Newport County, the non-profit foundation that operated many of Newport's mansions. The outcome was still undecided. Though Marianne had the authority of the will on her side, Paul had assembled a lot of high-powered talent on his: namely, the trust department of the prestigious New York corporate law firm in which he was a senior partner, and the resources of the politically powerful Preservation Society, which was anxious to acquire a house that had already been restored. For a while, Paul had even talked about adopting Nadine's sons as his heirs in order to prevent the property from ending up in Dede's hands. The idea made Marianne livid, of course.

"Believe me, I'm not burying the hatchet," Paul replied. "It's all in the service of the festival. I want to introduce Okichi-*mago* to the family. After all, she is a distant relative."

"I suppose she is, isn't she?" said Aunt Lillian. "I'm looking forward to meeting her. Is she as beautiful as everyone says?"

"Even more so. It may be my imagination, but I think I can even detect a resemblance to the Old Tycoon." The Old Tycoon was the name that Harris was known by after his return from Japan, he explained. He turned his attention back to the scrolls. "Are these your translations, Aunt Lillian?"

"Yes. From fifty years or more ago now."

Their conversation was interrupted by a Japanese man who greeted Aunt Lillian. They chattered away in Japanese for a few minutes and then she excused herself. "Someone needs a translator," she explained.

"Ninety-six and still going strong," said Paul after she had gone. "I hope I'm as sharp at that age." He turned back to the section of scrolls in front of them, which showed a row of cannons on deck. "I think they should have called this exhibit 'Trade Talks the Old-Fashioned Way.' "

Charlotte smiled. "I think there are some people here who would just as soon see the United States send out the black ships again," she said. "Especially after Mr. Tanaka's speech this morning."

"Well, at least it kept everyone from falling asleep. How do you like the scrolls?" he asked. "Of course, they're hardly Utamaro, but they're fun."

Utamaro was a Japanese artist who was famed for his woodblock prints of the everyday life of the geishas. Charlotte had first come across these colorful prints when she was filming *Soiled Dove* in Japan. A display in a Tokyo art dealer's window had caught her eye. They depicted the geisha dancing, singing, putting on their makeup, preparing for the bath. She was so entranced that she had eventually become something of a collector.

"Are you a collector?" she asked, sensing a shared interest.

Paul replied that he was. Not only a collector, but a very knowledgeable authority. He worked as a consultant for various auction houses and art galleries on the Japanese woodblock print, or *ukiyo-e*.

Charlotte explained how the *ukiyo-e* had helped give her insight into the customs and manners of the floating world: the world of wine, women, and song that was the province of the rich merchant-class. Barred from government and forbidden from the material display of wealth (such privileges being restricted to the aristocratic samurai class), the rich merchants turned their energies to the hedonistic pursuit of pleasure.

In many ways, the floating world reminded Charlotte of Newport. Except for a few survivors of the old guard like Spalding, there was little sense of the obligation of wealth among Newport's mansion dwellers. Public achievement, service to one's community, charitable contributions—all these had little or nothing to do with power and prestige. The index of social standing was money—or, if not money itself, an appreciation for the social prerogatives of wealth.

For a few minutes, they chatted away about Japanese woodblock prints with the fervidness of fellow enthusiasts who have discovered one another. Then Paul checked his watch. "Do you have some spare time this afternoon?"

Charlotte replied that she did.

"If you'll risk associating with the other side of the family, I'd like to show you my collection. Plus I'd like to show you something else, something that only you can appreciate."

"What is it?" she asked.

"A surprise."

· 3 ·

AFTER A SANDWICH at a luncheonette, Charlotte headed down Bellevue Avenue toward Paul's house. Although she had a car, she preferred to walk. She had looked forward to this moment. Much of Newport's appeal for her lay in the romance of this elegant avenue, which was lined with the grand mansions of the Gilded Age. She loved the ornate wrought-iron gates, the glimpses of mansions behind high brick walls, the expanses of sun-dappled lawn. But most of all she loved the trees. Just as the Newport socialites had vied to build the biggest mansions, to host the most lavish parties, and to wear the most stylish gowns, they had also vied to grow the most exotic trees. A century ago teams of oxen could be seen hauling young trees up from the harbor, trees that had been gathered from around the world to grace the grounds of these elegant mansions. Now these trees had come into their full maturity. She had once heard it said that this single avenue boasted one of the finest collections of specimen trees in the country. As she left the shops of central Newport behind, she reacquainted herself with her favorites: the pollarded beeches on the lawn of the The Elms, clipped to form dense, erect columns; the London plane tree on the lawn of Chateau-Sur-Mer, with a trunk that was seven feet around; the forty-foot-high rhododendrons; and everywhere enormous specimens of the graceful fern-leafed beech, Newport's most elegant tree.

At Narragansett Avenue, she turned left toward the ocean. On her right was another famous mansion, this one still in private hands: Bois Doré, another replica of a French chateau.

And again, the trees: a double row of pollarded planes lining the long approach to the door. The trees at Bois Doré were the subject of one of her favorite Newport stories: for a party, the then-owner of the mansion, a Harrisburg millionaire, had hung them with artificial fruits that were plated, like the faucets in his bathrooms, with fourteen-carat gold. She could imagine how they must have glittered in the lamplight. It was decadent, yes, but it was also magical. Not unlike Hollywood, not unlike the floating world. Newport was full of stories like that: the notorious dogs' dinner, in which a hundred dogs in fancy dress were served stewed liver and shredded dog biscuits by English footmen in full livery, or Mrs. Astor's jewel party at which five hundred guests dug in sand piles with miniature sterling silver shovels for diamonds, emeralds, sapphires, and rubies—theirs to keep as party favors. It was also Mrs. Astor, the high priestess of Gilded Age society, who was the subject of one of Newport's saddest stories. The lavishly gowned queen of the Four Hundred spent her last days in her mansion on Bellevue Avenue giving elegant parties for imaginary guests at which no rule of etiquette, no nuance of fine manners was ignored. It was a pathetic end for a woman whose husband's grandfather had made his fortune skinning beavers.

Such had been the fate of many of Newport's fortunes: the robust wealth that had come from trading furs or mining coal or laying rails had ended up in the hands of people who, treating their inheritance as their admission pass, had spent their lives denying admission to others, until, undermined by their lack of contact with reality, they degenerated into madness or dissipation.

At the far end of Narragansett Avenue, the sea glittered in the midday sun. Near the end, Charlotte turned right onto Ochre Point Avenue. Shimoda, as the house was called, was situated on the stretch of shoreline between two of Newport's biggest mansions: Ochre Court, a replica of a French palace, complete with turrets and gargoyles, and The Breakers, the seventy-room replica of an Italian Renaissance palace that was Newport's most fabulous summer "cottage." Shimoda was built by Townsend Harris upon his return from Japan. Before he became consul general, he had been in the China trade.

Many of his fellow China traders had retired to Newport, and it was only natural that he would too. He had lived out his years writing his memoirs while his niece, Lavinia, ran his household. Upon his death, he left the property to Lavinia, who lived to be nearly a hundred. As Newport became more fashionable, the early wooden cottages such as Shimoda were replaced by mansions like The Breakers. But Lavinia refused to sell the property, or, for that matter, even a lot. When she died, the property was rescued from the auction block by another Harris relative who left it in trust to Connie and Paul.

Although she had never been in the house before, Charlotte had seen it from the Cliff Walk and had even driven by several times. The house wasn't grand, but it was architecturally unique, the finest example of early Gothic Revival in Newport. It was also highly picturesque, with its steep, gingerbread-trimmed gables, mullioned windows, balconies, bay windows, and verandas. Unlike its white-elephant neighbors, it was a house to be lived in.

Turning in at the gate in the tall fence of wide wooden palings with a Gothic arch (painted dark gray to match the house), Charlotte walked up the winding gravel driveway to the front door, which was flanked by ornate cast-iron urns planted with yellow hibiscus.

Paul met her at the door. Again, he bowed slightly. He was wearing a patterned kimono of indigo-dyed cotton of the type the Japanese favor for informal wear in the summer. A frisky red and white spotted spaniel hugged his ankles. "Come in, come in," he said, ushering her into a foyer whose walls were paneled in dark wood carved in a Gothic motif. Facing the door was a suit of medieval Japanese samurai armor. "A gift from the shogun to Townsend Harris," he explained. "It's very valuable, one of the most important examples of medieval Japanese armor in the West."

Charlotte admired the menacing-looking suit of armor, with its horned iron helmet and leather breastplate stenciled with a fierce-looking monster.

Paul leaned down to pick up the spaniel, which was whining for attention. "Be quiet, Miako," he said. "Miako is a descendant of one of the two Japanese spaniels that the shogun gave

Townsend Harris. Japanese spaniels were always part of an Imperial present. Harris named them Miako and Edo after Japan's two capitals, Kyoto and Tokyo. Miako and Edo were the feudal names. We used to have an Edo too, but she died last year. Miako misses her very much." He ruffled the dog's mane. "Don't you, Micky?"

"He's beautiful," said Charlotte, reaching out to pet the dog. He was similar to a cocker spaniel, with a short muzzle, a mane around his neck, and a long, silky coat; but he was more exotic-looking. It struck Charlotte that he bore more than a slight resemblance to his master: he was small, spruce, and proud, with large, dark, protuberant eyes and an alert, intelligent bearing, but he also possessed the effete quality that goes with being overbred.

The dog wagged his tail vigorously in response to Charlotte's attentions.

"They're related to the King Charles spaniel. Of course, Perry was the first to own one in the West. Quite a few descendants of Perry's dogs are still around Newport, as well as quite a few descendants of Perry himself."

"Kind of like Harrises," joked Charlotte.

"Yes, I guess you could say that," Paul replied, his brown eyes smiling. "Well, are you ready for the Cook's tour?"

"Yes," Charlotte replied. "I'm honored."

She was also curious. Not so much about the art, though she always liked to look at Japanese prints, but about the appointments. She had once seen articles on Shimoda in two decorating magazines in the same month: one had featured Paul's rooms, the other Marianne's. They had been vastly different.

As Paul led her across the red-and-black-tiled floor of the foyer, he filled her in on the family dispute. She was already familiar with much of it from Connie, but he gave her his side of the story. At the back of his effort to break the trust by buying the house and donating it to the Preservation Society was his fear that Marianne or Dede would some day sell the property to a real estate developer. The fear was a real one: huge mansions on small lots were typical of Newport; Shimoda was a small house (by comparison) on a huge lot, a forty-acre promontory of tableland jutting out into the Atlantic with unsurpassed views of the ocean on three sides.

"Marianne doesn't need the money, but she isn't very attached to the house, either," Paul explained as they entered a parlor. "To her, it's just a stage-set for her lavish parties, and keeping it up is a lot of work. If somebody offered her the right price, I'm sure she'd sell in a minute. *If* I'd already gone to my final reward, that is."

Charlotte recognized the room from the magazine: it was decorated with heavy, dark Gothic furniture, tall built-in Gothic-arched bookcases, and Japanese paintings and antiques.

"Most of the furnishings are original to the house," Paul explained.

From the floor-to-ceiling windows the view was of smooth green lawn stretching out to the sea. Perched on a knoll at the edge of the cliff was a Japanese temple surrounded by pines whose limbs had been contorted like bonsai by the driving winds off the ocean.

"The Temple of the Great Repose," said Charlotte.

The cliff-top temple was a replica of the temple in which Townsend Harris had lived with Okichi. It was a simple rectangular building with a low, hipped roof with overhanging eaves surrounded by a wooden gallery. But its simplicity was deceiving: the balance of its proportions and the beauty of the natural materials used in its construction gave it tremendous power and elegance.

"Does it look familiar?"

"Very." Seeing the temple brought back vivid memories of filming *Soiled Dove* on location in Japan. "If we'd made *Soiled Dove* thirty years later, we could have used it as a set."

Paul smiled. "The Old Tycoon had it built here. Once the memories of his isolation faded, he started remembering the place fondly. After Lavinia died, it was boarded up. I pulled it out of the ocean five years ago. The hurricanes had nearly destroyed it. Part of the cliff washed away in the hurricane of 1938 and the rest in the hurricane of 1954. I had it completely restored."

"It must have been very expensive."

"Almost as much as restoring the house. It had been essentially without maintenance for years. The sun, the wind, and the salt air had really taken their toll. Nothing remained of the gallery and very little of the roof. The interior was covered with graffiti. Fortunately Lavinia had saved every document relating to its construction: plans, photos, bills—you name it. But it still took two years. I had to import all the workmen from Japan."

"I remember seeing it years ago from the Cliff Walk," Charlotte said. "I used to wish that someone would take the trouble to restore it. Though I didn't realize then that it was a replica of the Temple of the Great Repose; it was hard to tell what it was in that condition."

"It was a mess," said Paul. He stared out at the temple, which looked as if it were suspended in the air above the glittering sea. "Fortunately, it's one part of the property that my dear cousin once-removed and her low-life friends can't defile," he said. "The court has barred her from the premises."

"Though she'll be there tonight."

"But that's by *invitation*." Turning away from the window, Paul led Charlotte back through the parlor, the frisky Miako at his heels. "Now for the rear parlor, *her* parlor. Are you ready?" he asked, as he paused next to a pocket door leading to the adjoining room.

As Charlotte nodded, he ceremoniously rolled back the door.

The room was identical to the first, but instead of antiques, it was decorated with an eclectic riot of furniture and *objects d'art*: New Guinea fertility masks, an Egyptian mummy portrait, a Tibetan *thangka* painting, huge blowups of models wearing Marianne's fashions, a gigantic stuffed gorilla—the hide-away horde of a slightly mad and grossly acquisitive personality.

"Do you believe this?" he asked. "Michael Rockefeller meets Lawrence of Arabia meets Dr. Livingston meets the Dalai Lama. This is the place where she stores her possessions before she gets rid of them." His voice had taken on a complaining tone. "She goes through her African phase and her Egyptian phase and her Tibetan phase, and I have to live with the consequences."

Charlotte didn't quite believe it. "It's like those decorator show houses in which one room is decorated like a Moorish palace and the next like an English country house, except that it's all in one room."

Paul shook his head in disgust. "I think she does it just to annoy me. Now she's taking me to court again. She's trying to prevent me from giving house tours." He explained that he sometimes opened the house to house tours to raise money for charitable organizations. He continued: "She wants to prevent me from giving house tours, but she hasn't the least compunction about giving a party for four hundred people in honor of a rock star."

"Rock star?"

"Some British drummer. She says her parties are okay because the trust reserves the house for the private use of the family, and the house tours aren't, because they're attended by strangers. As if the people who attend her parties aren't strangers." He pointedly picked up a glass that had left a white ring on the glossy surface of a table. "She also objected when I allowed the filming of a historical documentary about the life of Townsend Harris."

His comments about the family made Charlotte think of Marianne's brother Billy, who was ten years younger than Marianne. As Connie's son, he should also have been entitled to the use of the house, but Charlotte had never heard Connie say anything about him in connection with it. "What about Billy?" she asked. "Does the trust entitle him to use the house, or is he just not interested?"

"Both of the above. Marianne got him to sign away his rights for a million dollars eight or ten years ago. She said the house and property were worth ten million, which meant that his half of their half was worth two-and-a-half. In her eyes, a million was a fair price—it was a cash deal. But even then, I'd been offered thirty million, and I've been offered much more since."

"She deliberately cheated him?"

Paul shrugged. "She says she was doing him a favor. He wanted the money to buy a boat. He's since gone through that and a lot more. Do you know Billy?"

Charlotte shook her head.

"He's boat-crazy. Anyway, this boat that he wanted came up for sale—a classic yacht. I don't know the first thing about boats myself. He wanted the money to buy it and he wanted it now. Marianne took advantage of the situation. I don't blame her completely. Billy should have known better. He's the kind of guy who people take advantage of. Including his ex-wife. He lost the boat in a divorce settlement a few years ago."

"Does he resent Marianne for taking advantage of him?"

"Oh no. They get along fine; they always have. He was grateful to her for coming up with the money. He'll be here tonight; you'll get to meet him. He has his own peculiar brand of charm—of the 'I'll never grow up' variety. People like Billy are a common type in the never-never land of Newport. They have two goals in life: party as much as they can and work as little as they can. He's succeeded pretty well at both."

From the rear parlor, Paul led her into the dining room, Miako nipping at his heels. "Here it is," he said with a wave of his arm as they entered the room. "Court-dictated schizophrenia."

The room was divided into Paul's section and Marianne's section. Over the intricately carved Gothic mantel on the north side of the room (Paul's) was a *trompe l'oeil* fresco of fruits, vegetables, and wild game, above which were painted the words of the doxology: "Praise God from whom all blessings flow . . ."

"The fresco is original to the house," Paul said. "It's considered a superb example of American naive art."

On the south side of the room (Marianne's) was a gigantic spatter painting à la Jackson Pollack.

"Ridiculous, isn't it?"

It was, but it was also fascinating. And, although Charlotte never would have said so to Paul, it kind of worked.

"Last spring, the surrogate judge ordered us to stop engaging in brinksmanship and to launch a new era of cooperation. Quote, unquote. When you see this dining room, you can see what a tall order that was."

"Like demanding an end to the Cold War," commented Charlotte.

"I wish it were as easy as that," he replied as he led her through the dining room into the service wing. "Here's what I wanted you to see," he announced as they entered.

The room was a memorial to Townsend Harris. A huge, ornately framed portrait of him hung on one wall. He'd been a handsome man with a fleshy face and a bushy mustache and sideburns. Around the room were mementos of Harris's years in Japan. At first glance, Charlotte took in a campaign trunk, a telescope, and a collection of lacquerware.

"Aunt Vinnie's shrine to the Old Tycoon," Paul announced. "No one's allowed to make any changes in this room except for the addition of new historical materials." He carefully straightened the portrait. "It's a good thing too. Otherwise the Old Tycoon would probably be hanging next to a portrait of Marilyn Monroe or some other artistic monstrosity."

Charlotte wandered around the room, looking at the mementos: a pencil sketch of the Temple of the Great Repose; a set of pipes on a pipe rack; a woodcut of two Japanese spaniels; a worn and tattered American flag, the first foreign flag to fly on Japanese soil. Each exhibit bore a label with an explanation carefully printed in an old-fashioned hand.

"I'm fascinated," said Charlotte. "I wish I'd seen this before we filmed *Soiled Dove*." Although she had studied the history books for her role, Aunt Vinnie's display made history come alive.

She was especially taken by a mannequin wearing the impressive gold-embroidered uniform that Harris had worn on his visit to the shogun's palace. Linc Crawford had worn an identical costume in the movie, right down to the cockaded hat with the gold tassels. She remembered their laughing about how funny he looked in it. Lillian was right: he should have stuck to Westerns.

"Wait until you see what's next."

"The surprise?"

"This is it," he said, opening the door into an adjoining room.

Entering, Charlotte found herself facing a faded sepia-toned photograph of a young Japanese woman. She was elegant and dignified, with dark, limpid eyes, and a long, oval face. Although she wore a kimono, she didn't look Japanese. In fact, she might have been a young Victorian beauty. The label next to the picture read, "Okichi at twenty-eight." Charlotte was spellbound. Although she had played Okichi, she had never seen a photograph of her. In her hair, she wore the camellias that were her symbol. They were tinted a deep red.

"She was very beautiful, wasn't she?" said Paul.

"Yes," Charlotte replied. "I hadn't expected it."

"You believed the historians."

She nodded. The historians had written Okichi off as little more than a street prostitute. If she had really been the geisha of beauty and talent portrayed in the legend, they argued, she would have left Shimoda to seek her fortune in the nearby capital of Edo.

"Historians are always trying to shatter legends," said Paul. "But they always find out in the end that the legends have a basis in fact. Okichi-*mago* looks very much like her, as you'll see when you meet. She's still resting upstairs; otherwise I'd introduce you to her now."

From the photo, Charlotte's attention shifted to a glass-topped mahogany case of the kind used by the Victorians for displaying collections of butterflies and minerals. Inside was a shallow, wide-mouthed sake cup, fired with a luminous sea-green glaze. "The cup!" Charlotte exclaimed. She looked up at Paul. "There really *was* a cup."

He smiled. "Yes, there really was."

It was the sake cup that Harris had given Okichi. The cup from which she had drunk for the rest of her life. The cup that she had left at the edge of the cliff when she had plunged into the ocean exactly a hundred years ago.

"I always thought it was a screenwriter's invention," she said. Next to the cup was a yellowed, half-burned calling card. She could just make out the words 'Harris. Consul and Plenipotentiary.' "The calling card too!"

Before taking her life, Okichi had built a fire at the edge of the cliff and burned all her papers. Found among the charred remains after her death was Harris's half-burned calling card. Like the cup, Charlotte had thought the calling card was the product of a screenwriter's imagination.

"There's more," said Paul, directing her attention to another case.

Inside were an ornamental comb and a round hand-mirror. Both were made of gold lacquer inlaid with mother-of-pearl in an intricate camellia pattern; both were exquisitely beautiful. Okichi had also left the comb and mirror at the edge of the cliff before taking her life.

"Where did you get these things?"

"Aunt Vinnie picked them up in Japan. She's the one who set up these rooms. The keeper of the flame. She went over to Shimoda after Okichi died. Someone must have given them to her there." He turned to the wall. "Here's something else I thought you'd be interested in."

Hanging on the wall was a framed piece of paper on which a text was written in Japanese characters. The label said simply "Raven at Dawn."

"I don't believe it," Charlotte said, shaking her head in amazement. "The screenwriter must have been here."

Okichi had been famed as a strolling singer of *shinnai*, or love ballads. She was especially renowned for her rendition of "Raven at Dawn," a bittersweet ballad about the ill-fated love between a courtesan and a young man. Charlotte had sung the song in *Soiled Dove*.

"Shall I translate it for you?"

She shook her head. "I think I remember the words." Fragments drifted out of her memory: " . . . of last night's vows of love, of lately whispered tales of tears and sighs, of a dear lover from the past . . ." And then, the refrain. She sang the words softly: "Sleeves wet with weeping, bosom torn with cares and sad regrets. The past will ne'er return: will drinking bring forgetfulness? Forget and drink—besides that, only to pluck the samisen with muffled fingertips. Once more I hear the raven's cry at dawn: that memory . . . Night deepens on Shimoda's waterfront. Tears falling, drop like red camellias."

For a moment, there was silence. A lump rose in Charlotte's

throat as she thought of Linc, her own "lover from the past." It was as if the opaque screen that shielded those memories from her consciousness had been rolled back on the runners of her mind, just as their old Japanese housekeeper had rolled back the sliding wood-and-paper walls of their little villa overlooking the seaside village, to let in the morning air. Indeed, it was the mornings of those idyllic weeks in Japan that she remembered best: waking up in Linc's arms on their silk futon under the gauze mosquito netting, golden threads of light seeping through the bamboo blinds; the sound of the cocks crowing and the wavering falsetto of the housekeeper's voice as she chanted her monotonous incantations to the Shinto spirits; and, once the screens had been rolled back, the magnificent view of Mt. Fuji across the bay, serene and gleaming.

Paul broke the silence, smiling with his warm brown eyes. "That was lovely," he said. "Would you like to see the prints now?"

"Yes, I would," she replied, following him into an adjacent room.

The room was a gallery of woodblock prints. Charlotte wandered from print to print: lovers, courtesans, actors, sumo wrestlers—the denizens of the floating world. Each a triumph of two dimensions, relying solely on line and color to create a sense of movement and form. In their avoidance of perspective and shading, the Japanese had anticipated the modernists by two centuries.

"I'm stunned," said Charlotte. "This is a collection worthy of a great museum." It must also have been very valuable. Although *ukiyo-e* now cost a lot more than they once had, they had never been cheap. They had been in fashion since the end of the last century. Even Van Gogh and Degas had been collectors.

"I've been collecting for years," Paul said proudly. "It's my hobby, or rather, my obsession."

On the far wall, she stopped to admire an Utamaro print of a young couple drinking tea. She loved the tall, willowy figures, the delicate features of the elongated faces, the brilliant colors of the elegant silk robes, the sensual curves of the folds in the fabric.

"From the 'Poem of the Pillow,' " commented Paul.

The "Poem of the Pillow" was a famous album of erotic prints showing couples in various positions of love. The print on display was a cover sheet, an innocuous print suitable for public viewing.

"Yes, I know. When I was filming *Soiled Dove,* I used to visit an art gallery in Tokyo where they sold *ukiyo-e.* The dealer kept the *shunga* in a drawer under the counter. He used to show them to me."

Shunga was the Japanese word for erotic prints, a subcategory of *ukiyo-e.* But unlike Western pornography, *shunga* were works of art: except for some of the later ones, there was nothing sordid or vulgar about them.

"I imagine that you can buy them in the open now," she continued. "But they were considered pornographic then." It had always struck her as ridiculous that a great artist was suddenly scorned as a pornographer the minute he applied his genius to the subject of love.

"Things haven't changed all that much. I have the other eleven prints from the 'Poem of the Pillow,' but I wouldn't display them here."

"You do!"

"In the next gallery. Would you like to see them?"

Charlotte replied that she would.

"The court order says that I'm allowed to use her rooms and she's allowed to use mine, but we each have one room reserved to ourselves," Paul said as he reached into his pocket for a key. "This is mine—God only knows what's in hers." He opened the door to reveal yet another gallery, at least as extensive as the first. The walls were lined with *shunga.*

Charlotte was amazed. Her Tokyo dealer had kept a few prints hidden away. Here was a whole roomful: print after print by the most famous of the woodblock artists. She wandered among them, marveling at the distortions of the limbs, the exaggerated sizes of the genitals, the lovely patterns of the bedclothes. They were a far cry from "Mount Fuji in Clear Weather."

Harris stood by, his arms crossed smugly over his chest. "What do you think?" he asked. "I want you to know that you are one of the few people to whom I've ever extended an invitation to view my collection. It's a pleasure that I usually reserve for myself." He bowed slightly. "However, how could I do otherwise for the former Okichi?"

Charlotte smiled.

In retrospect, she supposed that her discovery of *shunga* had had a lot to do with the passion of her affair with Linc. For a woman brought up in New England in the twenties and thirties, the *shunga* had been a sexual revelation. To the Japanese, sex was a natural event, and a beautiful one. The *shunga* displayed this casual attitude in the beauty, sensuality, freshness, and even humor with which sex was depicted. But then again, maybe it had been the warm ocean breezes, the forests of camellias, and being young—or younger. Certainly she had never experienced those same feelings again, on screen or off.

"I have thousands of *shunga* in my collection, but only the finest are on display here. There aren't a lot of them, but"— he smiled—"what there is, is choice, to paraphrase one of your colleagues."

"You must have one of the world's most extensive collections," she said.

"It's hard to say. I suspect there are still some sizable collections out there that haven't surfaced yet. Like myself, a lot of collectors have amassed their collections in secret. It's only been in the last twenty years that *shunga* have become even remotely respectable."

It was an odd feeling, being led by Paul through these interconnected rooms in the servants' wing. Charlotte had the impression that each room represented a deeper layer of her host's psyche: preservationist, descendant of Townsend Harris, art collector, and now—the hidden side of the public persona.

He led her over to the left-hand wall. "They're arranged chronologically," he explained. "Starting with the earliest, which dates back to 1660 and ending with the Meiji Restoration."

The earliest prints were lyrical portraits of young couples, most of them done in black and white. By the mid-eighteenth century, the subject matter had become more sexually explicit and the prints were in full color. These were her favorites: they were bold and modern, but still pretty.

"Do you like Shunchō?" asked Paul, as she stopped to admire an elegant series depicting a young couple making love, the bold patterns of their kimonos contrasting with their naked limbs and flesh.

"Yes. He's my favorite."

"I confess to liking the later ones myself," Paul said. "It must be the perverse streak in me."

By contrast with the early prints, the later ones that Paul favored were more abandoned, more primitive, and often more brutal. Even Utamaro had included a rape in his "Poem of the Pillow" album. Charlotte wasn't a prude: the pan from the bed to the window wasn't her style, but neither did she go in for brutality. But she could also see why Paul liked the later prints. They had a sense of force, vigor, and majesty that the earlier prints lacked.

Passing the "Poem of the Pillow" series, Paul paused at the last print. "My masterpiece," he announced. "Hokusai, 1814. A book illustration."

Charlotte knew the print; it was very famous. Famous, and disturbing: a nightmarish sexual fantasy. If the gallery represented the hidden side of Paul's public persona, this print was the dark core of that inner self.

The print depicted a young geisha lying naked on her back on a rocky shore, green with algae. Between her open legs an octopus sucked greedily, its bulging eyes staring over her pale belly, its slimy tentacles enveloping her body. A smaller octopus was attached to her mouth. One of its tentacles was wrapped around her nipple; another, her neck. At her sides, her small, delicate hands gripped the tentacles of the big octopus.

What disturbed Charlotte about the print was the ambivalence of the expression on the geisha's face. Her head was tilted back against the slimy rocks. Her eyes were closed, and her mouth was slightly open, revealing a row of tiny white teeth that gently bit the octopus's tentacle. Was she racked with pain?

Was she swooning in ecstasy? Or was she already a corpse, half-drowned and beyond all feeling?

Her expression summed up the ambivalence of the floating world. For all its freedom and beauty, it was also a harsh and depraved world, a world in which one person fed upon another, a world in which pleasure was fleeting, in which there was little room for tenderness or romance.

What would be left of the geisha when the octopus had had its pleasure with her? Charlotte wondered. Would she be an empty shell, washed up on a rocky shore? It was how she thought of Okichi.

· 4 ·

CHARLOTTE SAT WITH Connie in the living room at Briarcote, Connie and Spalding's house on the Cliff Walk. Briarcote had been built in the twenties on land owned for generations by Spalding's family, and was probably one of the most comfortable houses on the Cliff Walk. Unlike the mansions at the northern end, it was relatively small. But it was elegant: a white-columned Georgian densely furnished with well-worn antiques inherited from Spalding's forebears and a mishmash of *objets d'art* collected from his diplomatic postings around the world. At the rear, a wall of French doors led onto a terrace overlooking the ocean. At this time of day, the setting sun reflecting off the water cast a golden glow over the room, warming the faded Oriental carpets and polished wood surfaces of the furniture.

They were having a drink while they awaited Marianne and Lester, who were staying at a neighbor's guest house. They would all be leaving shortly for the geisha party. Spalding was talking on the telephone in the adjoining library, making last-minute arrangements for the Mikado Ball the next evening.

"I really don't understand it," Connie was saying. "He hasn't spoken to us in five years, and now he's inviting us to his geisha party. Maybe I do understand why he would invite us. After all, Spalding *is* president of the Black Ships Festival. Keeping up appearances and all. But why on earth would he invite Marianne?" Her brow creased in perplexity. "Would you like another, dear?" she asked, noticing that Charlotte had finished her drink.

"Thank you, I would. But don't call Mimi. I'll get it myself," Charlotte replied as she got up to fix herself another Manhattan at the bar tray. As she mixed her drink, she offered her explanation: "Maybe he's trying to get on the good side of the surrogate judge in order to enhance his chances of winning his case," she said. "He said today that the judge had ordered him and Marianne to cease hostilities, or something to that effect."

Her drink mixed, she resumed her seat on a chintz sofa facing the fireplace. Over the mantel hung a nineteenth-century seascape of a view almost identical to the one from the Smiths' terrace. It was called "Twilight on the Seashore."

"Maybe you're right," Connie said. "But that was last March, and he's never made any friendly overtures before this. And to invite Dede too! The thought that Shimoda might ever go to her is enough to . . . I don't know, to make him hysterical or something. He can't have changed that much. Only six weeks ago, he was accusing Lester and Marianne of trying to kill him."

Charlotte raised an winged eyebrow in an expression of skepticism that was her screen trademark, along with her long, leggy stride and her clipped Yankee accent. "Kill him?"

"It was a ridiculous incident. It happened on a Wednesday, the day they switch occupancy. Marianne and Lester had just arrived and Paul was just leaving. They'd been fighting about something: where to hang a painting, I think. Paul wanted it in the foyer, Marianne somewhere else. Instead of driving around back to the carriage house, Lester drove around the driveway and came up behind Paul's car and nudged it from the rear. Paul accused him of attempted murder."

"In court?"

Connie nodded. "Surrogate's Court. The judge didn't pay any attention, of course. The last I heard, Paul had reduced the charge to vehicular assault, though I don't think he ever filed any official charge. It was more like name-calling. Of course, Lester shouldn't have done it, but . . ."

"Lester shouldn't have done what, mother?" said Marianne. She had entered the room with a teenaged girl. Her daughter Dede, Charlotte assumed.

"Tried to kill cousin Paul," Connie replied.

Marianne laughed. "Oh that." She was dressed in a traditional kimono of flowered navy blue silk. On her head she wore a wig in the formal geisha hairstyle, complete with hair ornaments. With her white skin and brown eyes she might have passed for a geisha were it not for her height and for her nose, which was good-sized even by Western standards.

"You look lovely, my dear," said Connie. "You can always depend on Marianne to dress up for the occasion," she continued, addressing Charlotte. "I like to think it comes from having an actress for a mother." She neglected to pay a similar compliment to the teenager, who looked like an Eighth Avenue hooker. She was dressed in skintight black shorts, a skimpy halter top, and high heels.

The girl went over and kissed her grandmother on the cheek.

"Where's Spalding?" asked Marianne. "Lester's out in the car. You know Lester. He doesn't like to be kept waiting."

"He's on the phone. He'll be off in a minute," replied Connie. "Hello, darling," she said, giving the girl a big hug. "I want you to meet an old friend of mine, Charlotte Graham. You've probably seen her in the movies. My granddaughter, Dede Montgomery."

As Dede crossed the room to shake hands with Charlotte, Connie stared disapprovingly at her outfit, and then addressed Marianne: "I hope you're not letting her go to the party dressed like that."

"Yes, Mother, I *am* letting her go to the party dressed like that. One, she's old enough to make her own decisions; two, I don't want to discourage her fledgling sense of fashion experimentation; and three, I don't give a damn what she wears to a party given by cousin Paul."

Connie shrugged.

Dede shook hands politely with Charlotte. She was a petite blonde with blue eyes and a sweet smile. Although her father, whom Marianne had never married, had been a Greek, she had inherited none of his dark good looks. Nor did she resemble her mother, but rather her beautiful grandmother.

"Come sit here next to Nana," said Connie, patting the sofa. Then she turned to Marianne: "We were just speculating about why cousin Paul's invited us to his geisha party," she said as

Dede sat down beside her. "Charlotte's been fraternizing with the enemy. Paul gave her the grand tour this afternoon."

"Did you see the *shunga*?" asked Marianne with a concupiscent leer as she helped herself to a cracker and cheese from the tray on the coffee table.

Charlotte replied that she had.

"Aren't you the lucky one! Naughty cousin Paul keeps them hidden away from the rest of us. His own private obsession. I think it's rather strange to keep a gallery full of pornographic pictures locked up for your own private amusement. I don't think he's even showed them to Nadine. But then, we all know that cousin Paul is a very strange person."

The *shunga* weren't pornography, but Charlotte didn't want to bother explaining that to Marianne. Furthermore, when it came to sexual obsessions, Marianne was hardly one to cast stones.

"Charlotte thinks he might be trying to earn points with the surrogate judge," said Connie.

"Could be. But I have my own theory." She smiled mischievously. "It's based on an accident I heard about when I lived in Africa. Do you want to hear it?"

"Marianne lived in Rhodesia for five years," Connie explained.

Charlotte remembered that particular point of light on Marianne's path to artistic enlightenment—the African nationalist who inspired her "Uhuru" collection. For a while, every socialite in New York was wearing a *dashiki*.

"Zimbabwe, Mother."

"Sorry, dear. Zimbabwe. Anyway, what's your theory?"

"It goes like this: after Zimbabwe achieved independence, the government had all these armed rebels hanging around with nothing to do but get into trouble. Anyway, on the anniversary of independence, the government decided to have a reunion of revolutionaries. All the biggest troublemakers were invited. The reunion was held in a building next to a railroad siding."

"I don't see how a reunion of African guerrillas relates to cousin Paul's party," complained Connie, who over the years had developed a limited tolerance for Marianne's sympathetic accounts of various Third World struggles.

"Wait," said Marianne, raising a hand. "Unbeknownst to the revolutionaries, the government had brought in a railroad car that was loaded to the brim with dynamite."

"They blew them all up?" asked Charlotte.

"To kingdom come, amen. How to achieve governmental stability in one easy step—African politics at its most creative."

"What are you saying, dear?" asked Connie. "That cousin Paul is going to blow us all up?"

"Don't you think it's odd that he's assembling all the most troublesome members of the family in one place?"

"Then why are you going?"

"To see what happens," she replied. "Besides, I want to see the inside of the famed Temple of Great Repose. I've never been in it, or at least not since cousin Paul fished it out of the ocean."

The ride over to Shimoda took only a few minutes. They rode in Lester's big Lincoln. Though Lester had never said anything to that effect, Charlotte suspected that he was offended by Spalding's twelve-year-old Chevy. Spalding belonged to the breed of old rich who considered driving a new car an unseemly display of wealth. He also believed in turning off every light in the house except the one that was in use at the moment. Connie always said his obsession with the lights was the mark of a family that could trace its money back to the days before the invention of electricity. She also accused him of being as tight as a tick. But if Lester didn't think much of Spalding's Chevy, Spalding thought even less of the country-and-western music that blared from Lester's tape deck, serenading the ivied walls and graceful trees of Bellevue Avenue.

Lester dropped them off in front of the house, and then parked the car behind the carriage house. Once he had rejoined them, they were escorted by a young man in a kimono across the expanse of green lawn to the temple. Against the dark gray water and misty sky—it looked as if it was going to rain—the temple looked beautiful and mysterious. The pines had been strung with round red paper lanterns, the symbol of the floating world. As they walked, the boy babbled on about the Black Ships Festival.

"What's your name, young man?" asked Connie, who could always be counted on to be friendly to young people.

"Charlie," the boy replied with a smile.

"Are your parents on the Black Ships Festival Committee?"

"My mother is," he said. "My brother's going to the geisha party tonight. But my mother says I'm too young."

"And who is your mother?"

"Nadine Ogilvie."

Although the boy didn't seem to notice it, Charlotte caught the frown of disapproval that crossed Connie's face. Marianne was less subtle: she nearly fell off her *geta*. Grabbing Dede's wrist, she rushed on ahead.

As they drew near the temple, Charlotte could see how closely it resembled the rustic original in Shimoda. Next to the flagpole there was even a replica of the monument that had been erected after Harris's death, bearing an inscription of an entry from his diary describing the raising of the first American flag: " . . . at two and a half P.M. of this day, I hoist the 'First Consular Flag' ever seen in this Empire. Grim reflections—ominous of change—undoubted beginning of the end. Query—if for the real good of Japan?"

"The change is ominous all right, but not for Japan," Spalding grumbled as they stopped to read the inscription. "Maybe he should have said 'if for the real good of the United States.'" Still smarting from Tanaka's address, he looked as if he might smash a Toshiba radio at any moment, had there been one at hand.

"Better get it out of your system, dear," said Connie. "I think Mr. Tanaka's going to be here tonight."

Spalding harrumphed.

Past the monument, they climbed a stone path lit by the red paper lanterns. Wind chimes hanging in the pines tinkled in the breeze. As they passed the stone lantern that stood guard at the entrance, their host emerged and descended the stairs to the stepping stone at their base. He was wearing an informal brown-and-black-striped kimono. Welcoming them, he bowed deeply in Japanese fashion.

Marianne took the lead. "Hello, cousin Paul," she said as she marched up the stairs past her host, her daughter in tow. "Thank you for inviting us." The tone of her voice was acid.

"I would appreciate it if you would remove your shoes, please," said Paul as he caught sight of Dede's sharply pointed high heels.

"Oh, sorry," said Dede sweetly. But as she paused to take off her spike heels, she was jerked forward by her mother, who made a production out of clomping up the stairs to the gallery, *geta* and all.

Ignoring Marianne's bad manners, Paul turned back to the other guests and welcomed them to the party.

After removing their shoes and leaving them next to those of the earlier arrivals, they donned the one-size-fits-all slippers that had been provided for them, and climbed the stairs to the gallery.

Skirting the building, Paul led them around to the rear of the gallery, which jutted out over the cliff. Several guests had already gathered, among them a Japanese woman who stood at the railing, gazing out to sea. The collar of her kimono dipped backward as if it were going to fall off, revealing the nape of her neck, which was coated with the traditional white makeup of the geisha.

"I'd like you to meet my house guest, Okichi-*mago*," said Paul, introducing the famous geisha who would host the Okichi Day celebrations.

Okichi-*mago* slowly turned around, and then bowed to the new arrivals. Her slightest movement was possessed of infinite grace.

Charlotte was taken aback at her beauty. Like the Okichi of the faded photograph, she had the long, oval face of the classical Japanese beauty. But even four or five generations hadn't obliterated her Caucasian blood. Although she had the high cheekbones of the Oriental, her features were bolder than those of a pure Japanese and she had the round eyes so desired by stylish Japanese women, which they paid plastic surgeons hefty sums to create. They were also of a remarkable color: a rich, luminous sea-green flecked with turquoise, as deep and lustrous as the glaze of the sake cup displayed in the mahogany case inside the house.

"It is a great pleasure for me to meet you," she said. Her American accent was perfect, right down to the *l* in pleasure.

She was made up in formal geisha style: her face was coated with thick white makeup and her heart-shaped mouth was outlined in carmine red. A circle of rouge marked the center of each cheek. Her kimono was one of the most beautiful Charlotte had ever seen. It was made of a shimmery navy blue silk embroidered with gold and silver seashells that were being lightly tossed by waves imprinted in gold leaf. Her brocade obi was tied with a cord of deep celadon-green and fastened with a clip ornamented with a huge baroque pearl. In her hair, she wore a cluster of red camellias.

It was easy to see why she had become the most famous geisha in Japan.

For a moment, they were all slightly dumbstruck. Spalding finally took the lead, greeting her in Japanese. Then he introduced Charlotte: "Okichi, meet Okichi," he said. After Okichi-*mago* had chatted briefly with Charlotte, Paul introduced her to the other new arrivals.

As he introduced her to Marianne, Charlotte noticed Marianne taking in every detail of her appearance—and for once, not critically.

"Your kimono is very beautiful," said Marianne.

"Thank you," Okichi-*mago* replied. "It's very old."

And probably very valuable, thought Charlotte. Beautiful antique kimonos were considered works of art and were fabulously expensive. She wondered whether Tanaka had paid for it.

Once they had all met Okichi-*mago*, Paul introduced them to the other guests, who included Tanaka; Tanaka's assistant, a handsome young man named Takeo Hayashi; and Just-call-me-Ken. Just-call-me-Ken was taking pictures of Okichi-*mago*, who had resumed her place, with Marianne at her side.

Another legacy of Okichi-*mago*'s Caucasian blood was her height. She was as tall as Marianne. In fact, from the back, they looked very much alike: both were tall, both wore navy blue kimonos, and both wore their hair in the smooth, upswept, bouffant style of the geisha.

Connie, too, was intrigued by the beautiful geisha.

"Paul, she's exquisite," she said. "How on earth did you ever find her? Did you *know* that Okichi and Townsend Harris had a descendant?"

"I heard about her two years ago when I was in Kyoto, or rather I heard about a geisha who went by the name of Okichi-*mago* and who was said to be a descendant of Okichi and Townsend Harris's love child. But I thought then that she was just someone trying to take advantage of a famous name. Then I met her . . ." He looked wistful. Charlotte wondered if he was in love with her himself. "It turned out, of course, that she was for real."

"What's her background?" asked the ever-inquisitive Connie.

"She's the great-great-granddaughter of Okichi's daughter. Her mother, who was also a geisha, died in childbirth, and she was raised by a guardian in a geisha house in Kyoto. Beyond that, her background is somewhat mysterious. Her guardian had no money, but she was brought up as if she was from the finest of families. Apparently there was a mysterious benefactor in the background somewhere. She's been trained from her youth in the traditional geisha arts."

"Judging from her English, it looks as if she received a good education in other subjects as well," said Connie.

"Oh yes. She's had a topnotch education. All the best schools. She's one of the few geishas to have attended university."

"Has she ever revealed who her mysterious benefactor was?"

"No. It was always assumed he was her father, whoever he might be. Of course, Mr. Tanaka's been paying the bills in recent years, but I understand that his relationship with her is over now." He looked over at Shawn, who had just arrived, and who had already lured Marianne away from Okichi-*mago*.

He wore a formal kimono jacket, with crests on the shoulders and sleeves, over a long, culotte-like skirt of the type worn by samurai warriors. As before, his hair was pulled back into a topknot.

As Lester seethed in silence, Marianne affixed herself to Shawn's side like . . . Charlotte was reminded of the greedy octopus.

For a while, everyone took in the view, which was magnificent. With the exception of a single pine—which had managed to take root in the face of the cliff, and whose wind-contorted silhouette lent just the right Oriental note—the view of the ocean was unobstructed on all three sides.

Charlotte walked over to the railing. Sixty feet below, the waves lapped gently against the rocks at the base of the cliff.

After a few more minutes of chatting and exchanging business cards—the favorite social pastime of the Japanese—they removed their slippers, and went inside to the temple hall.

Inside, as well, the temple was an exact replica of the Shimoda temple. The hand-hewn beams were made of cypress aged to a warm honey tone, the movable walls of paper stretched on wooden frames. The smell of sandalwood from an incense burner mingled with the sweet smell of the tatami mats.

"It's beautiful," Connie exclaimed as they entered.

One by one, Paul seated the guests on square, flat cushions on either side of a long, low lacquer table with a black and gold checkerboard surface. To Charlotte's surprise, her host steered her to the seat of the guest of honor at the end of the table. "In recognition of Okichi Day," he said.

Charlotte suspected, however, that it was simply the most politic solution. He'd scarcely bestow such an honor on a family member, nor was he likely to bestow it on Tanaka, who had managed to aggravate even a Japanophile like Paul by his anti-American remarks.

In Japanese rooms, the guest of honor was seated in front of the *tokonoma*, an alcove in which a flower arrangement and a scroll painting were displayed. In this case, the theme was camellias: a simple cluster of red camellias in a shallow black ceramic bowl and an ink painting of a single camellia blossom.

"I see that you've put a lot of thought into the *tokonoma*," Charlotte said as he showed her to her seat. "Did you arrange the flowers yourself?"

"Yes," Paul replied. "In honor of Okichi-*mago*." His words had a bitter ring, as if she hadn't lived up to his expectations in some way, though how that could be, Charlotte couldn't imagine.

After thanking him, Charlotte slowly lowered herself into a kneeling position on the cushion. She dreaded the effect the position would have on her joints. Even in her youth, she'd found it hard to maintain for more than a few minutes.

As they were being seated, more guests arrived: Aunt Lillian, looking like an angel in a gossamery taffeta kimono the color of spun sugar; Marianne's brother Billy, who, like Dede, had inherited Connie's good looks; the mayor of Shimoda and his petite wife; and Justin Ogilvie, Nadine's handsome older son.

"This isn't going to be easy," said Connie as Paul showed her to her seat next to Tanaka, who was seated at Charlotte's left. Spalding had already been seated at the other end of the table between the mayor's wife and Tanaka's assistant, Hayashi, where his fluent Japanese would be put to good use.

The seat at Charlotte's right had been assigned to Shawn, who lowered himself effortlessly onto his knees, sitting with his legs slightly apart and his hands resting on his thighs. A position that it would have taken Charlotte several awkward adjustments to achieve was accomplished in one fluid motion.

"I envy you your flexibility," she said. "I always thought wrestlers were supposed to be muscle-bound."

"Not sumo wrestlers. We do exercises to increase our leg flexibility," he replied. "Eighty percent of a sumo wrestler's power is in his legs. Every sumo wrestler does sumo splits every day, which consist of sitting with your legs in a spread-eagle position and bending forward until your chest is on the ground."

"It sounds painful," said Charlotte.

"It is, at the beginning. But you get used to it—you have to. We'll be demonstrating some sumo training exercises at the match tomorrow. Will you be coming?"

"Yes, with Spalding. He's followed your sumo career very closely. He tells me that you've been interested in Japanese culture since you were a teenager. What originally prompted your interest?"

"It's funny that you should ask me that question," he replied. "Actually, my interest was prompted by a rerun of an old movie

I saw on television." He smiled—he had perfect white teeth.
"A movie about Japan."

"*Soiled Dove*?"

Shawn nodded. "I saw it when I was about thirteen, and fell
in love with everything Japanese. Fortunately, my parents supported my interest: they enrolled me in aikido classes, bought
me all kinds of books . . ."

Charlotte wasn't surprised. The lavish production had
launched a mania for Japanese culture. It was hard to
understand now, when there was a sushi bar on every
block, but at that time Japanese culture was still exotic to
most Americans.

"It was also when I saw *Soiled Dove* that I decided Okichi
was the woman for me. Unfortunately, the beautiful actress
who played Okichi was a little too old for me"—he smiled
again—"but I was lucky enough to end up with her suc-
cessor."

They both looked over at Okichi-*mago*. In keeping with her
role as geisha, she knelt to one side of the host's seat at the
head of the table, and slightly behind it.

"I would say you're a lucky man indeed," said Charlotte.
"Pity that the actress who played Okichi was a little too old
for you."

"Pity indeed," said Shawn. "Anyway, I spent my junior
year in high school as an exchange student in Osaka, where
I studied calligraphy. Then, when I went to Yale, I majored
in Asian studies."

"He's also translated several books of classical Japanese
poetry," interjected Marianne, who had plopped herself down
beside Shawn in the seat that Paul had reserved for Aunt
Lillian, forcing him to seat her elsewhere.

Obviously, Connie still hadn't told Marianne that Shawn
was already taken. Or if she had, Marianne was ignoring it.

By ten past seven, all the guests were seated. After sliding
the wooden doors shut, Paul lit the candles in the low wrought-
iron stands on the floor. Then he took a seat at the far end of
the table next to Nadine, his arm resting on a padded armrest.
"I guess we're ready to begin," he announced, clapping his
hands softly. At his summons, a parade of soft-footed Japanese

waiters appeared from behind a screen, bearing hand-towels in little wicker baskets which the guests used to wipe off their hands and faces. The washcloths were followed by lacquer trays with sake and beer. Charlotte was familiar with the geisha party routine from the time she had spent in Japan. Though a squeeze or a pat here and there wasn't unusual, the geisha party wasn't an erotic affair, but rather an opportunity for a wealthy businessman to entertain his friends or clients. It hadn't been common thirty years ago, but, today, Charlotte knew, it wasn't unusual for women to attend geisha parties, as they were this evening.

Once the drinks were poured, the geishas arrived. Sliding the wooden doors aside, they sank onto their knees in a low bow. When they stood up, it was as if the barren room had burst into bloom, so lovely were the colors of their kimonos. Like Okichi-*mago*'s, their lacquered jet-black hair was piled high on their heads and ornamented with various combs, hairpins, and flowers. But unlike Okichi-*mago*, who looked to be around thirty, these geishas were very young. They were also petite: none of them topped five feet.

After greeting the guests, they rose and glided into the room with a rustle of silk. Their names were Keiko, Fujiko, and Sumire. Keiko took a seat between Charlotte and Shawn, kneeling with her feet tucked under her. She was the only geisha, besides Okichi, who spoke English. She had a round face with no chin and tiny slits for eyes, which reminded Charlotte of the face of a tiny white kitten.

"I am very pleased to make the acquaintance of the other Okichi," she said demurely. As she bowed her head, the silver ornaments in her hair flashed in the flickering light from the candles. "May I pour you some sake, please?" Her English was perfect.

"Thank you," said Charlotte, holding out her cup.

Keiko proceeded to pour the sake, each movement practiced to graceful perfection. In contrast to her face, which was whitened with the traditional geisha makeup, her hands were lightly tanned.

"Okichi-*san* is my big sister," said Keiko, in a soft, high-pitched voice. "Perhaps you would like to be my big sister too. I would like very much to have a big sister in America," she added sweetly.

Under the geisha system, each geisha was introduced to the intricate etiquette of this special world by an older and more experienced geisha, her older sister. Ideally the older sister was both mentor and friend.

"I would be delighted," said Charlotte.

Keiko bowed her head again. Then, getting up as gracefully as she had knelt down, she moved on to Shawn and Marianne.

"Tell me," said Marianne as Keiko knelt beside her. "Is it true that the nape of the neck is the most erotic part of a woman's body to a Japanese man, just as the breast might be to an American?" As she spoke, she reached back with one hand and pulled down the collar of her kimono to display her long white neck.

Keiko giggled, revealing a charming set of dimples and an equally charming snaggletooth. She had a high-pitched, girlish giggle. "I'm afraid I don't know the answer to your question. I think you will have to ask a Japanese man."

"How about an American man who lives in Japan?" Marianne replied, staring brazenly at Shawn. "Would he do as well?"

It was ironic that someone whose fashion designs were the epitome of understated style and sophistication could be so coarse. She had all the subtlety and reserve of a kamikaze pilot.

"I wouldn't know," said Shawn curtly. "I'm a leg man myself."

Meanwhile Lester was quietly seething in his seat across the table. Connie was chatting with Tanaka on one side of him and Justin was flirting with Dede on the other, which left Lester with nothing to do but watch Marianne and Shawn.

Once the geishas had poured the drinks, the first course was brought out: a rich, delicious miso soup. After the soup came the appetizers: smoked fish, pickled vegetables, raw oysters, seaweed, and caviar. The foods were served in dainty little dishes that reminded Charlotte of a doll's tea party.

For some time, the guests ate and chatted, the geishas using their considerable skills at drawing people out to get the party off to a good start. Language didn't seem to matter: the geishas who didn't speak English were doing just fine with pantomime and pidgin English.

After the appetizers, the sashimi course was brought out: squid slices in green nests of seaweed strands, sea urchins in cucumber baskets, tuna fillets cut to resemble multi-petaled flowers—all almost too pretty to eat. Then there was another round of beer and sake followed by a baked quail course accompanied by a side dish of two tiny hard-boiled quail eggs.

Once the guests had finished the quail course, Paul gave a discreet signal and the three young geishas glided up to the front of the room. Sumire knelt at the center, Keiko and Fujiko to one side. Keiko held a small drum, and Fujiko a samisen, a long-necked stringed instrument. As Keiko and Fujiko played, Sumire removed a fan from her obi and began to dance.

By now Lester, who was drinking Scotch, had given up being angry—even Marianne's suggestive remarks about the aphrodisiac properties of raw oysters hadn't provoked him— and was getting drunk instead. "Brava, brava," he shouted as Sumire's deft hands transformed the fan into a falling leaf, a rippling waterfall, a branch waving in the wind.

"Brava, brava," echoed the mayor of Shimoda.

After Sumire's dance, Paul tapped a chopsick against a porcelain cup and called for his guests' attention. "Fujiko is now going to sing a classical Japanese love song called 'Rain on the Willows,' about Okichi," he announced.

Kneeling with her samisen, Fujiko proceeded to sing the melancholy song. After the audience had applauded, Paul translated the words for the benefit of the English-speaking guests:

"Rain falls gently on the lighted stream. Is it Okichi who goes in the palanquin along the Shimoda street wet with spring rain? Her tears run down her cheeks like the falling petals of the flowers of the camellia. The sad street song and the willows, weeping, keep company with her heart."

Returning from the front of the room, Fujiko took a seat between Lester and Justin. Justin ignored her—he was still too busy talking with Dede, but Lester made the most of the situation to take his revenge on Marianne. As Fujiko poured his Scotch, Lester made a great show of studying the nape of her neck.

Charlotte had to admit the nape of her neck was intriguing. Like her face, it was covered with white makeup except for three flame-shaped areas that hung down from her hairline like long, thick locks of hair. These were the deep yellow shade of her natural skin.

"I don't know about Japanese men," Lester said loudly as he hung over the back of her neck like a bloodthirsty vampire, nuzzling it with his beaky nose, "but to us Texas men, these napes are pretty damned sexy."

Marianne gave him a dirty look, but Fujiko took no notice at all: she was obviously used to being ogled by drunken men.

By now, in fact, most of the guests were drunk or getting there. The mayor of Shimoda was lunging at Sumire, sending his wife into a fit of giggles. Billy was bragging loudly to Nadine about his boat, as he had all through the song. Even their host was beginning to look a little glassy-eyed.

After the next course, the geishas changed places again. This time, it was Okichi-*mago* who sat between Charlotte and Shawn. First she filled Charlotte's sake cup, then Shawn's. As Shawn filled the geisha's sake cup in return, Charlotte noticed that it was a shallow, wide-mouthed cup of a deep sea-green color.

Okichi-*mago* noticed Charlotte's gaze. "It's a replica of the sake cup that Townsend Harris gave Okichi," she explained. "I always drink from this cup, just as my great-great-great-grandmother Okichi did."

"But how did you know what it looked like?" asked Charlotte. It was supposedly the original that was on display inside the house.

"I saw the movie," Okichi-*mago* replied. She smiled, pressing her lips together to avoid showing her teeth. As a part of the skeleton, the teeth were considered a reminder of death, and it was considered impolite to show them.

Charlotte wasn't bound by any such restraints: she threw back her head and laughed, the deep husky laugh for which she was famous. "You saw the movie!" It struck her as very funny: life imitating art come full circle. Perhaps the sake had gone to her head as well.

"Who else was I to use as a role model?" said Okichi-*mago*.

"Is the idea of wearing camellias from the movie too?"

"Yes," she replied. "I have to admit that I've capitalized shamelessly on the legend. I wouldn't have chosen the camellia myself. It isn't a popular symbol in Japan. Its tendency to drop prematurely from the branch is considered an omen of death. But it was Okichi's symbol, so I wear it."

As they spoke, another parade of dishes was brought out: a palate freshener of fresh vegetables followed by lobster and crabmeat tempura, and then a grilled chicken dish. For a while there was silence as the guests ate the main dishes. Then Tanaka volunteered to sing.

"I am going to sing a short song called a *kouta*," he said as he took his place at the head of the room. "Like Fujiko's song, it is about Okichi." He looked out at Okichi-*mago*, who averted her eyes. He sat with his hands on his knees, the eyes behind his gold-rimmed glasses half-closed. His white hair glowed in the candlelight. He sang the brief song in a pure, clear voice, accompanied by Keiko on the samisen.

As he sang, Charlotte could sense Okichi-*mago* tense up. She thought of Okichi's bitter words from *Soiled Dove*, in which the geisha's lot was likened to the sake cup, which was passed around to be pressed against the lips of any man, no matter how repulsive. "Even wives are like sake cups, sake cups that are carried to the lips only when there is still sake in them," Okichi had said. She wondered if that's how Okichi-*mago* thought of herself.

"Bravo, bravo," cried the mayor of Shimoda as Tanaka finished. They seemed to be the only English words he knew.

After bowing to the audience, Tanaka resumed his seat, and Paul translated. The *kouta* was the song equivalent of the *haiku*, or brief Japanese poem, he explained. The song was called "The Marionette," and the words were simple: "Your heart flip-flops and changes like a marionette. There's someone in the shadows pulling your strings."

As he spoke, Charlotte realized that the song was an indictment of Okichi-*mago*. The person in the shadows pulling the strings was Shawn.

Shawn had sat quietly through the song and the translation. Now he also volunteered to sing. He explained that his song was also a *kouta*; it was called "Evening Rain."

Charlotte could see the surprise among the Japanese guests as Shawn rose and went up to the front of the room. Singing *kouta* was considered an art. Although it was a common avocation of wealthy Japanese businessmen, it was an unlikely one for an American sumo wrestler.

Like Tanaka, Shawn sat on his knees with his hands resting lightly on his thighs. Before starting to sing, he looked over at Okichi-*mago*, who looked up at him lovingly before lowering her eyes into her sake cup.

Shawn's voice was deep and resonant—not beautiful, but compelling. As he sang, Charlotte could see the Japanese guests' look of surprise change to one of admiration. The exception was Tanaka's assistant, Hayashi, who had been making sheep's eyes at Okichi-*mago* all evening, and who clearly resented Shawn.

Shawn provided his own translation: "Rain tonight it seems. Drifting out of the clouds. Even the moon is haloed. Resigned to a drenching, the two of us, moored together. The rendezvous tree."

After Shawn's song, a dessert of Japanese persimmons was served. Then came the fun and games: rock, paper, scissors; paper-folding tricks, magic tricks, fan tricks. But despite the best efforts of the geishas, the evening dragged. The only live wires were Billy and Nadine, the veteran Newport party-goers.

Charlotte attributed the lack of party atmosphere to her host, who seemed dejected. If he'd thrown the party to satisfy the judge, it would explain his lack of enthusiasm. But then why the lavish presentation—the paper lanterns, the arrangement of camellias, the elaborate dinner? It didn't make sense.

As the evening drew to a close, the mood grew even more subdued. The mayor of Shimoda had piped down at last; the sake had finally gotten the better of him. Mori had stopped clicking his camera. The raindrops falling on the shingled roof sounded a monotonous tattoo.

Finally Okichi-*mago* took the stage with her long-necked samisen. "I will sing Okichi's famous song, 'Raven at Dawn,' " she announced. She sang in English in a clear soprano: "Dozing and softly aroused, lost and disheveled through love, the courtesan Urazato wonders: by what strange affinity did I love him so from our first meeting?"

She looked up at Shawn, and then continued: "Ah, now mingled with my sorrow, the sound of that samisen from the second floor. Some time ago it was that Tokijiro stayed on with me, day and night; we embraced each other all the time, we talked together with such joy. My love for him filled my whole body with an unbearable longing. But tonight, what contrast! I know not even where he may be—we two, who can never become man and wife. Oh, for the man I love, my life I'd gladly give. What could I regret, leaving this evanescent life? Oh, what a pitiless floating world!"

As she sang, teardrops drifted down her ghostly white face. Finally she sang the bittersweet refrain: "Sleeves wet with weeping, bosom torn with cares and sad regrets. The past will ne'er return: will drinking bring forgetfulness? Forget and drink—besides that, only to pluck the samisen with muffled fingertips. Once more I hear the raven's cry at dawn: that memory . . . Night deepens on Shimoda's waterfront. Tears falling, drop like red camellias."

The melancholy notes hung in the still air. The rain had stopped. The only sounds were the tinkle of the wind chimes and the splash of the waves against the rocks below. The candles flickered, creating shadow patterns in the rafters. For a few minutes, they sat silently. Then, the waiters reappeared with pickles, tea, and bowls of rice signaling that the party was over.

By the time they had finished with the bowing and leave-taking, it was just eleven. A light wind was blowing the rain clouds away. As they left the temple, a full moon was emerging from behind the clouds. It was surrounded by a luminous ring—a haloed moon.

· 5 ·

CHARLOTTE AWOKE EARLY early the next morning. She checked the hands of the clock on her bedside table: five o'clock. Much too early. She tried to go back to sleep, but it was no use. Seeing that the sky was clear and that it was going to be another gorgeous day, she decided to stroll the Cliff Walk. Strolling the Cliff Walk was something she did every time she came to Newport; it was her way of saying hello to the city-by-the-sea. Besides, she needed to get the kinks out: her hips were stiff from sitting on the floor for so long the night before. She was dressed in five minutes. After grabbing a slice of toast and a glass of orange juice, she was out the door. She joined the Cliff Walk at the foot of Briarcote's lawn. The Cliff Walk ran right across the Smiths' property, as it did the properties of the other Cliff Walk residents. Which is what gave it its appeal: it had often been called the most beautiful walk in the country—the gray-blue ocean on one side, the awesome façades of some of the world's largest mansions on the other. Years ago, some oceanfront property owners had tried to bar the public from the Cliff Walk, but the Supreme Court had ultimately ruled in the public's favor based on an old fisherman's right of way. Briarcote was located at the tail end of the Cliff Walk, which was the least-traveled section. Not many tourists made it to the end of the entire three-mile stretch. It was also Charlotte's favorite: here, the Cliff Walk was a narrow footpath that meandered across low ocean headlands between the head-high banks of wild roses from which Briarcote took its name. As she walked, Charlotte inhaled their wonderful perfume: it was particularly strong this morning, perhaps because of the rain the night before. Past Briarcote, the trail opened out onto rocky ledges. Two doors down was the first of the big mansions at this end: The Waves, a low, rambling English Tudor "cottage" on a rocky promontory. Beyond The Waves was Land's End, the black-shuttered stucco mansion where the writer Edith Wharton had spent her summers. Wharton had loved Land's End. Charlotte could easily see why: from this rocky promontory the ocean seemed to stretch all the way to Ireland. The view was directly east: the rising sun had tinted the horizon a rich orange and cast a wash of peach over the landscape. Past Land's End, the path curved around a promontory at Rough Point, where an elderly heiress lived in seclusion in a Gothic mansion. The high walls surrounding the property, topped with matted coils of barbed wire, forced Charlotte to walk on the rocks below. She loved the rhythm of walking on the rocks: the process of looking for the next place to put her foot cleared her brain. As she walked, she thought of her husband, Jack Lundstrom, from whom she'd been separated for several years. He had been attracted by her glamor, as she had been by his worldly success, but despite their best intentions, the marriage hadn't worked out. As the widower of a traditional wife, he'd found it too hard being Mr. Charlotte Graham. But they'd remained on good terms, and neither of them had filed for divorce. Recently she'd had the feeling that he wanted to get back together, and she suspected Connie and Spalding, who were old friends of his as well as of hers, of some kind of plot. She had half-expected him to show up on Briarcote's doorstep (she could just hear Connie: "What a coincidence," she would exclaim, "Charlotte is visiting us too!"), but so far it hadn't happened. She wasn't sure if the prospect made her happy or not.

Beyond Rough Point, the ocean became more tame and the coastline curved in upon the land to form a little bay. Instead of a rough path across a rocky shore, the path here was paved with asphalt. It was this section of the Cliff Walk that was most favored by tourists, though so far Charlotte had seen no one else other than a fisherman at Rough Point. No longer forced to mind her step, she was free to take greater notice of the architecture. The houses here were even more grand. The first mansion on this stretch was Marble House, the ostentatious marble palace built by William K. Vanderbilt. Taking her cue from Townsend Harris, Mrs. Vanderbilt, who by that time had become Mrs. Belmont, built a Chinese teahouse at the edge of the cliff, which was the scene of suffragist rallies in the early part of the century. "Brace up, my dear," was the oft-quoted advice she had once given a dejected suffragette. "Pray to God. *She* will help you." After Marble House came Beechwood, where Mrs. Astor had held the parties for her imaginary guests, and then Rosecliff, a replica of the Grand Trianon, Louis XIV's pleasure palace at Versailles. After this peaceful stretch came the most dramatic section of the Cliff Walk. The low shoreline of smooth, greenish-gray rocks gave way to craggy, dark gray bluffs that reminded Charlotte of Bermuda. Rivulets of clear, cold water trickled over the edge of the cliff to the ocean below. The sun was higher in the sky now: it was beginning to burn the dew off the wildflowers that clung to the cliff's edge. On the sea, flocks of birds flitted over the wavetops. Rounding a turn after a series of Victorian cottages, she found herself on the final section of her walk. Though the Cliff Walk continued for some distance, she would turn off at Narragansett Avenue. As the temple at Shimoda came into sight, she found herself thinking about the geisha party. She had left with the feeling of business uncompleted. Paul must have had a purpose in giving the party, but whatever it was, it hadn't been realized. Marianne had said she was attending because she wanted to see what would happen. Nothing had happened. As American businessmen who were dragged to geisha parties in Japan often complained, it was a total bore. A lot of people had gotten mildly drunk, and that was all.

Just past the turn was The Breakers, which looked oddly deserted in the morning stillness. Usually the huge pile of limestone was crawling with tourists. After The Breakers came Edgecliff, the Japanese-owned mansion that would be the scene of the Mikado Ball. She was nearly at the end of her walk. As she crossed the lawn at Edgecliff, she came upon the first sign of life aside from the fisherman at Rough Point: it was Miako, Paul's frisky Japanese spaniel. He was running toward her at full speed. Reaching her, he began barking furiously. Then, still barking, he ran ahead, and then back. And again: ahead, and then back. He wanted Charlotte to follow. Charlotte complied: she was going in that direction anyway. The temple stood above her, on top of the Cliff Walk. When Paul Harris had pulled it out of the ocean, he had built a tunnel under it to keep the Cliff Walk traffic out of sight. It wasn't a unique idea: several other Cliff Walk property owners had done the same thing. Charlotte couldn't blame them: although the Cliff Walk traffic at Briarcote was light by comparison, Connie and Spalding were still reluctant to sit out on their terrace because they didn't like being on display.

Just past Edgecliff, Miako stopped at the head of one of the pebbly channels that had been carved out of the cliff by water runoff, and began barking again. Charlotte followed him down the channel, which was overgrown with underbrush. It ran sideways across the cliff toward a promontory, and then turned downward. As she rounded the promontory, Charlotte saw what Miako had been barking about. She found herself looking out over a small shingled cove that stretched from the promontory above her to the one on which the temple was perched. At the far end of the cove, a body lay on the shingle beach at the foot of the temple. From this distance, it looked like an elegant porcelain Japanese doll. But, she realized with alarm, it wasn't a doll, it was a geisha. Following Miako, she scrambled down the channel to the foot of the cliff, hoping that whoever it was, wasn't dead, only injured. A few minutes later, she had crossed the cove. Even from some distance, she could tell that the geisha was dead, but it wasn't until she got up close that she saw it was Okichi-*mago*.

She was lying on her back, slightly twisted to one side, with her knees bent. The tide had covered her lower legs. She was still wearing the seashell kimono; the clams, whelks, and periwinkles seemed to shimmer under the pale pink surface of the water. Catching sight of her broken ankles, Charlotte realized with a pang what had caused her death. Glistening white shards of bone had punctured the heels of her white socks. She had jumped from the temple gallery, landing feet first. Stepping over a piece of driftwood, Charlotte moved closer, and touched a hand lightly to the dead geisha's face. Her skin was ice-cold and her jaw was stiff: rigor mortis had already begun to set in, indicating that she had been dead for some time. Charlotte shivered; the balmy air suddenly seemed cold and malevolent. Though the shards of bone protruding from her heels were grotesque, there was surprisingly little blood. Maybe it had been washed away. Her left hand lay under her body and her right was stretched out. Lying on the rocks near her right hand were several broken pieces of green porcelain—the sake cup. Charlotte also noticed that the lustrous surface of the baroque pearl on her obi clasp had been scraped off. But apart from the broken cup, her obi clasp, and her ankles, there was no other evidence of a fall. The surface of her white makeup was cracked from the dampness, but the rest of her makeup was still perfect. She was as beautiful in death as she had been in life; even her camellias were still fresh.

But in spite of the neatness of the body, Charlotte was shocked at its appearance. There was something about it that was deeply disturbing, apart from its being dead. Charlotte had seen dead bodies before. What was it? Her head was tilted back and her mouth was open, exposing small white teeth that next to the porcelain white of her makeup looked more yellow than they actually were. Her sea-green eyes stared vacantly at the dawn sky. The seaweed, that was it! Entwined around her long, white neck was a slimy greenish-brown filament of ribbon weed. The seaweed looked like the tentacle of an octopus.

The body reminded Charlotte of the geisha in the ghoulish Hokusai print.

She remembered her sense of unfulfilled expectation from the night before. Was this what fate had had in store? The anticipated climax of the evening's events? Tomorrow would be the hundredth anniversary of the day on which Okichi had plunged into the sea. She remembered what Okichi-*mago* had said about the camellia being considered an omen of death because of its tendency to drop prematurely from the branch. She also remembered Okichi-*mago*'s tears as she sang the ballad about the pitiless floating world. "Ah, for the man I love, my life I'd gladly give—what could I regret, leaving this evanescent life?" It must not have been long afterward that she had jumped; she was still wearing the seashell kimono.

But Okichi had had good reason to commit suicide. What was Okichi-*mago*'s? Charlotte checked her watch; it was just after six. She would have to notify the police. Leaving the body as it was—she had learned that much from police work—she clambered back up the cliff, hanging onto the vines that clung to the lichen-studded rocks. Miako followed at her heels. She would call the police from Shimoda. She was about to cut through the Edgecliff property out to Ochre Point Avenue, when Miako showed her a shortcut. After charging between the posts of the balustrade and across the lawn, he disappeared through a hole in the hedge between the two properties. Charlotte followed, and found herself emerging at the rear of the Shimoda property, near the temple. Though she knew she should notify the police, she found herself being drawn to the temple. She wondered whether Okichi-*mago* had left a note, and if so, what it said. After crossing the lawn, she climbed the stone path to the temple. The tinkling of the wind chimes hanging from the pines sounded otherworldly in the morning stillness. The temple looked just as it had the night before except for a single pair of unclaimed shoes on the stepping stone at the foot of the stairs: Okichi-*mago*'s delicately rounded black-lacquered *geta*.

The morning dew was still wet on the polished boards as Charlotte made her way around the building to the rear of the gallery. The spot from which Okichi-*mago* had jumped was on the south side, near the old pine tree whose branches stretched out so splendidly over the face of the cliff. Peering over the railing, she could see the body far below. A fresh scar on the wooden surface of the railing marked the spot where the pearl on Okichi-*mago*'s obi clasp had scraped against it as she went over. Turning away from the railing, Charlotte took off her shoes and entered the temple hall. The room had been cleaned up, but otherwise it was unchanged. The only evidence that a party had taken place there was the indentations that Dede's heels had made in the tatami matting. And the smell: the sharp odor of stale beer hung in the air along with the faded scent of sandalwood incense, and . . . something else. It was the acrid smell of a charcoal fire. Looking around again, Charlotte noticed that the square

tatami-covered board that concealed the sunken charcoal pit
had been removed. A straw basket of charcoal sat on the
floor next to it. Circling the low, lacquered table, she walked
over to the pit. Arranged on the floor next to it were three
objects: a green-glazed sake cup, and a gold lacquer comb and
mirror, both inlaid with a camellia design in mother-of-pearl.
Charlotte recognized them as Okichi's mementos from the
display cabinet inside the house. Inside the lacquered frame
of the charcoal pit were the remains of a fire: a few blackened
pieces of charcoal on a bed of white ashes. Among the remains
was a singed business card with Japanese characters. Picking
it carefully out of the ashes, she turned it over. The other side
read: "Hiroshi Tanaka, president and chief executive officer of
Yoshino Electronics, Inc."

It was a re-staging of Okichi's death, right down to the
business card. Charlotte remembered the scene from *Soiled
Dove*: carefully laying the fire on rocky headlands, then burning her few possessions and her personal papers, including
Harris-*san*'s business card. Setting out the sake cup, the comb,
and the mirror. And finally, plunging off the edge of the cliff.
In the final scene her things are discovered by a village official.
"What does it mean?" asks a baffled onlooker. "The comb
is the symbol of leave-taking, the mirror is the symbol of
the soul," the official replies. "These symbols mean Okichi
has left us forever." Pan to the waves lapping against the
rocks at the foot of the cliff. "What does it mean?" Charlotte asked herself, just as the baffled onlooker had asked
in the movie. Why had Okichi-*mago* burned Tanaka's business card? Had she taken her life because she was ashamed
at having humiliated the man who was her patron? If so,
why hadn't she stayed with him in the first place? And why
make such a production of her suicide? She remembered what
Okichi-*mago* had said about capitalizing shamelessly on the
Okichi legend. Was she taking advantage of the legend even
in death? Leaving the brazier, Charlotte went back out to
the gallery to retrieve her shoes. Then she headed toward
the house, Miako trotting along purposefully beside her, his
agitation allayed now that his mission was completed. As she
walked along the gravel path, she imagined the sensation

the Japanese scandal sheets would make of Okichi-*mago*'s suicide. In Japan, there was a long history of appreciation for suicide as an art form. It was said that the Japanese were as obsessed with suicide as Americans were with murder. She thought of the novelist who had committed ritual disembowelment after an impassioned appeal for the revival of Japan's ancient heroic spirit. According to the ritual, a second was supposed to have stepped in and chopped off his head with a sword, but the second had botched it, and a third had finally had to finish the job. It was forty minutes or more before he finally died. At least Okichi-*mago* had had style enough to succeed. For that matter, her death had style enough to land her a permanent place in the annals of Japanese suicide.

As Charlotte approached the rear of the house, Paul emerged from the front parlor. He was wearing a cotton kimono and holding a mug of coffee. He awaited her on the long wisteria-shaded veranda with a look of bewilderment.

"What is it?" he asked as she drew near, seeing from her manner that something was wrong.

"It's Okichi-*mago*," Charlotte replied. "She's dead. I found her body lying down on the rocks below the temple a few minutes ago. It looks as if she jumped from the gallery."

The blood drained from his face. "Are you sure it's her?" he asked. "Maybe it was one of the others." His brown eyes searched her face, not wanting to see the truth.

"I'm sure," she replied softly. "She still had the camellias in her hair. Her ankles were broken in the fall. I'm very sorry," she added.

His hand shaking, he set his coffee mug down on a table, and then seemed to lurch from one piece of furniture to another, like a drunk hanging onto the wall of a building. Finally he headed over to a hydrangea bush at the end of the veranda and quietly threw up.

Charlotte took a seat and waited. His vomiting was probably as much hangover as it was shock.

After a few minutes, he returned and slumped into an old-fashioned wrought-iron garden chair. For a few minutes, he stared quietly at the floor. Then his face crumpled in sorrow, and he began to cry. Wrenching sobs racked his small frame. Sitting at his ankles, Miako whined in sympathy.

"Can I get you a drink of water?" she asked once he had stopped.

He shook his head. "When?" he asked.

"I'm not sure. I think it must have been last night, after the party." She waited for his response, but there was none. He stared blankly at the floor, his hands clasped tightly between his knees. "We'll have to notify the police," she continued. "May I use your phone?"

He waved an arm vaguely toward the inside of the house.

Charlotte found the phone on an antique desk in the front parlor—Paul's parlor—and, after making the call, rejoined him on the veranda. He was still staring blankly at the floor.

"Someone will also have to notify the family," she said. "I understand from what you said last night that there's a guardian in Japan."

"Yes," he said quietly. He sat motionless for a moment. Then he shook his head, and started to cry again.

He seemed oddly affected for a man who barely knew her. But then, people often reacted to death, especially sudden death, in strange ways. Charlotte had seen more than one family become unhinged in such circumstances. If he was in love with her, as everyone else seemed to be . . .

She sat quietly, looking out at the sea, which was framed by the wisteria vines. Although most of the flowers had already bloomed, a few tardy blossoms lingered, and bumblebees hovered around the long, fragrant flower clusters.

"Did she leave a note?" he asked after a while.

"Not a note exactly." She described finding Okichi's mementos and the half-burned business card. "I thought she might have been distraught over the scandal involving Mr. Tanaka," Charlotte said. "Do you have any ideas?"

He shook his head.

In the distance, they could hear police sirens wailing.

After lunch, Charlotte set off with Spalding in his old Chevy down Bellevue Avenue. They were heading to the Newport Casino, the scene of a Meet the Sumos reception, which would be followed by the sumo tournament, the second in the two-day exhibition match. Connie had elected to stay at home. In her opinion, watching a sumo match was like watching "two elephants wrestling each other to death." Bellevue Avenue was slow going: on weekends—starting on Friday afternoons—Newport was crowded with day-trippers and weekenders who came to go to the beach or to visit the half a dozen or more mansions that were open to the public. Long lines of people waited for admission to Marble House, Beechwood, and Rosecliff. Ahead, a tour guide blared out anecdotes about Newport's Gilded Age over a public address system to a busload of tourists. It reminded Charlotte of Beverly Hills. As the tour guide described the dogs' dinner, Charlotte and Spalding talked about Okichi-*mago*. Now that she was dead, Spalding had spent the latter part of the morning conferring with the other members of the Black Ships Festival Committee on what to do about the Afternoon of Japanese Culture scheduled for the next day. Finally they had decided that the show must go on: the other geishas would perform without her. Charlotte had been drafted to take her place as mistress of ceremonies. With the practical matters out of the way, Spalding was now trying to explain Okichi-*mago*'s suicide in terms of the cultural concept of *giri*.

"*Giri* means obligation," he explained. "To the Japanese, no act is ever an isolated event; every favor must be repaid in kind. To fail to fulfill one's obligation is the worst sin a self-respecting Japanese can commit. The whole country runs on the principle of *giri*: *giri* to your boss, *giri* to your family, *giri* to your business clients."

"And Okichi-*mago* failed to fulfill her obligation to Tanaka?"

"She certainly did," Spalding replied. "Tanaka was her *hanna*, her patron. He showered her with magnanimous gifts, as he was expected to. He set her up in her own teahouse. She in turn was supposed to reserve her sexual favors for him; or, if she did take a lover, to be discreet about it. Not only was she indiscreet, she was practically shouting about her affair from the rooftops."

"The press was shouting about it from the rooftops," Charlotte corrected. She spoke as one who was sensitive to having her private affairs splashed across the front pages of the scandal sheets.

Spalding shrugged.

"I'll grant you that she was indiscreet, but at least she was honest," Charlotte continued. "Obviously she must have been conscience-stricken about continuing to accept Tanaka's patronage in the face of her relationship with Shawn. Instead of carrying on in secret as someone else might have done, she accepted the responsibility for her actions and publicly severed her relationship with Tanaka. I think that's commendable."

"She may have thought she was behaving responsibly and you may have thought she was behaving responsibly, but to most Japanese, she was being irresponsible, disloyal, and selfish. That's why she was vilified in the press. To the Japanese, style is more important than substance: it didn't matter that she had a relationship with Shawn as long as she kept up the *appearance* of loyalty to her patron."

"She made Tanaka lose face."

Spalding nodded.

"But Spalding, he didn't seem to me to be acting like a humiliated man. Did he to you? In fact, he struck me as a man who was handling the situation with tact and sophistication, even humor."

"Which is what made the burden of her obligation to him all the greater. If he'd publicly denounced her or publicly attacked Shawn, she would have lost face in return, and they would have been returned to an equal footing. But he behaved like a perfect gentleman." Spalding harrumphed. "I wish he'd displayed the same degree of tact when he gave his talk at the opening ceremonies."

"His only reproach was the marionette song," Charlotte said, remembering Tanaka's high, clear voice singing the song about the marionette whose heart "flip-flops and changes."

"Exactly," said Spalding. "Not only did he behave like a perfect gentleman, he behaved with impeccable style."

"Giving her no out but to take her own life, leaving his half-burned business card as the only clue to the reason why."

"Yes. To atone for her debt of honor. A modern young

woman wouldn't even consider atoning for her disgrace in such a situation—look at the bar hostess who was blackmailing a cabinet minister to keep their relations a secret—but geishas in general, and Okichi-*mago* in particular as one of Japan's foremost geishas, are different. The world they inhabit is an anachronism; they are the guardians of traditional values."

" 'To die with honor, when it is impossible to live with honor,' " said Charlotte. She explained: "The words that Butterfly reads before she takes her life: the words inscribed on the blade of her knife." Charlotte had played Butterfly in the screen version of Puccini's opera. After *Soiled Dove*'s success, she'd played Oriental women in a whole string of films. That was the Hollywood recipe for success: if it worked, repeat it *ad nauseam*.

"Ah yes, another story based on the Okichi legend," said Spalding.

As they rode, Charlotte looked out the window. She never tired of this lovely avenue. But this afternoon she saw a sight that disturbed her. The enormous fern-leafed beeches in front of a sprawling Victorian were being cut down. Their beautiful sculptured gray trunks bore huge white scars where limbs had been amputated in preparation for felling the entire tree. They looked like mutilated bodies.

"Spalding, why are they cutting down those trees?"

"Sickening, isn't it?" he said. "I can hardly bear to look at it. It's Nadine Ogilvie's property, Strawberry Lodge. She's selling off a lot on Bellevue Avenue. She's planning to move the entrance to her house from Bellevue Avenue to the side street. Several others have done the same thing. They make money from selling off the lot, plus they save on their real estate taxes as a result of no longer having Bellevue Avenue frontage."

"What a shame," she said.

"Yes. I'd rather have seen her sell off the entire property to someone who could afford to keep it up, and move to a smaller place. But people will do anything to hang on to their houses on Bellevue Avenue, even if they have to enter from a side street. They sell off a lot, they sell off the furnishings, they fail to keep the place up, until eventually all that's left is a big run-down house on a tiny lot with nothing of substance left in it."

"You'd think the developer would have the good sense to at least try to save the trees," said Charlotte.

"Several have tried, but it doesn't work. They start to die when they dig the foundation hole. Beeches are shallow-rooted, which makes them very sensitive to any ground disturbance. The Preservation Society's trees are dying too, either from old age or from ground compression caused by the footsteps of all the tourists. They have a program to replace them with young trees, but it will be a long time before they reach full maturity."

"What does Paul think about Nadine's cutting down the trees?" asked Charlotte. She imagined that an ardent preservationist like Paul would be horrified at the prospect.

"I don't know," replied Spalding. "As you know, Connie and her cousin aren't that close," he added, with his usual talent for understatement. "But I've heard from other members of the Preservation Society board that it's been a source of contention between them."

Charlotte nodded. She would miss these graceful trees whose airy, delicate foliage turned Bellevue Avenue into a leafy bower. Nadine's trees were only three or four among dozens, but their absence would make a difference.

As they rode, Charlotte's thoughts turned back to the idea of *giri*. It was a concept that she still had trouble with, though it helped to think of it as an informal system of IOU's.

"Let me see if I've got this straight," asked Charlotte.

"What's that?" asked Spalding.

"Oh, *giri*," she said. "I'm back on that. If Okichi-*mago* committed suicide because of her obligation to Tanaka, and if she was forced to do so because of her affair with Shawn, then what kind of an obligation does that impose on Shawn?" she asked. "And what does Shawn then have to do to free himself of the burden of that obligation? Is he obligated to redress the balance by taking his own life because their affair forced her to take hers?"

"You're getting the hang of it. The answer is 'maybe.' The ramifications and counter-ramifications of *giri* can get pretty Byzantine, to say the least."

"But if Okichi-*mago*'s commitment to tradition was so great that she took her life on account of it, why didn't she conduct her affair in secret, as you suggested that tradition dictates she should have?"

"Ah, now you're getting into another aspect of Japanese culture: *ninjo*, or the demands of the tenderer feelings. She was carried away by *ninjo*, by love. The conflict between *giri* and *ninjo* is a major theme in Japanese literature. The story usually involves the illicit love between a geisha and a young actor or sumo wrestler. Sumo wrestlers in particular. The worlds of the geisha and the wrestling ring have always been closely associated."

"Why's that?"

"The geisha and the sumo wrestler lead very similar lives. They both have an appreciation for the traditional arts. They both serve long apprenticeships, and they both undergo arduous training. They both live in a closed society, and they both are expected to behave in a particular fashion. Also, they are both readily identifiable from their appearance."

Charlotte hadn't thought about it before, but he was right.

"They even share some aspects of technique," said Spalding, looking over at her with a twinkle in his eye. "They say the forty-eight traditional winning techniques in sumo correspond to the forty-eight positions of love."

Charlotte arched an eyebrow. Then she giggled as she thought of a four-hundred-pound sumo wrestler contorting himself into some of the positions she had seen depicted in Paul's *shunga*.

"That's why their romance has gotten so much attention in the press. To the Japanese, they're larger than life: they could be Romeo and Juliet or Tristan and Isolde."

"Somehow I have the feeling that these love stories don't have a happy ending," said Charlotte, thinking again of *Madame Butterfly*.

"You're right. They usually end like *Romeo and Juliet*, as a matter of fact," Spalding replied. "With a double suicide. Caught between *giri* and *ninjo*, the lovers choose to be reborn together in another life."

At the end of the string of mansions, Spalding turned the car into a shopping-center parking lot across the street from the casino. In a city that was being taken over by day-trippers and the ice cream stands and T-shirt shops that catered to them, the casino was a relic of a gracious time when people still had the leisure to spend an entire summer doing nothing. Originally built as a country club—it had once been considered the most exclusive private club in the nation—it was a long, rambling structure sheathed in weathered wood shingles and adorned with a multitude of porches, gables, and verandas. The former club rooms on the upper story were now the home of the International Tennis Hall of Fame and Museum. Considered the masterpiece of the renowned architectural firm of McKim, Mead, and White, it was a combination of Victorian charm and Oriental elegance. If the Newport of the Gilded Age could be compared to the floating world, then the casino was its most popular teahouse, the center of its social life.

"Spalding, what does *Tojin* Okichi mean?" asked Charlotte as they headed across the street to the casino.

He frowned. "Where did you hear that?"

"At the geisha party," she replied. "I heard Hayashi whisper it—actually, it seemed more like he hissed it—into Okichi-*mago*'s ear as the party was breaking up. It seemed to upset her."

"It's a derogatory term for a Chinese—we would translate it as *chink*—but in the larger sense it applies to all foreigners. Before Perry opened Japan, the only foreigners the Japanese were familiar with were the Chinese."

"But Okichi-*mago* wasn't a foreigner; at least, she didn't have enough foreign blood in her veins to make a difference."

"No. But she consorted with a foreigner. *Tojin*-Okichi or 'Foreigner's Okichi' was one of the taunts that the townspeople hurled at Okichi because of her relationship with Harris. At that time, foreigners were ranked on the same level as animals. Some Japanese don't think any better of foreigners today."

Charlotte nodded. She remembered the stricken expression on Okichi-*mago*'s beautiful face.

· 6 ·

THE CASINO'S STREET façade was relatively simple—the ground floor housed chic boutiques and galleries—but once one passed under the green awning and through the arched, wood-paneled passageway, one was in another world, another century. It was on the uneven brick sidewalk outside this dim passageway that the townspeople had once gathered to catch a view of the summer colonists taking their afternoon tea on the Horseshoe Piazza. Rubber plants, these stargazers were called. A few rubber plants were planted there now, trying to decide whether or not to pay their admission to the International Tennis Hall of Fame. The passageway opened onto an oval courtyard of smooth, green grass surrounded by one- and two-story piazzas enclosed by latticework screens pierced by round openings, like the moon gate in a Japanese wall. A fat clock tower bulged near the entrance, the white clock face contrasting with the weathered shingling. Beds of roses edged with boxwood surrounded the courtyard, and baskets of brightly colored flowers hung from the piazzas. Over all grew sheaths of old ivy. Beyond the courtyard lay the working—or rather, playing—part of the casino: a dozen or more immaculate grass tennis courts, an indoor court for the sixteenth-century game of royal tennis (one of only a handful in the United States) and a theatre. Although Charlotte had been there before, the place always struck her anew with its magic. It was as if this vivid oval of emerald green was the heart of the floating world that was Newport. On the green, a croquet match was in progress. In addition to housing the International Tennis Hall of Fame, the casino was the home of the New England Regional Croquet

Association. Players in starched white trousers carefully lined up their shots while diners in the adjoining restaurant looked on.

The Meet the Sumos reception was being held on the Horse-shoe Piazza. Walking down a gravel path at the side of the courtyard, Spalding and Charlotte climbed the stairs to the U-shaped piazza, where members of the Black Ships committee and other guests were mingling with the sumo wrestlers, who were readily identifiable by virtue of their size, their bathrobe-like kimonos, and their distinctive topknots. One sumo wrestler who wouldn't be present was Shawn. He had been discouraged from attending because he might hear about Okichi-*mago*'s suicide. Her death was being kept from him until after the match.

At the head of the stairs, they were greeted by an extraordinary man. He was at least six foot four and must have weighed four hundred pounds. He wasn't handsome—his deeply lined face was framed by long, bushy sideburns and several layers of fleshy chins, and his dark skin was pockmarked by a bad complexion—but he had a warm, infectious smile. Unlike the other sumo wrestlers, he was formally dressed in a kimono jacket over a culotte-like skirt.

As Charlotte looked on, he enveloped Spalding in a bear hug. Spalding introduced him as Lani Kanahele, the Hawaiian sumo wrestler whom Spalding had written the book about and the first American to make it big in sumo. Despite their disparate backgrounds, the two men had a similar mission: the promotion of sumo wrestling. During his years in Japan, Spalding had developed a love of sumo, and was considered one of the foremost Western authorities on the sport.

Spalding's face beamed: he was obviously very fond of this amiable bear of a man. "Lani retired several years ago to serve as the international good will ambassador for the Japan Sumo Association. His job is promoting the internationalization of sumo," he explained. "This tournament is his baby, one of the first professional tournaments to be held on American soil. We're hoping to make it an annual event, aren't we, Lani?"

"Yes, we are," the wrestler agreed.

"If it weren't for Lani, I doubt we'd be having a sumo tournament here today," Spalding continued. "Lani's the one who made all the arrangements from the Japanese end. And you can take it from me that arranging to import thirty-four of Japan's top professional sumo wrestlers wasn't easy."

"Nor was it easy from this end," said Lani. His voice was surprisingly soft for so large a man. "Spalding made all the arrangements for room and board. And sumo wrestlers can pack away a lot of food. The meals have been supplied by the local restaurants, and they've been very good."

Charlotte had seen an account in the local newspaper of one meal: five courses, several tubs of rice, and as much as twenty cans of soda—per sumo wrestler. To say nothing of beer, sake, plum wine, and tea.

"The food wasn't a problem," Spalding replied. "It was the damned dirt. We had a devil of a time finding fifteen metric tons of just the right kind of clay for the ring. To say nothing of getting it here."

"Is it unusual for sumo wrestlers to travel outside Japan?" asked Charlotte.

"It used to be," Lani replied. "Five years ago, you could only see sumo in Japan. But it's becoming more international. The Japanese would like to see it become an Olympic sport. In the last few years we've held exhibition tournaments in Korea, Brazil, Argentina, Mexico, France, Germany, Great Britain, and, of course, the United States."

"I'm afraid I don't know much about sumo," Charlotte said.

"That's okay, most Americans don't. But it's easy to catch on. The goal is simply to get your opponent out of the ring or down on the ground. Out or down—it's that basic. Whoever steps out of the ring or touches the ground with any part of his body except the bottoms of his feet loses. It's very fast—the average bout only lasts thirty seconds."

"But sumo is much more than just wrestling," said Spalding. He was speaking in part for the benefit of a reporter who had appeared at Lani's side, notebook in hand.

"Oh yes," Lani replied. "The history of sumo goes back two thousand years. It's deeply rooted in the Japanese national religion, Shinto. Originally sumo was a fertility ritual. As you'll see, elements of Shinto still figure heavily in sumo. It's the ritual that appeals to Westerners. Except maybe for the lighting of the Olympic torch, Western sports are pretty devoid of ritual."

The reporter introduced himself as being from a local newspaper. By now, a knot of listeners had gathered around Lani. The other sumo wrestlers stood nearby in little clusters, isolated by their lack of English. Among the listeners was Marianne, Lester at her side.

"Is that the reason for the peculiar hairstyle?" the reporter asked.

"The *chommage*," said Lani. "Yes, the *chommage* is worn by *rikishi* . . ."

"*Rikishi* is the preferred name for a sumo wrestler; it means strong warrior," Spalding interjected.

Lani continued: "It's worn by *rikishi* in the top two divisions. Wearing the *chommage* is synonymous with being a sumo wrestler. The *chommage* was once the universal hairstyle of Japanese men, but today only *rikishi* still wear it. It's a symbol of a way of life in which the *rikishi* follows a strict code of conduct and ethics similar to the samurai's code of *bushido*."

"A *rikishi* can never go incognito the way even a movie star"—Spalding nodded at Charlotte—"or a politician sometimes can. The *chommage* always identifies him as a *rikishi*, and as long as he's wearing it, he's expected to behave in accordance with the sumo creed."

"The first sentence of which is 'Carry yourself with pride at all times because you are a *rikishi* in Japan's national sport of sumo,' " Lani added.

Charlotte thought of Shawn's dignified responses to Marianne's advances. Anyone else would have shown annoyance—if they hadn't been interested, that is—but Shawn had behaved like a perfect gentleman.

"In fact," Spalding continued, "the *chommage* is so important to the *rikishi* that one of the few forbidden methods of attacking your opponent is by pulling his hair. If a *rikishi* pulls his opponent's hair, he automatically loses. Likewise, fans are permitted to touch the *rikishi*—it's a way of vicariously sharing in his power—but they may not touch his hair."

"Ordinarily, the *chommage* is tied in a topknot and then pulled forward, but for tournaments, the *chommage* of *rikishi* in the two top divisions is fanned out into the shape of a gingko leaf," Lani added.

Charlotte noticed that the sumo wrestlers at the casino wore their hair differently from the way in which Shawn had worn his at the party. The front part was fanned out stiffly, almost like a hair ornament. She also observed that Marianne was taking note too; it was an easy bet that the models in her next big show would be wearing their hair in the gingko-leaf style.

"Why don't you have a *chommage*?" the reporter asked Lani, whose dark brown hair was combed straight back.

"My *chommage* was cut off in my retirement ceremony," he replied. He proceeded to describe the day-long ceremony before an audience of twelve thousand fans in which his *chommage* was cut off strand by strand by the hundreds of people who had been part of his sumo career, from the lowliest worker to the master of his sumo stable.

Producing a wallet from the leather pocketbook that hung from his wrist, he showed the reporter a photo. "This is my stable master making the final cut," he said. He then showed the reporter another picture. "And this is my *chommage*." The photo showed a shiny *chommage* dressed in the gingko-leaf style displayed on a red velvet cloth in a Plexiglas box.

Charlotte thought it was grotesque-looking. Had the skin been attached, it could have been mistaken for an Indian scalp.

"It was the saddest day of my life," Lani continued, still speaking of his retirement ceremony. "But I wasn't in shape anymore. I was losing most of my bouts. I couldn't go on forever." Flipping once more through his photographs, he turned up one of a pretty young Japanese woman and her baby. "My wife and daughter," he said, showing the picture to the reporter.

"Mr. Kanahele, can you tell us a little about this tournament?" asked the reporter, after admiring the photograph.

"Well, this is a *jungyo*, an exhibition tournament. What happens here in two days is similar to what takes place in fifteen days every other month in Japan. Technically what happens here doesn't count in the official rankings. But just because it's an exhibition tournament doesn't mean the *rikishi* don't take it seriously. I think we can expect to see some exciting sumo."

"Are there any wrestlers we should be keeping an eye on?"

"Well, of course everyone's eye is going to be on Akano-hana."

"Is that Shawn Hendrickson?" the reporter asked.

"Akanohana is his professional name," Spalding explained. "It means red flower. Sumo wrestlers' names often end with the suffix *hana*, which means flower. In Japan, the word flower carries the connotation of perfection. *Akano* means red, which stands for the red stripes in the American flag." He continued: "As you probably know, Akanohana is Mr. Kanahele's protégé."

To Charlotte, the sumo wrestlers' names all sounded like the names of sushi bars on New York's upper East Side.

"Yes," said Lani. "One of my missions as foreign minister for the sumo association is to find foreign wrestling talent. I discovered Shawn Hendrickson at an Ivy League wrestling tournament three years ago. He was a natural for sumo. A lot of Western wrestlers who try sumo drop out—the discipline is too rigid—but Shawn took to it like a duck to water."

More like a water buffalo than a duck, thought Charlotte.

"Naturally, I'm very pleased that he's done as well as he has," Lani continued. "It's every scout's dream to discover a star."

"Why is everyone's eye going to be on him?"

"Akanohana has advanced through the sumo ranks more quickly than any *rikishi* before him. Last month, he was promoted to *ozeki*, which is the second-highest rank in sumo. He's only the second foreigner to reach such a high rank. And there's a very good chance that he'll be the first foreign *yokozuna* in the history of sumo."

"What's a *yokozuna*?" asked the reporter, still writing away.

"*Yokozuna* means grand champion; it's sumo's highest rank. There have been only sixty-one *yokozuna* in the three-hundred-year history of professional sumo. At the moment, there are two *yokozuna*, but only one, Kotoyama, is participating in the Black Ships Festival Tournament. The other wasn't able to attend because of an injury."

"What does Hendrickson have to do to become a *yokozuna?*"

"He has to win two consecutive grand tournaments. He's already won one: the grand tournament earlier this month. As I explained, the Black Ships exhibition tournament doesn't count toward his ranking. But it does offer a preview of the kind of performance that can be expected of him at the fall grand tournament. One of the men he has to beat is his rival *ozeki*, Takafuji."

"What about the *yokozuna*, Kotoyama?" asked the reporter. "Wouldn't a grand champion be favored to beat a lower-ranking sumo such as Akanohana?"

"Akanohana is a *rikishi*, not a sumo," Lani corrected with a warm smile. "Or, you could call him a sumo wrestler. Never just a sumo. To call a sumo wrestler a sumo is a little like calling a baseball player a baseball."

"Sorry. I thought this was a Meet the Sumos reception."

"That's all right. That's my job, to promote the international understanding of sumo." He looked over at Spalding, his warm black eyes smiling. "Looks like I still have some work to do."

"We talked about calling it a Meet the *Rikishi* reception, but somehow it didn't have the same ring," said Spalding.

"To answer your question," Lani continued. "Not necessarily. Unlike the *rikishi* in the lower ranks, a *yokozuna* can't be demoted. Kotoyama hasn't been performing well for some time. He's thirty-three, which makes him the oldest wrestler in the top division. Let's just say that it's about time he started planning for his retirement."

"You mean, it's about time for the *rikishi* to cut off his *chommage*," said the reporter, proud of his use of sumo jargon.

Lani's warm black eyes crinkled in a smile.

"What are the chances that Akanohana will beat Takafuji?" the reporter continued.

"Very good, I'd say. As you may know, Akanohana won his last forty-three consecutive bouts. He's also favored to win the match today. If he does, he'll be pitted in the playoff against

Takafuji, who won yesterday's match. Takafuji has pledged
to beat Akanohana in the playoff, breaking his winning streak.
We'll see what happens; it's bound to be a very exciting
event."

The tournament began shortly after the reception. After a
drink at the casino restaurant, Spalding and Charlotte, along
with Marianne and Lester, joined the throngs that were pouring
into the casino for the event. The match would be held in the
casino's Center Court, usually the site of professional tennis
tournaments. The capacity of the stands was nearly five thousand, and it appeared that they would be full. In addition to
Americans who were curious about sumo wrestling, the event
seemed to have drawn every Japanese or Japanese-American
in New England. Having thirty-four of Japan's "best and the
biggest," as the posters put it, wrestling on American soil was
an event that was not to be missed. Outside the entrance to
the stands, the Black Ships committee members were doing
a brisk business in commemorative T-shirts emblazoned with
the red handprints that sumo wrestlers called *tegata*, and that
were the sumo equivalent of the autograph. Also on sale were
the *tegata* themselves: the red handprints of a *rikishi* on a piece
of square white cardboard, signed with a brush in black ink.
Not surprisingly, it was Akanohana's *tegata* that were selling
the most briskly.

Inside, the smooth grass of the Center Court had been
covered with the sumo ring: a two-foot high, eighteen-foot
square of hard-packed clay coated with a thin layer of sand.
Embedded in the surface was a circle of straw rope that delin-
eated the ring, which was fifteen feet in diameter. The ring
was sheltered by a vaulted wooden roof similar to those of
Shinto shrines. Supporting the roof were four colored poles
symbolizing the cardinal directions and the seasons of the year:
green to the east for spring, red to the south for summer, white
to the west for autumn, and black to the north for winter. Apart
from the ring and roof, it was like a sports stadium anywhere.
In addition to the flags of the United States and Japan, the
stadium was decorated with banners representing the sponsors
of the Black Ships Festival: Suntory, All Nippon Airways,

Honda, and Tanaka's Yoshino Electronics, whose logo was a branch of cherry blossoms. Television equipment was set up everywhere. Fuji Television would be beaming the match back to Japan.

Charlotte noticed many familiar faces in the front rows, among them those of Tanaka and his young assistant, Hayashi, who had called Okichi-*mago* "foreigner's Okichi." Like Shawn, Tanaka and Hayashi were still in the dark about Okichi-*mago*'s suicide. If the eyes Hayashi had been making at Okichi-*mago* at the geisha party were any measure of his feeling for her, he would be just as shocked at the news of her death as his rival. Brightening up the front row next to them were Fujiko, Sumire, and Keiko. Unlike Okichi-*mago*, who had been staying at Shimoda, the other geisha were being put up at Edgecliff, courtesy of Tanaka. At Lani's urging, Spalding had notified them that morning that Okichi-*mago* wouldn't be attending the match. He had used the jet-lag excuse. Otherwise they would have wondered about her absence. He would tell them about her death after the match. If they knew she was dead, they couldn't have helped giving it away to Shawn, with predictable consequences for his performance. Fortunately, none of the those who were staying at Edgecliff had been up early enough to witness the drama that was being played out beneath their windows: the police had come and gone long before seven, eager to have Okichi-*mago*'s body out of the way before the morning joggers, dog-walkers, and sightseers appeared on the scene.

As a television camera panned the audience, Hayashi decorously held aloft a small handmade sign printed with Japanese characters.

The Japanese audiences were a lot more subdued in the way that they displayed their enthusiasms than their American counterparts, Charlotte thought. "What does Hayashi's sign say?" she asked.

" 'Stop Akanohana,' " Spalding replied.

"I guess he doesn't want Shawn to win," she said drily.

"No," said Spalding. "Each of the sumo wrestlers has a corporate sponsor. Tanaka's corporation, Yoshino, is the sponsor of Shawn's rival, Takafuji. But it goes beyond simple corporate loyalties."

"The old xenophobia bit?"

"Carried to its most hysterical extreme. Shawn wasn't liked before on account of being a foreigner, but now that he's on the verge of attaining *yokozuna* status, the traditionalists are going berserk. Last week, one of the newspaper columnists speculated about strategies that might be used to prevent him from winning: deliberately inflicting a practice injury, lacing his food with sugar so that he'll develop diabetes, and so on."

"That's ridiculous."

"Yes. But some of these fans are beyond reason. One newspaper proposed calling off all sumo tournaments if Akanohana should become a *yokozuna*. To the Japanese, sumo is a reflection of their traditions, a vestige of a more chivalrous past. For a foreigner to have penetrated that world is almost unthinkable. It would be like the Japanese buying the Dallas Cowboys."

"Or Rockefeller Center," said Charlotte.

"Good point. I guess the Japanese aren't the only xenophobes around. But they're going to have to get used to the idea if they're truly interested in seeing sumo become an international sport."

"Connie was saying that they've made it difficult for Shawn all along."

"Very difficult," said Spalding. "The committees that determine the match-ups have always pitted him against the toughest opponents. I have to give him a lot of credit for sticking it out."

"I would think his perseverance would have earned him their respect."

"It has, among some. He has a big following among the young Japanese, and of course among fans from other countries, who are becoming more numerous. But some of the traditionalists hate to see a foreigner playing their game, and playing it better than they do. I sometimes think they'd like him better if he was the ugly American they expect him to be."

"They feel as if Shawn's showing them up?"

"Exactly. Especially when so many of the young Japanese wrestlers can't tolerate sumo's rigorous discipline. Like Taka-fuji, for instance. He has a reputation as a hothead. Once, he roughed up one of his attendants, and another time he kicked a member of his fan club. To the Japanese, such behavior is as unacceptable as stepping on a tatami mat with your shoes on."

Charlotte smiled at the reference to Dede's spike heels.

"To a lot of sumo fans, he embodies everything that's wrong with the modern generation, sumo wrestler or no."

"No respect for his elders, no respect for tradition, no self-discipline."

Spalding nodded.

The complaint was the same the world around.

The sumo match opened with a series of brief speeches by various officials: a representative of the Japan Sumo Association, the mayor of Newport, the governor of Rhode Island. After the speeches, Lani took the microphone and gave a brief explanation of the history and rules of sumo, a recap of what he had said at the reception. The match itself began with drumming: a ring attendant pounded on a drum suspended from a pole carried by two other ring attendants. After the drumming came the ring-entering ceremony. The procession was led by the referee, who was dressed in a traditional kimono and a pointed black court hat which was tied under his chin. After the referee came the *rikishi* from the east (the *rikishi* were divided into east and west sides). After filing into the stadium, they circled the ring in a counterclockwise direction. From the moment they entered the stadium, Charlotte could see the appeal of sumo. Despite everything she had been told, in some compartment of her mind she still linked sumo with the professional wrestling on Saturday afternoon television. But professional wrestling bore as much resemblance to sumo wrestling as an advertising jingle did to a Gregorian chant. Like the referee, the *rikishi* were colorfully dressed, each wearing a sumptuous embroidered silk apron. Spalding explained that the aprons, which cost thousands of dollars, were donated by the sponsors. As Lani announced their names, each *rikishi* mounted the raised ring and then turned outward to face the audience. Explaining that the wrestlers liked to hear their names, Lani urged the crowd to cheer for their favorites. "The more noise you make, the more they like it," he said.

The *rikishi* entered the ring in order of rank, the last to enter being Takafuji, the highest-ranked sumo on the east side. He was wearing an apron embroidered with a cherry branch, the emblem of Yoshino Electronics. As Takafuji entered the ring, Hayashi cheered loudly for his favorite. As sumo physiques went, Takafuji's was middling: he wasn't a butterball, but neither was he as lean as some. But he was ugly and mean-looking, with black eyebrows that formed a straight line across his forehead, a narrow, thin-lipped mouth, and slitlike eyes.

"Central casting's idea of the Japanese villain," said Charlotte.

"He is a mean-looking bastard, isn't he?" said Spalding. "He's said to have the most menacing stare in sumo. He's also considered one of the best showmen, of the bad-guy variety. Easy to hate, and fun to watch. The fans love him. His nickname is The Warthog."

"An apt description," said Charlotte.

Once all the *rikishi* had mounted the ring and shown themselves to the fans, they turned inward to perform the opening ritual, which included clapping their hands to summon the attention of the spirits, and raising their arms to show that they had no concealed weapons. After the *rikishi* from the east had departed, the ceremony was repeated for the *rikishi* from the west. Reflecting his rank at the top of his division, Akanohana was the last to enter. He wore a stunning light blue apron embroidered in gold with a magnificent cloud design and the logo of the American airline that was his sponsor. He stood out from the other wrestlers not only because of his Western features, but also because of the hair on his chest: the Japanese wrestlers were hairless. His physique was also quite muscular by comparison with many of the other wrestlers, who tended toward pendulous breasts and pudgy upper arms. As he mounted the ring, the crowd roared. He appeared to be especially popular with the Japanese-Americans, who probably saw a reflection of themselves in him: a hybrid of two cultures.

As he turned outward to face the audience, Charlotte caught a glimpse of Marianne's expression out of the corner of her eye: her nose was pointing, her nostrils quivering: she had that bird dog look again.

After the *rikishi* from the west had departed, the elaborate ring-entering ceremony for the *yokozuna* began. In addition to the chief referee, he had two other attendants, a herald and a sword-bearer. The thick white ceremonial rope belt that was the symbol of the *yokozuna*'s rank was wrapped around his waist and tied in an elaborate knot at his back. From it hung white paper strips cut in a zigzag pattern that represented symbolic offerings to the gods. Like the *rikishi* before him, the *yokozuna* performed the ritual of clapping and raising his arms, as well as foot-stomping, signifying the stomping of evil into the ground. After the *yokozuna*'s ring-entering ceremony, there was a brief exhibition of sumo holds and training exercises by the young apprentices who served as attendants to the wrestlers in the higher ranks. Then the first bout began.

Mounting the ring, the kimono-clad announcer slowly unfolded a white fan. Facing east and west in turn, he extended his fan and called out the names of the *rikishi* from each side. As the opponents ascended into the ring, Lani filled the audience in on their backgrounds. The *rikishi* on the east stood six foot two and weighed four hundred and fifty-five pounds. To Charlotte, he looked like a gigantic popover on stumps. He was known for his prodigious appetite, said Lani, who proceeded to describe his dinner-table record: six dozen bowls of noodles, thirty-six box lunches, and twenty-five bottles of beer. By contrast, the *rikishi* on the west was a pipsqueak, standing only five feet eleven and weighing just over two hundred and fifty pounds.

Marianne leaned across Charlotte to speak to Spalding. "Spalding, this seems so unfair. Isn't the big guy going to squash the little guy? After all, he's the size of four people!"

Spalding smiled, a twinkle in his eye. "Wait and see," he said. "The little guy usually has a few tricks up his sleeve."

Marianne looked skeptical.

"That's the appeal of sumo," Spalding explained to them. "Unlike Western wrestling, there aren't any weight classes. It's strictly man-to-man combat. Who wins depends more on factors like skill, guts, balance, intellect, and concentration than it does on size or brute force."

No longer wearing their aprons, the *rikishi* were clad only in a silk loincloth called a *mawashi*. As they warmed up, their names were called again, this time by the referee. Then they went to opposite corners of the ring and rinsed their mouths out with a dipper of water.

"Power water," said Spalding, explaining the mouth-rinsing ritual. "The idea is to enter the ring in as clean and pure a state as possible. You'll also see them wipe the sweat off their bodies just before the match begins."

After the mouth-rinsing, each contestant picked up a handful of salt and threw it into the ring, another act of ritual purification. Then they squatted facing one another at the center of the ring, and proceeded to fix one another with a piercing stare.

Charlotte thought of her Siamese cats, who often stared at one another like this before a fight. The one who looked away first always lost.

"Is this a psychological duel?" asked Marianne.

"Exactly," said Spalding. "The pre-bout staring contest often decides the bout. To stare your opponent straight in the eye demands a lot of concentration. If you're physically or psychologically off balance, your opponent is going to find out about it."

Lester leaned over to interject a comment: "Marianne is very talented at this, aren't you, honey? She knows just where a man's weaknesses lie."

Marianne gave him a dirty look. They were obviously still feuding over the night before, which had ended in a nasty quarrel. If Marianne had looked Lester in the eye, she would have seen a very red one; he was very hung over.

After the *rikishi* had repeated the squatting, standing, staring, salt-throwing ritual a few times, the referee signaled that their time was up and the wrestlers squatted for the last time. In her position at ringside, Charlotte was only a few feet from the action. Less than ten feet from her nose was the enormous, cellulite-pocked rear end of the gigantic popover. Then the bout began. As the crowd roared, the *rikishi* circled one another for a few seconds, and then charged like rutting hippos on the African veldt. Before Charlotte could figure out what had happened, the behemoth was on his back.

The referee pointed his fan to the little guy and announced his name. The bout had taken less than ten seconds.

"How did he do that?" asked a bewildered Marianne, as the gigantic popover bowed curtly to his opponent and then waddled out of the ring, his enormous back coated with the sand of defeat.

"The little guy used a technique called *uwate-nage*, or outside arm throw, to throw the bigger guy," Spalding explained. "As you watch some more, you'll begin to get a feel for it."

For the next hour, Charlotte watched in fascination. As Spalding had predicted, she began to develop a familiarity with the basic techniques, which included shoving your opponent out of the ring, lifting him up and carrying him out, and slapping him out: a peculiar technique in which one man slaps the other toward the edge of the ring, and then pushes him out. In addition, there were a variety of grappling techniques aimed at dumping the man within the ring. As the match wore on, the giants also took on their own individual identities. Charlotte became particularly fond of the aging *yokozuna*, Kotoyama, who, reconciled to losing most of his bouts, seemed to be wrestling just for the hell of it. Unlike some of the other stone-faced giants, he even seemed to have a sense of humor. Maybe it was just one old warhorse identifying with another.

But the real star of the show was Akanohana.

Charlotte was mesmerized as she watched him defeat one opponent after another, his intelligence radiating from every movement. Unlike the other sumos, who tended to favor a single technique, Akanohana varied his according to the strengths or weaknesses of his opponent. In one bout, he patiently wore his opponent down, gradually penetrating his defenses; in the next, he deftly grounded his opponent with an elegantly executed arm throw; in still another, he struck with the flashing impact of a lightning bolt. He was cunning, skillful, and cool. It was no surprise that his nickname was The Fox. Coached by Spalding, Charlotte found herself cheering him on with the phrase, *Ganbare*! the rough translation of which was "Go for it." Spalding cheered right along with her, and Charlotte was

pleased to see him abandon his customary reserve. Even Lester
cheered, temporarily forgetting Marianne's romantic interest
in Shawn. After four winning bouts, Akanohana predictably
emerged as the winner, and Lani announced a break before
the playoff with Takafuji.

As the audience resumed their seats for the playoff a few
minutes later, the atmosphere in the stadium was electric.
Once again, the announcer mounted the ring and called out
the names of the contestants. Then they mounted the ring:
Takafuji all strut and swagger, and Akanohana all cool and
concentration. He reminded Charlotte of Linc Crawford in
a cinematic shoot-out on Main Street. Lani announced their
statistics: The Warthog, Takafuji, was five feet eleven and
three hundred and eighteen pounds; The Fox, Akanohana,
was six foot one and two hundred seventy-five pounds. As
sumo wrestlers went, they were pretty evenly matched. Lani
went on to talk about the colors of their *mawashi*: as a purist,
Akanohana wore a black loincloth in keeping with official
rules that *mawashi* be black or a dark color like purple or
navy blue, but Takafuji's loincloth was a blinding chartreuse.
Since the introduction of color television, many *rikishi* had
chosen to ignore the unenforced rule on *mawashi* color, Lani
explained.

"In my book, the chartreuse *mawashi* alone is reason enough
not to like the guy," Spalding whispered in her ear.

After mounting the ring, the *rikishi* performed the opening
ritual, clapping their hands and raising their arms. Then they
went to the center of the ring and stomped evil into the ground.
Next came the salt-tossing ritual: drinking their power water,
wiping their mouths with a special paper towel, throwing the salt
into the ring, and finally taking up their positions at the center
of the ring, crouching like coiled springs. By now, the noise of
the audience was a roar, and Hayashi's placard was bouncing
up and down. They repeated the salt-tossing ritual several
times: Takafuji glaring and stomping; Akanohana behaving
with supreme disdain and Zen-like single-mindedness, as if
his opponent were too insignificant even for his contempt.
After some more posturing, the timekeeper signaled that the
time was up, and a ring attendant handed the wrestlers towels

to wipe off their sweat. Once they had braced for the opening charge, the referee raised his war fan from a horizontal to a vertical position, and the two *rikishi* came together with a bone-shattering thud. According to Spalding, the opening charge was the moment of truth. If the bout hadn't already been decided in the stare-off, it would be when the two *rikishi* came together. The key to victory was a strong belt grip.

By now, Charlotte had a better idea of what was going on. If what Spalding said was true, Akanohana had the advantage. After charging his opponent with lightning speed, he had succeeded in getting hold of Takafuji's chartreuse *mawashi* with both hands. For a few seconds, he skillfully pushed and pulled his opponent around as Takafuji tried in vain to free himself. Finally Akanohana succeeded in throwing Takafuji off balance and the match was decided. With Takafuji's belt firmly in his grip, Akanohana hoisted the squirming and kicking wrestler into the air and deposited him outside the ring as summarily as a bouncer throwing a lightweight-but-troublesome patron out of a nightclub. He nearly landed in their laps.

It was a spectacular display of strength and skill for Akanaohana and a humiliating defeat for Takafuji. The referee pointed his fan at Akanohana; it was a perfect record—he hadn't lost a single match.

"Unless anything unforeseen happens, Japan is about to see its first foreign *yokozuna*," said Spalding as the crowd went wild.

CHARLOTTE TOOK THE man's business card and tucked it into her purse. The card identified him as Mr. Junichi Kanazashi, chairman of the Shimoda Board of Education. He looked disappointed that she hadn't offered him one in return. She knew that the exchange of business cards was a major preoccupation of the Japanese, but a business card was something Charlotte had never needed. After fifty years in front of the cameras, her face was as familiar to most Americans as their best friend's. Failing a business card, she introduced herself as Charlotte Graham and explained that she had played Okichi in *Soiled Dove*.

With the reference to *Soiled Dove*, Kanazashi's face lit up. He stepped back to size up her full height. "Miss Graham, of course," he said, pumping her arm vigorously. "I'm very pleased to make your acquaintance. I'm sorry I didn't recognize you. You are so tall—much too tall for a geisha."

Thanks to *Soiled Dove*, Charlotte was famous throughout the Orient as well. Playing Okichi was to the Japanese what playing Joan of Arc would have been to the French, or Queen Christina to the Swedes. Almost without knowing it, she had become a cultural icon.

"I could never have played Okichi on stage," she agreed. With her white skin and black hair, she had made a fairly believable geisha as long as the camera camouflaged her height.

Kanazashi laughed. Reaching into his breast pocket, he withdrew a leather notebook. He ripped off a sheet of paper and extended it to her. "Please, may I have your autograph?" he asked.

Charlotte signed the paper with her round, bold scrawl. She was not the kind of star who scorned her fans. For fifty years, her fans had been her bread and butter, and she had been happy to oblige.

They were standing on the rear loggia of Edgecliff, the mansion that was the scene of the Mikado Ball. The light of the setting sun bathed the landscape in a tropical yellow light tinged with orange: an ochre light. She wondered if Ochre Point has taken its name from the light of the setting sun or from the ochre with which its fabulous mansions had been built.

She handed her autograph back to Kanazashi, who gazed at it as fondly as if it were a fifty-dollar bill that he'd just picked up off the sidewalk. "I'm going to frame this and hang it in the museum in Shimoda."

"I hardly think it's a museum piece," said Charlotte.

She was happy to have found this genial Japanese man. Since arriving at the ball, she'd been subjected to a series of lectures on what was wrong with America. One man she had talked with had even written a book called *The War Between Japan and America Is Not Over*. Apparently the Japanese trade group that owned Edgecliff was a hotbed of Japanese right-wing nationalism.

"You know, Miss Graham, because of *Soiled Dove*, Shimoda has gone from a sleepy fishing village to a major tourist attraction. I, for one, have grown rich from the Okichi legend," he added, explaining that the hotel he owned was the site of the annual Shimoda Conference, a gathering of Japanese and American intellectuals and businessmen.

Their conversation was interrupted by a young woman in a flowered kimono who offered them a tray of hors d'oeuvres.

"Have you been back to Shimoda since you filmed the movie?" asked Kanazashi as he helped himself to a cracker heaped with caviar.

Charlotte shook her head. She had always meant to return. The little fishing village at the edge of the mountain-rimmed harbor was one of the most beautiful places she had ever seen.

"Oh, you should see it now! We have"—he counted on his fingers—"three museums with displays on Okichi. Make that four—the new Shimoda Port Memorial Hall also has an Okichi exhibit." He held up the piece of paper. "That's where your autograph is going to hang. Even the restaurant that Okichi opened a few years before she died has a display. We also have an Okichi Festival."

"An Okichi Festival too?"

"Along with our own Black Ships Festival in mid-May. Not to criticize the way you do things here in the United States . . ."

That was all right, everybody else was, Charlotte thought.

" . . . but you could make a lot more of the Black Ships Festival than you do. We celebrate for three days: parades, parties, fireworks. The children are let out of school. It would be very good for the tourist business of Newport." A look of sadness crossed his face. "Of course, it is terrible about Okichi-*mago* committing suicide on the one hundredth anniversary of Okichi's death."

"Yes, it is," Charlotte agreed.

He continued: "But I don't think her suicide will hurt the Black Ships Festival in Newport. In fact, it will enhance it, just as the tragic story of Okichi's death has enhanced tourism for Shimoda. I think tourists will be very interested in seeing Townsend Harris's replica of the Temple of Great Repose and the place where Okichi-*mago* jumped off the cliff."

Japanese tourists might be interested, but Charlotte doubted that American tourists would. To say nothing of the fact that neither Paul nor Marianne would ever have anything to do with such a scheme.

"Maybe you could arrange a tour to Newport for the Japanese," Charlotte said. She was speaking half-facetiously, but he took her seriously.

"Yes, you're right!" he said, his face lighting up again. "That's a very good idea. I am going to look into it right away." Pulling out his notebook again, he made a notation.

"An Okichi tour to Shimoda's sister city. I think it would be a very big success."

They were interrupted by the whirring of a helicopter rotor. A helicopter was approaching over the ocean from the direction of Providence, to the north. Directed by national guardsmen, the helicopter landed on the lawn, and the governor emerged with his wife—he in black tie, she in a full-length gown.

"I guess the ball has officially begun," said Kanzashi.

Following the crowd, they drifted inside for the opening ceremonies, which were held in the Great Hall, a majestic gilt-encrusted arcaded hall rising three stories. From the outside, Edgecliff was undistinguished: a Gothic pile of red sandstone that Charlotte had mentally dubbed the Smithsonian-by-the-Sea. But the interior was palatial. As the usual dignitaries gave the usual speeches, she studied the surroundings. Overhead, an enormous mural depicted Zeus at the Banquet of the Gods. Above the windows, gilded figures in bas-relief represented the industrial and liberal arts. The curving staircase was lined with a balustrade of white marble dolphins and cupids. Like Marianne's parlor, nothing made any sense, but it had a kind of mad magnificence.

After the speeches, the guests headed toward the adjacent oak-paneled library, where dinner was to be served. Charlotte went in search of her table. A Black Ships committee member at the door had told her that she was assigned to table number twenty-three.

She found her table on the other side of the library. Her tablemates included a young couple who identified themselves as Japanophiles, several Newport city councilmen and their wives, and the city solicitor and his wife. Charlotte sat between the last couple: a handsome, light-skinned black man named Lewis Farrell and his beautiful Hispanic wife, Toni. They were a charming couple, and she was pleased to find herself in such pleasant company.

Charlotte had no intention of asking him how a black man had ended up in Newport, but he told her anyway. It appeared to be a favorite story. He explained that he was a descendant of slaves who were brought to Newport in 1690, a time when

Newport rivaled Boston as the country's busiest seaport, and was the center of the slave trade.

"I love to see the reactions of some of these snobby Colonial Dames types when I tell them that my ancestors have been in New England longer than theirs," he said, his eyes crinkling in a good-natured smile. He had a long, narrow face and a stylishly droopy mustache, and wore round glasses with gold wire rims that gave him a professorial air.

He also filled her in on his wife's ancestry: she was descended from Portuguese fishermen who had emigrated to Newport from the Cape Verde Islands.

It was this variety that Charlotte loved about Newport. Dozens of diverse groups—the blacks, the Portuguese, the socialites, the sailing crowd, the intellectuals, the artists, the Naval War College personnel, the college students, the fortune hunters, the day-trippers, the summer residents, and the merchants and shopkeepers—each existing in their own little world on this idyllic New England island.

From Lew and Toni's ancestry, the topic of conversation at the table shifted briefly to *Soiled Dove* and then to Shimoda, which the young couple who'd said they were Japanophiles had just visited.

"The chairman of Shimoda's board of education was just telling me that there are several museums there devoted to the memory of Okichi," said Charlotte.

"Not museums really," said the young man. "There are exhibits in several of the temples, but they don't really amount to much. There's a memorial museum with a few mementos in Okichi's family temple. Her grave is also there—just behind the temple. They still keep incense burning in her memory."

"What about the other temple?" prompted the wife.

The husband looked embarrassed.

"Tell them," she urged.

The husband took a breath. "There's another temple in which they have a display of Okichi's palanquin and some other mementos. Next to it there's another building in which there's a display of—I don't know quite how to describe them—they call them 'Buddhist images symbolizing ecstasy.' "

" 'In commemoration of Okichi's amorous exploits,' " the wife said, raising her fingers to indicate quotations marks around the words.

"What do Buddhist images symbolizing ecstasy look like?" asked Toni.

"Well. . . ."

"Like the male organ," interjected the wife, who clearly wasn't as reticent about such matters as her husband. "They're phallic symbols; some of them are really very beautiful, carved out of wood or ivory. Unfortunately, Bob wouldn't let me take any home. They sell them all over town."

"The town's really made a big deal of the Okichi legend," her husband added. "In addition to these . . . phallic objects . . . you can buy all sorts of other Okichi souvenirs: postcards, towels, key chains."

"Every time the tourist business starts to slacken, they think of some new angle of the Okichi legend to promote," the wife added.

The husband looked up. "Here comes our dinner," he said, obviously relieved to get off the subject of Okichi's amorous exploits.

A parade of waiters had appeared, and were serving the guests their dinners. The dinner was typical banquet food, but with an Oriental touch: lemon sesame chicken or a shrimp stir-fry, served with rice and shitake mushrooms and carrots and snow peas in a ginger sauce.

"Did you know that Okichi's descendant, the young geisha who was here for the Black Ships Festival, committed suicide this morning?" one of the city councilman's wives asked the young man, Bob.

The news was apparently out.

"Yes, we heard about it," Bob replied.

"I heard she did it because of her obligation to her patron, but I can't say I really understand it," said the woman.

"It's a difficult concept for a Westerner to comprehend," Bob said. "The Japanese call it *giri*, or obligation, but it's easier to understand if you think of it in terms of guilt. Every time you receive a favor, you're incurring a debt, which you're then obligated to repay in kind, or better."

The same story that Spalding had given her, Charlotte reflected.

"In Okichi-*mago*'s case, her obligations were so much greater than what she was owed that the only way for her to redress the balance was to kill herself," Bob continued. "If you consider the suicide in her family history, you have a pretty potent motive."

"But to take your life!" the councilman's wife said. "It seems very extreme."

It seemed so to Charlotte too, despite what Spalding and this young man had said. Yes, Okichi-*mago* was obligated to Tanaka. And, yes, she had seemed mildly depressed. She remembered the tears rolling down her white cheeks. But there was something not quite right about the suicide theory—something besides the point that it seemed like a drastic solution to a minor problem, *giri* or no *giri*. The image came to her mind of Okichi-*mago*'s body lying on the shingle beach, her green, turquoise-flecked eyes staring up at the pale dawn sky. And then it struck her what it was that wasn't quite right: the broken pieces of the sake cup lying on the rocks. Why would she have retrieved the sake cup from the house if she already had one in her hand? It didn't make any sense. As Okichi's descendant, Okichi-*mago* would have been more familiar with the legend than anyone. First Okichi built the fire at the edge of the cliff and burned her possessions and her papers. Then she carefully set out the comb, the mirror, and the sake cup Harris-*san* had given her—the sake cup she had been drinking from for more than thirty years—and then she jumped. She didn't set out one sake cup and then jump with another.

There was something else that wasn't quite right about the suicide theory too: the scraped surface of the baroque pearl on Okichi-*mago*'s obi clasp. If she were going to throw herself off the gallery, she wouldn't have leaned over the railing and kicked up her legs as if she were diving off a diving board. One, it would have been awkward; two, it would have been unpleasant: she would have been looking straight down at the rocks below; and three, it would have been difficult if not impossible to kick her legs up high enough to propel her over the railing. The natural approach would simply have been to climb to the top of the railing and jump. That's why people who plunged from heights were called jumpers. But picking up her legs would have been a natural way to *push* her over the railing. Charlotte imagined Okichi-*mago* standing at the railing, just as she had been earlier in the evening, her sake cup cradled in her hands. Then she imagined someone sneaking up on her from behind and pushing her over. Finally she imagined that person trying to make the murder look like a suicide. Not realizing that she was already holding a sake cup—she would have been holding it in front of her—the killer sets out the cup, the comb, and the mirror next to the fire, just as Okichi had a hundred years before.

Unlike the suicide hypothesis, this was a theory without any holes; all the pieces fit together. There was another element of the original hypothesis that didn't fit either, Charlotte thought. She had found Okichi-*mago*'s body lying several feet to the side of the place where her obi clasp had scraped the railing. If she had dived off the gallery, she would have landed directly below. But if she had been pushed, any twisting movement would have resulted in her landing off-center.

The conversation at the table had drifted off to the price of food in Japan—something about cherries costing sixteen dollars apiece and cantaloupes a hundred and twenty-five. As her tablemates talked, Charlotte turned the pieces around in her head, trying to fit them together in some other way. But they added up to only one conclusion: Okichi-*mago* had been murdered. But who would have wanted to murder her? she wondered.

Excusing herself, she went off in search of the geishas. She wanted to speak with Keiko, who, as Okichi-*mago*'s younger sister, might be able to give her some clues. Thank goodness it was Keiko and not one of the other geishas who was Okichi-*mago*'s younger sister. After the labored conversations she'd had with some of the other Japanese at the ball, she welcomed talking with a Japanese who spoke good English. Keiko had grown up on Okinawa, and had learned English at a United States military base. From the library, Charlotte wandered out to the Great Hall, where an orchestra was playing Cole Porter. For a moment, she stood and watched the couples dancing, and the people who were watching them. Not seeing the geishas, she headed over to the bar and asked the bartender if he had seen them. He directed her to a morning room adjoining the library. The room was empty except for Keiko, who sat despondently in a gilded armchair, drinking Scotch.

"Keiko?" she said. She hadn't really expected to find her at the party, but then parties were a geisha's natural habitat; she probably felt more at home with her grief here than she would have upstairs in her room.

The girl nodded. She was wearing the same gorgeous kimono as the night before, on which geishas embroidered in gold and silver thread strolled among the willow trees and teahouses of the floating world.

Charlotte took a seat next to her. "I'm very sorry about Okichi-*mago*'s death. I know you'll miss her very much."

Tears leaked from the corners of the narrow eyes of her round, white kitten's face, and she bit her carmine lip in an effort to keep from crying.

"Keiko, several people have suggested to me that Okichi-*mago* committed suicide because she felt that she had betrayed her patron through her love affair with Shawn Hendrickson. Do you think that's true?"

Keiko shook her head emphatically, the glittering pendants of her hair ornaments tinkling as she moved her head.

"Why not?"

"Tanaka-*san* didn't care. To him, it was strictly a business arrangement. He liked Okichi-*san*, but he will find another geisha. In what way did she betray him? For six years, she has been fulfilling her end of their agreement."

Perhaps Spalding had been naive in interpreting Okichi-*mago*'s death in terms of cultural stereotypes, Charlotte reflected. Okichi-*mago* had been a guardian of tradition, but she had also been a modern career woman.

"But then, why did she cry when she sang 'Raven at Dawn'?"

"I don't know," said Keiko. "Maybe she was sad. Everyone is sad sometimes. Okichi-*san* could be happy one minute, and sad the next. Why not? Life can change from one minute to the next. I'm sad right now"—she blinked her tears away—"but I'm not going to jump off a cliff."

"Okichi did."

Keiko looked almost angry. "Yes, but Okichi committed suicide because Townsend Harris deserted her, not because she deserted him. Also, she was a wreck of a woman when she died. An alcoholic, a beggar, and a cripple. She was paralyzed from syphilis, you know."

"I didn't know that."

"Okichi-*san* was the first person to take advantage of the Okichi legend. But she didn't like to be compared with her. Okichi-*san* thought she was pathetic." She paused to take a swig of Scotch, and then shook her head. "She would never have chosen to die in the same way."

"Then she didn't have a melancholy temperament?"

"Not at all," said Keiko. "She was very happy. She was in love with Shawn. They were going to be married."

Charlotte thought again of the Japanese novelist who had committed suicide, the only example she had to go on. But judging from everything she had read, he was a little crazy. By contrast, Okichi-*mago* was a model of stability: disciplined, dedicated, successful, and, as Keiko pointed out, in love.

"Besides," Keiko continued, "if she were going to commit suicide, she never would have done it by jumping. She would have taken pills. Jumping would have been too undignified for her. She couldn't even have been sure of succeeding. What if she'd just broken her legs?"

Keiko was right. Jumping wasn't the way Okichi-*mago* would have chosen to die. She was too neat: the perfect English, the perfect hair, the perfect makeup—Charlotte remembered the touch of gilding outlining her underlip. She would have wanted to die as immaculately as she had lived.

"Then if she didn't commit suicide, she must have been murdered."

"Yes," said Keiko quietly.

"Do you have any idea who might have wanted to murder her?"

Keiko shook her head.

Fujiko and Sumire were returning from the direction of the bar. Fujiko was carrying another Scotch for Keiko. After offering her condolences—with Keiko serving as translator—

Charlotte excused herself and wandered back to the bar. She felt as if she could use a drink herself.

After the dessert course, the orchestra started playing livelier music, and the older couples turned over the dance floor to the young. Manhattan in hand, Charlotte headed back out to the loggia at the rear of the house. In the distance, the sea was a deep blue green against a night sky tinged with pink. The lights of Middletown twinkled across the water. The view reminded her of another famous Newport story. A Newport hostess was giving a White Ball, a *Bal Blanc*. Everything was to be white: the china, the tablecloths, the flowers, the doves in white birdcages on the tables. The guests were asked to wear white gowns, white suits, and white powdered wigs. But despite the hostess's elaborate plans, the view at night over the ocean hadn't a glimmer of white. To remedy the affront to her color theme wrought by the orbiting of the heavenly spheres, the hostess decided to engage a fleet of twelve full-sized ships with white hulls and sails and order them to anchor offshore. But it proved impossible to anchor a dozen fully rigged ships in the Atlantic, so instead she had a dozen all white, full-sized ships anchored at the foot of the lawn, where they made a tableau of white against the deep blue sky. Looking out into the starry night, Charlotte could easily imagine how lovely they must have looked, floating down the Cliff Walk. Leaving the loggia behind, she wandered out to the lawn and down toward the cliff's edge. Behind her, the lights of Edgecliff blazed against a background of dark trees. Resting her elbows on the balustrade at the foot of the lawn, she gazed out to sea. From this position, she could just see the spot where she had found Okichi-*mago*'s body. It had only been that morning, but it already seemed like ages ago. The waves lapping at the rocks created ribbons of white on the shoreline. She thought again of the position of the body. She was sure of it—Okichi-*mago* had been murdered.

Turning back toward the mansion, she saw Lew and Toni heading toward her, arm in arm. A few minutes later, they joined her at the balustrade.

"Checking out the scene of the death?" asked Lew.

"Yes, as a matter of fact."

"I know all about your reputation as an amateur detective," he said with a smile. "I read *Murder at the Morosco*."

Nine years ago, Charlotte had solved the case of the murder of her co-star in the Broadway play *The Trouble With Murder*. She had shot him on-stage with a bullet that had been planted in a stage prop. The memory of seeing real blood oozing from the wound still gave her the shivers. Her role in solving the case had been publicized in a best-selling book called *Murder at the Morosco* (the play had been showing at the lovely old Morosco Theatre, which was torn down the next year despite the protests of the historical preservationists). Since then, she'd successfully helped solve several other murders.

"He's a crime buff," Toni explained, her lovely brown eyes gleaming. "He reads all the books about real-life crime."

"I work very closely with the police department, both as city solicitor and in our business: Toni and I run a security business, Viking Security. If you ever want to give a party in Newport, just let us know. We'll make sure that no one steals the guests' jewels or makes off with the silver."

"I'll keep that in mind," said Charlotte.

"I heard that it was you who discovered Okichi-*mago*'s body this morning," Lew continued. "We get a body at the foot of the cliff from time to time—accidental deaths. Kids partying on the cliff who drink too much and fall off. Or people walking along at night who mistake the edge for the path."

"They ought to fence it off in some places," Toni added. "The edge has caved away in spots, and it's not very well lit."

"I can see that," said Charlotte, looking out. "Maybe you can use your influence with the city government to get a fence put up."

Toni smiled, and looked up at her husband.

"Tell me," said Lew, "what do you think about Okichi-*mago*'s death?"

"What do you mean?"

"Do you think it was a suicide?"

"No," she replied bluntly. She explained about the sake cup and about her conversation with Keiko.

"I've got news for you. The police don't think it was a suicide either. The state medical examiner says the body was found too far out from the base of the cliff for it to have been a suicide. He thinks she was pushed."

Now that he mentioned it, Charlotte remembered that the body had been at least ten feet away from the base of the cliff.

"He's ordered a reconstruction of the fall. Apparently it's the only way to tell whether a fall was a suicide or a murder. He'll be using a dummy that's the same height and weight as Okichi-*mago*."

"That sounds *very* interesting," said Charlotte with a coquettish smile.

"I saw those eyes light up," Lew teased. "They're going to stage the reconstruction tomorrow morning. I'm going to be there. I can take a hint: would you like to come along?"

"I certainly would," Charlotte replied.

"Good. I'll pick you up at nine."

"Do the police have any leads yet?" Charlotte asked as she rode down Bellevue Avenue with Lew the next morning.

"They don't, but I do," Lew replied.

"You do!"

"Do you know about the feud between Marianne Montgomery and Paul Harris?"

Charlotte nodded.

"According to their great-aunt's will, the house and property pass to Connie's descendants, namely Marianne, and Paul's descendants. The only trouble is that Paul doesn't have any descendants."

"And the idea that Marianne's daughter will eventually inherit Shimoda is enough to drive him crazy," said Charlotte. She was reminded of his disgusted expression when Dede had entered the temple in her spike heels.

"Exactly," said Lew. "He's been talking for years about adopting Nadine's sons as his heirs. In my opinion, that's the only reason she's stuck it out with him. But he's never done anything about it."

They turned onto Narragansett Avenue and drove past the long buff pink walls of Bois Doré, the mansion where the coal magnate had hung gold fruits from the pollarded lindens lining the approach to the house.

Lew continued: "According to my confidential source, Paul had finally decided to do something about it, but it wasn't Nadine's sons that he was planning to make his heirs, it was Okichi-*mago*."

"Whew!" Charlotte exclaimed. "This is a new wrinkle. Who's your confidential source? Toni?"

Lew looked over at her in surprise. "How did you know?"

"Just a hunch, I saw her chatting with Nadine at the ball. They looked as if they were friends."

"They are. Her younger son and our son are on the same tennis team. Nadine told Toni that she'd seen a revised copy of Paul's will naming Okichi-*mago* as his heir, and some other papers designating her as his adopted daughter. She was very unhappy about it."

"I can imagine," said Charlotte.

"Promise me you won't tell anyone who told you this. I don't want to get into trouble with my wife, or get her into trouble with Nadine. I'm married to one of those hot-blooded Latin types."

Charlotte gave him her solemn word.

"I can't tell the police about it for obvious reasons, but I can tell you. You're close to the family. Maybe you can find out something the police can't—like who murdered Okichi-*mago*."

"Won't the police mind my interfering?"

"I'll make it their business not to mind. If anyone gives you any trouble, just tell them that you're acting on my authority. I'll introduce you to the chief this morning. He's an okay guy."

"Do you think it was Nadine who killed her?"

"Maybe," Lew replied. "She has a strong motive, but so do a lot of other people. Think about it."

Charlotte did. "Marianne," she said after a minute. "If Marianne killed Okichi-*mago*, then the house and property would go to Dede."

"Right. Marianne is crazy, as I'm sure you've realized by now. She is capable of dreaming up the wackiest schemes imaginable, and—more than that—of putting Lester up to carrying them out."

"Connie told me about how Lester nudged Paul's car from behind with his own. They were arguing over something. Paul accused him of attempted murder, and then reduced the charge to vehicular assault."

"Where did this happen?" asked Lew.

"In the driveway at Shimoda."

"In the *driveway*!" Lew shook his head. "Sounds like Lester. Paul too, for that matter. Probably neither one was going faster than six miles per hour. Newport has got to be one of the world's craziest towns."

"So far, we've got Nadine, Marianne, and Lester."

"What about on the jealousy front?" asked Lew. "I hear Okichi-*mago*'s Japanese patron wasn't too happy about her taking up with the wrestler."

"Tanaka," she said. "He didn't strike me as being too upset about it, but maybe that's just his Oriental inscrutability. I suppose he could have killed her in revenge. Then there's Hayashi."

"Who's Hayashi?" asked Lew as he pulled the car into the driveway.

"Tanaka's assistant, I think he was in love with Okichi-*mago* too. He might have killed her for the same reason." She explained about him hissing "*Tojin* Okichi" into Okichi-*mago*'s ear at the geisha party.

"That makes five," said Lew.

"Even Shawn, I suppose. Although it's farfetched, she could have rejected him too. Maybe the idea of inheriting Paul's millions opened up some prospect for her that made the idea of marriage to Shawn less enticing."

"Six," said Lew, as he turned off the ignition. "See what I mean? The murder suspects really multiply once you start thinking about it."

· 8 ·

THE CIRCULAR DRIVEWAY was crowded with police cars: there were several gray state police cars as well as the local black-and-white Newport police cars. In a state as small as Rhode Island, it didn't take long to get to the scene of the crime. The capital, Providence, was only forty-five minutes away, as was just about any other spot in the state. The knoll on which the temple stood had been sealed off with barriers joined by yellow plastic tape printed with the words POLICE LINE. DO NOT CROSS. On the gallery, half a dozen policemen stood around drinking coffee from white Styrofoam cups. It was a beautiful morning, cool and crisp. The low gray clouds that had been hanging over the ocean had been blown away by a stiff offshore breeze, carrying the oppressive heat and humidity with them. Sixty feet below, the waves splashed gently against the shingle beach. Lew introduced Charlotte to the police chief, a tall red-faced Irishman named Kilkenny, and to the burly local detective who would be handling the case, Detective-Captain Sullivan. But the star of the morning's proceedings was the state medical examiner, a tanned, dapper man named Ken Miller, with a gray crew cut and a red bow tie. He stood under the wind-contorted pine at the south corner of the gallery with two state policemen and a young reporter. By Miller's gestures, it was obvious he was talking about Okichi-*mago*'s fall. As Charlotte and Lew approached, the state policemen left, heading back toward the stairs to the gallery.

"They're going down the base of the cliff to see where you found the body yesterday morning, Miss Graham," said the medical examiner.

"I guess I don't need to introduce Miss Graham," Lew said. "Miss Graham, this is Doc Miller, the state medical examiner."

"Indeed not," said Miller, pumping Charlotte's hand. "I've known Miss Graham since I was a teenager. At least I feel as if I've known her that long," he added. "And been in love with her that long, too."

"Thank you," said Charlotte.

"I don't think there are many of Miss Graham's fans who haven't been in love with her," said Lew. "I invited her to witness this morning's procedures," he explained. "As you may know, she's had some experience with police work."

"Oh yes. I read *Murder at the Morosco*," said Miller. "Lots of interesting work there on cartridges. I also heard about that herbal poisoning case you helped solve up in Maine."

"You New England medical examiners must talk to one another."

"We do, we do," he said genially. "Actually, I think a lot more people die of poisoning than we know about. Hard to catch poisoners. If you want to do away with somebody, that's the way to do it."

"I'll keep that in mind at city hall," said Lew with a smile.

"This young man is from the *Newport Daily News*," said Miller, introducing the reporter. "I'm afraid our beautiful geisha's death is going to be the lead story in tomorrow's newspaper."

The reporter greeted Charlotte and Lew. "I was just about to ask Dr. Miller why he thinks Okichi-*mago*'s death wasn't a suicide."

"You mean autokabalesis," said Miller. "There, I've done it." He snapped his fingers. "I've always wanted to use that word in an interview. Thought I'd eventually have occasion to use it in connection with the Newport Bridge. We've had people try from time to time, but we've usually managed to talk them out of it."

"Autokabalesis?"

"The act of jumping from a high place for the purpose of killing oneself. Nope, don't think she was a jumper." He shook his head. "Several reasons. One: suicides usually jump facing out, which means that they land on their fronts. Miss Graham found Okichi-*mago* lying on her back, which means that she either pushed herself over the railing, or was pushed. If she pushed herself, it would have been a very awkward way to commit suicide."

It was the same conclusion Charlotte had come to.

"Two: she was too far out. If she had pushed herself over the railing, she would have landed directly below. Miss Graham found her eleven feet out from the base of the cliff. Here's a little known fact about the murder-versus-suicide issue with regard to falls: you can only propel yourself as far out in the air as you can on the ground. Suicides don't always realize this. They think they can soar out into the void like Peter Pan."

"You mean, she couldn't have pushed herself with enough force to land so far out," the reporter said.

"Exactly," Miller replied. "I'll show you." He looked Charlotte up and down. "I'd guess you're a couple of inches taller than our geisha, Miss Graham," he said. "Five feet eight or so. Am I right?"

Charlotte nodded.

"Let's see how far you can jump. Line your toes up with one of the cracks in the floorboards here," he directed. Bending over, he marked the spot with a pencil. Then he stood back and signaled for her to jump.

Charlotte did.

Producing a tape measure from the pocket of his crisply pressed khakis, he measured the distance.

"Four feet, one inch. Very good, Miss Graham—you must have been a broad-jump champ in high school. Our geisha was eleven feet out. Quite a difference. The two situations aren't strictly comparable: Miss Graham jumped and our geisha would have pushed herself, but it nevertheless illustrates my point. A lot of murderers don't realize this. Actually, this little-known fact helped crack the famous Bowery bums case."

Lew stood with his arms folded across his chest, primed for a story. "What's the Bowery bums case, Doc?" he asked.

"Six or seven Bowery bums who supposedly jumped out of windows. Autokabalesis. There, I've done it again. Only they were too far out. Turned out to be a ring of murderers: they were insuring derelicts, tossing them out of windows, and then collecting on their life insurance policies. The lesson of the story is, if you're going to heave somebody out of a window and you want to make it look like suicide, don't get too carried away."

"Something else to keep in mind at city hall," said Lew with a wink at Charlotte. "Any other ideas on how to do away with someone without getting caught? I need all the help I can get."

"Oh, lots," said Miller. "Lesson number one: do it on the spur of the moment. Unless you're killing someone obvious, like your wife—Evelyn, forgive me—murders committed in the heat of passion are harder to solve than those that are carefully planned. The reason is this: the carefully planned murder is the product of an abnormal mind that is going to make a mistake at some point. These guys have blind spots that will eventually do them in."

"What if I'm not overcome by passion?"

"Then you can hire a contract killer. The contract killer flies into town, identifies his victim, squeezes the trigger, and pockets the money. There's no connection except the money, no motive except the money. The killer and the victim are total strangers: there's no complex web of human interactions for a sleuth to unravel." He smiled at Charlotte. "Or, as I suggested earlier, you can always try poison."

"But if your enemies at city hall suddenly start turning up dead, you can bet that Dr. Miller will know where to look," said Charlotte.

"Just don't push your opponent over a railing and try to make it look like a suicide," Miller said. "I could be wrong, of course." He walked over to the railing and picked up a walkie-talkie. "We're going to find out." He leaned over and waved an arm. "How're you boys doing down there?" he said.

"All ready, Doc," came the reply over the walkie-talkie.

Like the temple, the section of the Cliff Walk that crossed the Shimoda property had been blocked off by police barricades. Charlotte could see the disappointed dog-walkers and joggers looking up at the temple and trying to figure out what was going on. Several stood at the cliff's edge, watching the policemen on the beach below.

"We'll just be a minute more," Miller said to the policeman below. He turned back to Charlotte and Lew. "We're just waiting for our dummy to arrive. Here's where she went over." He pointed to the fresh scar on the surface of the weathered railing. "There's a scrape on the railing that was made by the ornament on her obi. We found little bits of pearl embedded in the wood."

Charlotte was glad that forensic science had confirmed her conclusion.

"The scrape is five feet to the side of where the body was found, but we can account for that by normal deviation. The distance to the top of the railing is fifty-seven feet: at that height, a deviation of half an inch can mean several feet by the time the body hits the ground. The more significant fact is that the body landed so far away from the base of the cliff."

"Any chance that the body was moved by the tide?" asked Lew.

"No." Miller shook his head. "High tide was at six forty-four this morning, shortly after Miss Graham found the body. At that time, her legs were submerged up to mid-calf and that's as far as the water level got. The same goes for the wind: there was a light wind that night, but not enough to make any difference in where she landed."

He was interrupted by the appearance of a policeman carrying a life-sized dummy covered in white canvas. A crude face with large, slanted, black-pupiled eyes, a piquant heart-shaped mouth, and a tiny upturned nose had been drawn on the head with a black Magic Marker.

"Aha! The star of the show has arrived," said Miller. "Isn't she lovely? I got a guy I know who works in a sail loft to sew her up for me from yacht canvas. He's made dummies for me before. Drowning cases: to see where the currents might have taken the body. Hard to know where to look otherwise." He shouted over to Kilkenny. "Our dummy's here, Chief."

The police chief joined the group, accompanied by a young policeman with a video camera. As the young man filmed, Miller explained:

"She's constructed around a plastic skeleton. Precisely five feet six inches and one hundred and eighteen pounds, the victim's height and weight. Okay, young man," said Miller, turning to the policeman who was holding the dummy, "set her up." He walked over to the railing. "Right here." He tapped the spot where the obi clasp had left its mark.

The policeman placed the dummy where Miller had indicated.

"We're going to do this two ways," Miller continued. "First, we're going to have her push herself." He lifted the dummy up and draped it over the railing. The arms and head hung downward, the feet were on the floor. "Though how she could have held onto a sake cup in this position is beyond me. Anyway, we'll give it a shot. Okay, Chief," he said. "I guess we're ready."

The chief notified the group below that the reconstruction was about to begin. Another cameraman stood at the bottom of the cliff, waiting to film the dummy as it hit the ground.

"She would have had to kick up her feet to propel herself over the railing," Miller explained. Stepping forward, he grabbed the dummy's feet and flipped them upwards. As they watched, the dummy fell straight down and landed on its head at the base of the cliff. Miller looked up: "Well, I think we can say with some certainty that she would have suffered some head injuries had she tried to kill herself this way, which she did not."

"What *were* the results of the autopsy?" asked Charlotte.

"Well, she died at once as a result of internal injuries," he said. "I estimate that the body was moving at between thirty-five and forty miles per hour when it hit the ground. The aorta was ruptured, as were her heart and kidneys. Her backbone, pelvis, knees, and ribs were fractured, and her right lung was perforated by a broken rib. And, as you know from viewing the body, Miss Graham, both of her legs were broken at the ankles."

"I was surprised at how little blood there was."

"That's common in falls," Miller explained. "You can have a fatal cerebral injury with no external signs of injury at all."

"Do we know the time of death?"

"Sometime between twelve and two." Miller continued: "Now I'll tell you how I think it did happen." He took a position at the railing, pretending to hold a sake cup in his hands. "As I figure it, she was standing here under this crooked old pine tree looking out into the night. Why wasn't she in bed? I don't know—that's for you sleuths to figure out."

As he spoke, Charlotte suddenly remembered the words from "Evening Rain"—*The two of us, moored together. The rendezvous tree*—and it dawned on her why Okichi-*mago* had been standing there: she had been waiting for her lover! Charlotte thought that Shawn had chosen the song because it was raining, but she now realized that it was a cryptic message to meet him at the pine tree.

Miller interrupted her thoughts. "Miss Graham, would you like to play the geisha?" he said, with a courtly little bow. "I think it's a role that you're already familiar with."

She smiled in assent and stepped up to the railing.

"Now, as I figure it, the murderer would have sneaked up on his victim from behind. I imagine he would have clasped her with both arms around the legs and flipped her over. Like this." He demonstrated on Charlotte. "He must have done it very fast; she was caught entirely by surprise. Not only were there no marks of violence, she didn't even drop her sake cup." He unclasped Charlotte's legs. "She goes sailing off the cliff, and that's that."

"Sounds like you've got it all figured out, Doc," said Lew.

"I hope so. We'll see when we do the next reconstruction. I like these kinds of cases. Usually, the cause of death is clear. If there's a hole in the front of the guy and a hole in the back of the guy, you can be pretty sure that there's a hole through everything in between. But something like this takes some brain work"—he tapped his temple with a forefinger—"I look at it as a puzzle, like an acrostic or a crossword."

The two policemen who were carrying the dummy back up the cliff had finally reached the top; it couldn't have been an easy load to haul.

"Okay, fellas," said Miller, as they carried the dummy onto the gallery. "Put her right here."

The policemen propped the dummy up against the railing.

Standing aside, Miller gestured to Lew. "Would you like to do the honors, honorable city solicitor?"

"I'd be delighted," said Lew. "Where should I start from?"

"Let's say from inside. Although it's possible our murderer could have come from around the side of the building. He would have had to be more quiet that way, though." He stomped a foot on the floorboards. "These boards make a lot of noise when you walk on them. Then again, he could have been in his stocking feet. Probably was, if he had any brains. Though I've discovered over the years that a lot of criminals have no brains at all."

Lew leaned over and removed his shoes.

"Aha, I like a man who strives for authenticity," said Miller. Once again, he picked up the walkie-talkie and notified the men below that the reconstruction was about to take place.

After placing his shoes to one side, Lew crossed the gallery and took up his position just inside the sliding wooden doors. Then he stealthily tiptoed across the gallery. As he reached the dummy, he quickly clasped her around the abdomen and flipped her neatly over the railing.

Charlotte leaned over the railing to see. Propelled by the force of the push, the dummy's legs flew outward, whirling the body around in a flip. As the head came around, Charlotte could see the upside down eyes staring, as if in fright. It landed feet first, and then fell backward, coming to rest in exactly the same position in which she had found Okichi-*mago's* body: on its back with its head toward the cliff, about eleven feet out. The dummy had landed directly below, not off to one side as Okichi-*mago*'s body had. But according to Miller, that could be accounted for by a deviation in the force of the push.

"Perfect," said Miller, with an ear-to-ear grin. "I guess you guys—and gals"—he looked over at Charlotte—"had better start looking for a murderer."

"Dr. Miller," asked Charlotte, "would a woman have been capable of pushing Okichi-*mago* over, or would it have required the strength of a man?"

"I'll defer that question to the honorable city solicitor."

"Sure," Lew replied. "It was a snap."

* * *

As they were leaving, Paul drove up with Nadine in his Jaguar. After getting out of the car, they approached Lew and Charlotte. They were a striking couple. Although Paul was by no means handsome, he was always impeccably dressed and carried himself with an air of quiet authority. Nadine was lovely: a petite figure, glossy black hair worn in an elegant French twist, and a warm and gracious smile. Charlotte could easily see why Marianne hated her: it was the hatred of the ugly duckling for the beautiful swan. By contrast, everything about Marianne seemed forced, cold, and pushy. But Charlotte could also sympathize with Marianne. Although she didn't know Nadine, she shared the visceral distrust that the woman who has always supported herself has for the woman, be she wife or mistress, who rides graciously through life on the coattails of a wealthy man. Nadine was a modern version of Okichi: a sake cup which was carried to a man's lips only as long as there was still sake in it.

"I see the police are still here," said Paul, nodding at the string of police cars in the driveway. "We couldn't get here before. We had to attend a meeting of the Black Ships Festival Committee. How's it going?"

At closer range, Charlotte noticed that he looked drawn and haggard; purplish-red circles hung below his bulging brown eyes.

Lew explained the outcome of the reconstruction.

"Oh, how terrible," said Paul. "The police told me when they called yesterday that they doubted it was suicide. But I can't believe it. Who would want to murder her? She didn't even know anyone here."

But despite what he said, Paul looked quietly pleased at the news, as if he were relieved that her death was a murder and not a suicide.

"I've asked Miss Graham to help the police with the case," Lew continued. "As you may know, she's had some experience in solving murders."

"God knows, another head never hurts in these matters," said Paul. "I'm sure the police will be asking us plenty of questions, but if you have any you want to ask, Miss Graham, please don't hesitate."

"I just have a couple," Charlotte replied. "If Okichi-*mago* didn't commit suicide, that means someone else entered the house and removed the sake cup and the comb and mirror from the display cases."

"Yes, I guess it does," said Paul.

"Were you here at the time?"

"I must have been," he replied, glancing over at Nadine. "I gave Shawn Hendrickson a ride home, but that couldn't have taken more than twenty minutes. But I didn't hear anything, if that's what you're asking. I went to bed around a quarter past one. I read for a while, and then went right to sleep."

"You didn't even hear Miako barking?"

Paul tugged thoughtfully on his neatly trimmed reddish-gray beard. "No, I didn't hear him bark. But I'm not sure he would have barked at an intruder. He's not a barker. More of a lap dog than a watch dog, I'm afraid."

"Were the doors locked?"

"Yes. I locked them before I went to bed. But the burglar alarm wasn't turned on. The caterers had been going in and out all evening. I had turned it off and forgotten to turn it back on again."

"Any signs of forced entry?"

"None that I've noticed, but I haven't really checked."

"What about you, Mrs. Ogilvie?" Paul's glance had led Charlotte to think that Nadine might have spent the night with him.

"Paul asked me to stay until the caterers had finished packing up," Nadine replied. "But that only took a few minutes—ten at the most. Then I went home. I got home a little after eleven-thirty."

"Did your son stay here with you?"

"No, he went on ahead. It's only a five-minute walk."

Charlotte remembered that Nadine's house stood near the intersection of Narragansett and Bellevue. "Any servants?" she asked Paul.

"Just the housekeeper, Mrs. Engel. But she doesn't live in. Ordinarily, she comes in just during the day, but she stayed late last night to help with the party. She went home about ten-thirty, I think."

"Thanks, I appreciate your help," said Charlotte.

* * *

Lew dropped her off at the head of Bellevue Avenue, where she ate a quick lunch. Then she headed over to the casino. She was due at the casino theatre at twelve-thirty for the "Afternoon of Japanese Culture," which started at one. She would start looking for the murderer there. It looked as if Nadine was out of the picture. Her story was probably true: it was unlikely that she would have spent the night with Paul with her sons at home alone. As for gaining entry to the house: Charlotte had assumed that Okichi-*mago*, being Paul's house guest, would have had a key, but her murderer, if there was one, would have had to force his way in. The police would no doubt be looking for signs of forced entry, as well as for fingerprints on the sake cup, comb, and mirror, and the display cases from which they had been taken. The burglar alarm being turned off was a lucky break for the murderer. But if he hadn't known the alarm was turned off, wouldn't he have been taking a big chance by breaking in? It didn't take a criminal genius to figure out that the house would be equipped with an alarm system: there probably wasn't a house on the Cliff Walk that wasn't. Unless the murderer was someone at the party, who, seeing the caterers going in and out, concluded that the alarm had been turned off and assumed a tired host would forget to turn it back on at the end of a busy evening. But it was a chancy assumption. Or, the murderer could have been someone who knew how to turn off the alarm himself, namely Marianne or Lester. There was another reason Charlotte wanted to question them as well: Marianne's flirtation with Shawn had provoked a scene at the close of the party. Lester had called Marianne several unpleasant names, whereupon she had refused to ride home with him. After dropping Charlotte and the Smiths off at Briarcote, Lester had returned to Shimoda in search of Marianne. What had happened after that was anybody's guess, but it was likely that either or both of them were at Shimoda at around the time that Okichi-*mago* was killed.

Although Paul had been responsible for importing the geishas for the Afternoon of Japanese Culture, it was actually Marianne who was coordinating the program. The program consisted of three parts. The first was a charity fashion show of Marianne's "Geisha" collection sponsored by a Boston department store. The show was what was known in the fashion industry as a trunk show: the collection that had been unveiled to rave reviews in New York two weeks ago would be traveling across the country from Newport to San Diego, giving loyal customers in places like Chicago, Dallas, and Atlanta a chance to buy Marianne's designs on their home turf. The second part was an exhibition of traditional Japanese song and dance performed by the geishas. Charlotte assumed it would be similar to the performances at the geisha party. The third part was a performance of a traditional Japanese puppet play by a Japanese-American puppet theatre troupe from San Francisco. Charlotte was looking forward to the puppet theatre, which she had never seen. The puppets were half the size of a human adult, and each was manipulated by three men: one for the head, body, and right arm; another for the left arm; and a third for the feet. The puppets' ability to portray human emotions was said to be nothing less than miraculous. Overseeing these events would be the mistress of ceremonies, Okichi of *Soiled Dove*, otherwise known as Charlotte Graham. Under her arm, she carried the script that Paul had hastily revised from the one he had originally prepared for Okichi-*mago*. Apart from delivering the script, she had no idea what she was supposed to do. But that was okay: after fifty years in front of the cameras, she was used to improvising.

The theatre was located at the rear of the casino complex, next to the royal tennis court. The exterior was of the same unassuming shingle style as the rest of the building, but, as she discovered when she entered, the theatre itself was an ornate, if somewhat run-down, gem. Spalding had told her it was one of Stanford White's favorite designs. Charlotte was something of a connoisseur of theatres, having worked over the years in most of Broadway's most well-known houses as well as an untold number of obscure ones around the country. She could appreciate this one despite its cracked plaster and peeling paint. She had seen many a Broadway landmark in worse condition. On the stage, artists were busy putting the finishing touches on the backdrop, which was a reproduction of a Japanese landscape depicting a temple perched on a mountainside. It reminded her of the Temple of Great Repose. Leaving the empty theatre, she made her way down a corridor to the backstage area, which was humming with activity. People were adjusting lights, fiddling with the sound controls, dressing models, taking pictures. At the center of it all was Marianne, who was fluttering around as nervously as a playwright on opening night: pinning a hem, fussing with a model's makeup, and giving orders right and left.

Seeing Charlotte, she disengaged herself and clattered across the stage in her *geta*. "You're here!" she said. She was wearing a white kimono made of a light, airy fabric and dotted with enormous parti-colored polka dots. "We start at one. First, the fashion show. Then the geishas. Then the puppet play. Did Spalding give you any script?"

Charlotte nodded. "Paul sent it over this morning."

"Paul." She repeated the name with a grimace. "Ordinarily I can't stand the mention of that man's name. But we'll make an exception for Okichi Day. Let me see." She grabbed the script out of Charlotte's hand and looked it over. "Looks okay to me," she said, passing it back. "He may be a bastard, but he's an efficient one. As I found out in court. Do you have any questions?"

A reporter interrupted their conversation.

"This is a reporter for Jordan Marsh," Marianne explained. "They're sponsoring the show. She's doing some sort of publicity thing for the store. What did you want to know?" she asked.

"Can you tell us a little about the collection?" asked the reporter as an assistant with a video camera filmed Marianne's reply.

"The big news in this collection is the return of loose, unrestricted shapes. We've reached the end of the line when it comes to a certain kind of design: skirts couldn't get any shorter, or tighter. The time has come for a shift to a looser, more *dégagé* silhouette. These styles are all based on the kimono design: very light and modern, very colorful, very exciting."

"Isn't this a radical departure from your recent collections?" the reporter asked. "You were the designer most responsible for popularizing the miniskirt in the sixties, and for reviving it in the eighties."

"The point of creating is to change, to go elsewhere. I decided I wanted to create a mixture of Occidental and Oriental. The Occidental clothing tradition has become too tight. I wanted to make things that were free, both mentally and physically. But I wanted to avoid the drab Japanese colors. The eighties were the decade of black; the nineties will be the decade of color."

At a signal from the reporter, the cameraman set down his camera. "Thank you," the reporter said, and moved on.

"An excellent performance," said Charlotte.

"I'm an old pro," Marianne replied. "Now we have to get you dressed. You're going to wear one of the designs from my collection. Do you want something way-out or something tame?"

Charlotte looked at Marianne's outfit. It was stunning: original, dramatic, playful, but it wasn't Charlotte. "Something tame please."

"That's fine. I know my more colorful designs aren't for everybody. The Princess of Wales, the First Lady of the United States, the Queen of Jordan. But not for everybody. I'm only kidding. We have something that will be perfect for you— just your style." She called to a handsome young man who was fitting a model in one of Marianne's smashing kimono designs.

"Just a minute," said Charlotte.

Marianne swiveled her head around in surprise.

"Before you call him over, there's something I want to talk with you about—in private. Is there a place where we can talk?"

"Sure," Marianne replied. "But I can't talk for long. I have a show to put on." Signaling the young man to stay where he was, she led Charlotte toward a bank of office cublicles against the back wall. "Would you like a cigarette?" she asked as they sat down on two folding chairs. She removed a packet from the voluminous sleeve of her kimono, and offered it to Charlotte.

"Thanks," said Charlotte, taking one.

"What is it?"

"It's Okichi-*mago*. The police think she was murdered."

"Murdered!"

Charlotte nodded as Marianne lit her cigarette for her. "They think someone pushed her over the railing after the geisha party. The state medical examiner staged a reconstruction of the fall at the site this morning, with a dummy that was Okichi-*mago*'s height and weight. The dummy landed in exactly the same position as the one in which I found Okichi-*mago*'s body."

"I thought she committed suicide," said Marianne. "What about the comb as the symbol of leave-taking, and the mirror as the symbol of the soul? It was so romantic—I hate to think of that beautiful woman being just plain murdered."

"Someone planted them—to make it look like a suicide. There was also the sake cup that Townsend Harris had given her. Actually, there were two sake cups." Charlotte explained about the extra sake cup, and about the body being found too far away from the base of the cliff for the death to have been a suicide. She also explained about Lew asking her to look into the murder.

Lester stuck his head in the door. "Is this where you've been hiding out?" he asked in an accusing voice. "You'd better hightail it out here, because everybody is looking for you and I'm sure as hell not gonna answer all their questions." As usual, he was wearing a wide-brimmed felt hat and reptile skin cowboy boots that made him look taller than he really was.

"Come on in," said Marianne. "Okichi-*mago*'s been murdered." She gave him a brief recap of the story Charlotte had just told her. "I presume Miss Graham has some questions to ask us about where we were and what we saw."

Lester entered and sat down on another folding chair. He was a sharp-featured man with a hooked nose and brown eyes that were set too close together. He looked a little like Marianne, in fact. He also looked cranky and preoccupied. "Is there any doubt?" he asked. "What I mean is, could she have committed suicide, or is it definitely murder?"

"I suppose anything's possible," Charlotte replied. "But the state medical examiner is convinced that she was pushed." She explained again about the body being too far out from the base of the cliff. She addressed Marianne: "Where you were and what you saw is exactly what I'd like to know. What did you do after everybody left the party? I know Lester went back for you. Did you end up going home with him?"

Marianne turned to Lester. "You went back for me?"

Lester nodded.

"Isn't that nice." Her voice dripped sarcasm. It was clear that all was not well with the Montgomery/Frame relationship. She turned back to Charlotte: "I walked home—on the Cliff Walk. It was a beautiful night: the moon was full and the stars were yellow, as the old song goes. Haven't walked the Cliff Walk at night since I was a kid."

"In a kimono, wearing *geta*?"

"I took off the outer kimono and the *geta*. Left them in one of those little closets in the temple. I just wore the under-kimono. I went back yesterday to pick them up." Looking over at Lester, she licked her lips provocatively. "The nice young policeman who was guarding the place let me in."

Lester pretended to ignore her.

If the story had come from anyone else, Charlotte would have doubted it, but walking the Cliff Walk alone on a moonlit night wearing nothing but an under-kimono was just the kind of thing Marianne would do. She would probably have done it stark naked. "Did you see anything unusual?"

"Nothing."

"What about you, Les? Did you see anyone when you went back?"

"Not a soul. I walked out to the temple looking for Marianne. But she wasn't there, so I left. I don't know what time it was when she got back. I was asleep by then."

"How long were you there?"

"Ten minutes, at the outside."

Charlotte nodded. She turned back to Marianne. "Did you know that Paul was planning to make Okichi-*mago* his heir?"

"He was!" Marianne nearly dropped her cigarette. "His heir—that's great! Paul is so . . . so *Gothic*." She looked at Charlotte. "Let me guess. You think I killed Okichi-*mago* so that Shimoda will go to Dede. Am I right?"

"Let's say that it's a possibility."

"I love it. A suspect in a murder! But forget the motive." She waved the hand holding the cigarette dismissively. "Contrary to what you may think, I have no objection to sharing Shimoda with Paul."

"Then why have you been fighting him?"

"The operative word is 'share.' My great-aunt's will says that Shimoda is to be *shared* between my mother and Paul and their descendants. Just because Paul had the place to himself for ten years, he thinks it's his. In fact, not only do I not have a motive, I have a counter-motive. If I'd known he was going to make Okichi-*mago* his heir, I would have been standing down on the rocks with a safety net."

Charlotte raised a skeptical eyebrow.

"I don't mind sharing, but I do mind who I share with," she explained. "Unless Paul manages to dig up some other obscure relative, he's going to end up adopting Nadine's sons and making them his heirs. Actually, they seem like nice boys. Dede seems to have a thing going with the older one. I have nothing against them; it's their mother I can't stand."

"She's putting it mildly," said Lester. "She hates her."

"Okay," Marianne agreed, "I hate the bitch."

"Why?"

"She's a phony, a snob, a social climber. She writes under the name of Nadine de Goncourt. Supposedly it's her maiden name, but it sounds made-up to me. She says she's from Paris, but she's really from some hick town in Quebec. It's like that. I don't know who I hate more, him or her. The person who you *should* be investigating is her. Now, there's a woman with a motive. Have you seen the trees on Bellevue Avenue?"

Charlotte nodded.

"She won't give up her house on Bellevue Avenue, but she'll cut down some of the oldest trees in town to save it. Now *that's* desperation. The only people I know who are more desperate than she is are the ones who turn the whole place into condos and end up living in an apartment in their former house."

They were interrupted by the handsome young man who informed them that there were only fifteen minutes left until show time.

"I've got to go," said Marianne, jumping up. "So do you. Mark will take care of you. Mark, fit Miss Graham in the gold silk suit. Sorry I wasn't able to help. If you want to ask me anything else, you know where to find me."

A few minutes later, Charlotte was delivering the speech that Paul had prepared for her. It described the history of the relationship between Townsend Harris and Okichi, and Paul's meeting with Okichi-*mago* in Kyoto last year. Finally it described Okichi-*mago*'s tragic death, and ended with a prayer.

Nothing was said about the suspicion that she'd been murdered.

After that came the fashion show. As an announcer from the department store reeled off the names of the designs—"Court Lady," "Madame Butterfly," "Samurai Woman"—the tall, thin models paraded down the runway to the accompaniment of electronic New Age Japanese music. Charlotte was amused to see that several of the models wore their hair in the gingko leaf hairstyle.

Although the show had already opened to rave reviews in New York, the fashion press had turned out en masse for the road show. They couldn't resist the temptation of photographing the Japanese collection against the splendid Newport backdrop. Which was exactly Marianne's idea.

The show lasted only half an hour: close to a hundred outfits, ending with "Scarlet Empress," a ball gown of iridescent red. After the show, Marianne strode confidently down the runway in her parti-colored polka-dot kimono to thunderous applause, blowing kisses to the photographers. She had added a huge hat with an abstract Japanese flower arrangement on top.

"The hat is great, but who except Marianne would ever wear anything like that?" commented Connie, who was sitting in the front row next to Charlotte.

Spalding leaned over: "Only another exhibitionist like your daughter."

Connie smiled.

After the fashion show came the geishas' exhibition of traditional Japanese song and dance, and then the puppet play, which was titled *The Love Suicides at Sonezaki*. According to

Charlotte's introduction, the playwright was Chikamatzu, who was known as the William Shakespeare of Japan, and the play was considered his first great love suicide play.

The play was short, lasting only half an hour. But it was very moving. The story, which was based on an actual event, involved a young soy-sauce merchant and his geisha lover who kill themselves because they cannot marry, vowing to be "husband and wife for eternity." The theme was the conflict between *ninjo* and *giri* that Spalding had spoken of.

"No one is there to tell the tale," the narrator sadly announced as the merchant stabs himself in the throat in the last scene after killing his beloved, "but the wind that blows through Sonezaki Wood transmits it, and high and low alike gather to pray for these lovers who beyond a doubt will in the future attain Nirvana. They have become models of true love."

Charlotte noticed that the deaths of the amazingly lifelike cloth-and-wood puppets brought tears to the eyes of many in the audience.

After the puppet play, the audience withdrew for a reception on the Horseshoe Piazza. As she helped herself to cheese and crackers, Charlotte was joined by Aunt Lillian, who looked as if she had just walked off a blue-willow plate in a kimono with a pattern of willow trees and teahouses. The cobalt blue of the kimono exactly matched the blue of her eyes.

"Wasn't the play wonderful?" she asked, "I love the idea of experiencing eternal bliss together in paradise." She quoted a line: " 'In the world to come, may we be reborn on the same lotus.' It refers to the lotuses growing in the lake before the Buddha's throne in paradise."

"I suppose it helps make the whole idea of double suicide more palatable," said Charlotte. "Though I must confess that I still find the whole idea farfetched. Why couldn't they just elope?"

"That's because you put too much store in your earthly existence, my dear. They'd rather be released from their unfortunate lot in this world and take their chances in the next. Besides, by committing suicide, they also achieve eternal fame. The Sonezaki Wood is a famous place of pilgrimage for lovers."

"Immortality in this world and the next."

"Yes. I thought you did an excellent job of explaining the play in your introduction. But you did make one mistake in your opening speech about Okichi-*mago*," she said, her cobalt blue eyes twinkling.

"What's that?"

"Paul Harris didn't just discover Okichi-*mago* at a Kyoto geisha house last year. He's known her since she was a girl."

· 9 ·

CHARLOTTE WANTED TO talk with Shawn before he went back to Japan: if he'd had a rendezvous with Okichi-*mago* as she suspected, he would have been the last person to see her alive. And Spalding had told her he was scheduled to leave Newport with the other wrestlers on a flight out of Providence the next night. The only formal event on the wrestlers' schedule today had been a children's sumo workshop that morning (part of Lani's effort to promote the internationalization of sumo), but the Black Ships committee had been keeping them busy in their free time. Tour buses had been taking them all over: a harbor cruise, wine-tasting, a visit to the mansions, a tour of Boston, and several radio interviews, with Lani serving as translator. The local press had been charting their every move. They were probably off doing something now. But Charlotte doubted Shawn was among them. First, he'd probably already seen the tourist attractions, and second, he probably didn't feel much like playing. No doubt he would have heard that the police were no longer considering Okichi-*mago*'s death a suicide. They might even have interviewed him already. Charlotte checked her watch. It was just after four. If she left now, maybe she could catch him before dinner. The sumo wrestlers dined early in order to give them enough time to finish their enormous meals. Spalding and Connie, who had eaten with them on their first evening in Newport had been astounded at the amount of food they had consumed: one sumo wrestler—probably the gigantic popover from the first sumo match—had tucked away fifteen lobsters. Slipping away from the gathering, she hastened back to the theatre and quickly changed back into her own clothes. In a few minutes, she was heading down Bellevue Avenue.

Shawn and the other sumo wrestlers from his stable were staying at The Waves at the south end of the Cliff Walk, two houses down from Briarcote. The four houses shared a common road. Like many of Newport's other mansions, The Waves had been chopped up into condos. Newport was a city of condominiums: new condos and old mansions converted into condos occupied by weekenders from Boston and Providence, boat owners who wanted a place to stay overnight, officers attending the Naval War College, college students working in bars and restaurants, and families taking their annual week at the beach. The sumo wrestlers were occupying two of the largest condos at The Waves, along with a cook who had been hired to prepare their enormous breakfasts and lunches. Dinners were eaten out, courtesy of local restaurants. Because of his senior rank among the wrestlers from his stable, Shawn had a condo to himself, which he shared with Lani. His stablemates were housed dormitory-style in the other. The condos in The Waves were among Newport's most luxurious by virtue of the mansion's dramatic location on a rocky promontory at the southern tip of the island. The Waves was one of Charlotte's favorite Newport mansions. Built in the twenties by John Russell Pope, the architect of the Jefferson Memorial, as a summer house for himself and his family, its rambling half-timbered gables and undulating slate roof were meant to be reminiscent of an English country cottage. Despite its enormous size and the way it loomed fortresslike above its windswept site, it nevertheless projected a feeling of warmth and coziness.

It didn't take Charlotte as long as usual to travel the length of Bellevue Avenue. She was driving her own car, an ordinary Oldsmobile. When it came to cars, she was in Spalding's camp: pretentious cars weren't her style. At the end, she turned onto Ledge Road and from there onto the private road leading to The Waves. The house was built in the form of a U surrounding a walled inner courtyard. Inside the courtyard, apple trees flourished and flower beds bloomed, protected by the building from the driving winds off the ocean. As she entered the courtyard through a low door in the wall, she saw a gardener working in a rose bed, and asked him where she could find the sumo wrestlers. "The important sumo wrestlers, or the rest of them?" he asked. "The important sumo wrestlers," she replied. The gardener directed her to a door opening off the courtyard. She should have been able to figure it out for herself: outside the door was a simple pair of rope thongs.

Shawn answered the door and bowed, Japanese style. He was wearing only a *mawashi*, a practice *mawashi* made of heavy canvas, rather than silk. In texture and size, it resembled a fire hose. He was shining with sweat.

"I thought you were Lani," he said, apologizing for his appearance. "Won't you come in?" He gestured toward the interior.

Once she had removed her shoes, Shawn ushered her into a huge wood-paneled room with giant windows overlooking the ocean. The oversized modern furniture had been moved aside to make room for futons that had been rolled up for the day. Shawn maneuvered a chair into position for her. "Why don't you sit here?" he said. "I'm just going to put on a kimono. I'll be right back."

The room was immaculately neat. Apart from the rolled-up futons and a couple of lacquered wickerware trunks, the only sign of the sumo wrestlers' residency was a small shrine that had been set up at the side of the room. Above the shrine hung a scroll that was decorated with ink-wash calligraphy.

Shawn returned a minute later wearing a summer kimono in shades of green that emphasized the deep green of his eyes.

"I'm staying here with Lani," he explained. "In Japan, we usually stay at temples when we're on tour so we can practice on the grounds. Most of the *rikishi* are staying in condos in the mansions for the same reason."

"It's beautiful," said Charlotte, but she didn't really mean it. The setting was beautiful, but the ultramodern furnishings seemed out of place, more suited to a New York penthouse than a vacation retreat by the sea.

"Too luxurious for me," he said. "Are you familiar with the Japanese idea of *wabi*? The rough translation is refined poverty."

Charlotte shook her head.

"It means the absence of excess. Not wanting what's lacking. Making do with what's at hand. Enjoying simple austerity. It's a concept that's always appealed to me." He smiled. "But I guess I can live with excess for a while."

"For the bachelor residence of two men, it's very neat," she commented.

"It's part of the sumo way of life," said Shawn. "Always keep your surroundings neat so that you won't be ashamed if you die while you're away."

Charlotte raised an eyebrow in surprise.

"Readiness for death is one of the pillars of the code of the samurai. It's recommended that you meditate on death every morning and every evening. If you die every day in your mind, you won't fear death. Death sharpens life, just as discipline sharpens pleasure."

Despite a hefty dose of native New England common sense, Charlotte had a superstitious belief in the power of mental images; to her way of thinking, if you imagined something powerfully enough, it might come true.

"It's a hard concept for Westerners to understand," Shawn continued. "Most Westerners think it's morbid, but actually it's the opposite. By dying every day in your mind, you're freeing yourself to live in the moment."

"I don't think it's morbid. I think it's dangerous: by dying every day in your mind, aren't you opening the door to death?"

"Aha! That's another difference between East and West. To the Oriental, tempting fate is impossible because your fate is preordained."

"Karma?" said Charlotte.

Shawn nodded and leaned against the back of a chair. "I saw you at the match yesterday," he said. "How did you like it?"

"I loved it," she replied. "I didn't really expect to. I'm not a very sports-minded person. But I liked the swiftness of it. The immutability. It's like acting in that respect: you only get a few minutes for your big scene; if you flub it, there's no second chance."

"That's what I like about it, too. Only one chance to win or lose. It's very Eastern, very Zen-like. Of course, you need a certain amount of strength and size, but the important thing is concentration: to me, it's more like ink-wash painting than wrestling."

Charlotte nodded at the calligraphy above the shrine. "One of your paintings?" she asked.

He nodded. "Ink-wash painting is very much like sumo: the inspiration has to be transferred to the paper in the quickest possible time; you have to be entirely in the moment. If you hesitate, you'll tear the paper. There's no deliberation, no retouching, no repetition. Once executed, it's irrevocable."

He gestured to French doors leading out to a grassy terrace where a canvas mat with a green circle outlined on it—a practice sumo mat—was spread out on the grass. A long black *mawashi* was draped out over a makeshift clothesline. "Would you like to sit outside?" he asked.

"Yes," she replied.

On the way out, her eye was caught by an object sitting on a small table beneath the shrine. It was a *chommage* in a Plexiglas box, just like the one Lani had showed her the photo of. "Is this Lani's *chommage*?" she asked.

"No," Shawn replied. "It's mine."

Charlotte glanced up at Shawn's hair, but his *chommage* was still intact.

"Someone sends me one before every tournament. It's their way of saying that it's time I should retire. It's a subtle form of harassment, one of many that I've had to put up with."

"Do you know who sends them?" she asked as she looked again at the *chommage*. It looked like the shiny pelt of a dead muskrat.

"No. I have some ideas. But it doesn't really matter—I look forward to getting them now. I use them in my meditations as a reminder of death, a *memento mori*. For a *rikishi*, retirement *is* a form of death."

He led her through the French doors to the terrace.

As she followed, Charlotte noticed his peculiar gait: it was almost as if he were ice skating. Then she remembered something Spalding had said about sumo wrestlers sliding their feet to prevent stepping accidentally out of the ring. The gait must have become as habitual as a ballet dancer's turnout.

"This is where I practice; it's also where I meditate," said Shawn, as they reached the center of the grassy terrace. "It's totally private. In Japan, we like to have sumo fans watch us practice. But outside of Japan, people stare at us as if we were freaks."

As many times as she had walked by The Waves, Charlotte had never noticed this terrace. From below, the wall surrounding it looked like part of the huge stone foundation that anchored the sprawling mansion on its rocky promontory. She said as much to Shawn.

"I know," he said. "I like that about it. We can see them, but they can't see us," he explained, looking out at the tourists who were picking their way across the rocks below. "Unless they're looking directly at us."

Charlotte looked out, too. At the end of Ledge Road, a police scooter was ticketing illegally parked cars. The rocky ledges at the end of the road were a popular spot for fishing, diving, and rock-combing, and a problem with too many cars had led to the no-parking ordinance.

"Did you ever notice the stairs?" asked Shawn.

"No," said Charlotte. "What stairs?"

He led her over to a gap in the wall where stairs led down to an overgrown path that meandered across the rocks to join the Cliff Walk. "Every once in a while, a tourist strays off the Cliff Walk and ends up here. They're always very surprised. Suddenly they're practically in someone's living room."

"They'd be very surprised indeed if they happened upon a couple of sumo wrestlers," said Charlotte. "Especially in your skimpy *mawashi*."

Shawn smiled. "I'm used to wearing a *mawashi*," he said, "but I forget that other people aren't. Someone once told me it looked like a diaper."

Charlotte laughed.

For a moment, they looked out at the ocean, where the surf surged against the rocks, sending plumes of spray into the sky. In the distance, an excursion boat was rounding the point, beginning its tour of the Cliff Walk from the sea.

"I'm here about Okichi-*mago*," said Charlotte, as they turned back toward a pair of lawn chairs that sat side by side, facing the sea. She explained about Lew Farrell asking her to look into the geisha's death.

"May I ask you a question?" Shawn said hesitantly as they sat down. The sumo creed dictated that he not show emotion, but there was a heaviness in his manner and a dullness in his deep green eyes that betrayed his grief.

"Certainly."

"Did you see her?"

Charlotte knew immediately what he meant. It was the survivor's craving for the details of death, the details that were needed to fix the final picture of the dead person in the mind, to grasp the awful reality.

"How did she look?" he asked.

"She looked beautiful," Charlotte replied. She described how, except for her broken ankles, there were no signs of injury. "Even the camellias in her hair were still in place," she said.

"Thank you," he said. He leaned back, his tense shoulders sinking with relief. "I know it would have meant a lot to her not to have looked"—he paused to think—"ugly, grotesque. The police couldn't tell me. They tried, but . . ."

"I'm sorry," said Charlotte.

"The camellias. The symbol of premature death." He smiled bitterly at the irony. "The police were here this morning," he continued. "I couldn't tell them anything. I don't think I can do any better for you, but I'll try."

"I remember the *kouta* you sang at the geisha party."

"'Evening Rain'? Are you asking if I was making an appointment to meet Kichi after everyone had gone home?"

Charlotte nodded.

"Yes, I was. *Kouta* are known for their hidden meanings, but the hidden meaning in that one isn't all that subtle. Paul Harris gave me a ride home; after he dropped me off, I turned right around and came back."

"You walked?"

Shawn nodded. "It's only a mile and half. It was about eleven forty-five when I got back to the temple. I was supposed to meet Kichi at the rendezvous tree—the pine at the corner of the gallery. But she wasn't there, so I left."

"Did you see anyone?"

"Not at the house. But when I was standing at the railing, I saw a man in a kimono on the Cliff Walk. He was walking away from the temple, in the direction of The Breakers. It looked like Tanaka—he was short and slight, with white hair—but I couldn't say for sure."

"Did you look down? If you looked down and didn't see the body, it would help us pinpoint the time of death."

"I really don't remember." He shook his head in uncertainty. "I remember looking out: that's when I saw Tanaka, but I don't remember looking down."

"Do you know of anyone who might have wanted to kill her?"

"No. The only person I can think of is Tanaka. But I don't think he would have killed her. He wasn't that upset by our relationship. In a way, I think he actually liked it. He considered it a status symbol that his geisha was having an affair with a sumo wrestler."

"Reflected glory?"

"Something like that. A liaison with a geisha has more to do with manners than it does romance or sex; it comes from the ambition to be known as a gentleman. It would be comparable to a gentleman's owning a fine collection of leather-bound books or a renowned painting."

It was the same observation Keiko had made.

"It's not uncommon for a geisha who has a patron to have an affair with an actor or a sumo wrestler," Shawn continued. "To use the same analogy: it would be the equivalent of a gentleman's loaning out his famous painting to be put on display at a prestigious museum."

"Except that your relationship with Okichi-*mago* wasn't just a casual affair. At least, I didn't think it was."

"No, it wasn't," Shawn agreed.

"Which meant that the painting wasn't going to be returned."

Below, a scraggly-haired tourist in a yellow windbreaker and navy blue baseball cap, with a pair of field glasses hanging from around his neck, had lost the Cliff Walk and was wandering up the path toward the house.

"A wandering tourist," said Shawn. "The path is hard to follow across the rocks." He ice-skated across the grass to the head of the stairs, and hailed the tourist. "Excuse me, sir," he shouted. "This is private property." He pointed over at the rocks. "The Cliff Walk is over there."

The man raised his field glasses to look at Shawn. Then he looked down at a piece of paper in his hand, probably a map. Waving an arm in acknowledgment, he headed back down the path.

Shawn ice-skated back to his chair. "The man who owns this condo told me that a tourist once walked right into his living room, and said, 'Nice place you've got here.' Where were we? Oh, Tanaka. Yes, he could have done it, I suppose. In anger over his painting not being returned. But I don't think so."

"Did you know that Paul was planning to make Okichi-*mago* his heir?"

"No," he replied with surprise. "She never said anything about it."

"I guess he didn't have a chance to talk with her about it before she died. But it does provide a motive—several other Harris relatives have a stake in inheriting Shimoda."

Shawn stared out at the shining sea. "I'm sorry," he said as he caught Charlotte waiting for a response. "It seems so inconsequential to me—who did it. In the face of her being gone. I think about other things: like whether she died well— dying well is important to the Japanese—but I don't think about who did it."

"I understand," said Charlotte. "Just one more question."

"Sure," said Shawn.

"What about Takafuji as the murderer?" Admittedly it was farfetched, but why not ask as long as she was here?

"What would be his motive?"

"He hates you."

"Yes, he hates me, but I don't think he'd kill Kichi on account of that. If he were going to kill anyone, he'd kill me. I've always suspected him of sending the *chommages*. He's going to hate me even more if I win the fall tournament and become the first foreign *yokozuna* in the history of sumo."

"Are you going to win?"

For a moment, the fighting spirit flashed in his dull green eyes. "Yes," he replied softly. "For Kichi."

* * *

The next event on the busy Black Ships Festival program was
a reenactment of Perry's landing at Shimoda. A black-hulled
steamship similar to Perry's flagship, the *Susquehanna*, had
been borrowed from Mystic Seaport for the occasion. Drama students from the University of Rhode Island would be
reenacting Perry's presentation of the letter from U.S. President Millard Fillmore to the shogun's representatives. The
reenactment would be followed by a Dixieland jazz concert
and a display of Japanese fireworks. But Charlotte decided to
skip this event and visit Aunt Lillian. Her brief exchange with
Aunt Lillian that afternoon had left her curious: what had she
meant by saying that Paul had known Okichi-*mago* for years?
And if this were so, why had he gone to such great lengths to
make the point that he had met her just last year? He had said
so when he'd spoken with Connie at the geisha party, and had
reiterated the point in the speech she had just delivered. Then
again, Aunt Lillian was nearly a hundred years old. Maybe she
was mistaken. But it was worth a visit to find out. After leaving
The Waves—it had been a long shot anyway, but she was now
convinced that Shawn had nothing to do with Okichi-*mago*'s
death—she returned to Briarcote, and called Aunt Lillian. She
was in, and she would be delighted to have a visitor. Connie
gave Charlotte directions.

A few minutes later, Charlotte was headed down Bellevue
Avenue once again. Aunt Lillian's house was located at the
other end of town, near the Newport Bridge. It was the un-chic
end, but it was also the oldest part of town. Her house, which
was called Old Trees (did every house in Newport have a name?
Charlotte wondered), was a gracious old Greek Revival mansion dating from the early nineteenth century. "One of the finest
examples of Greek Revival architecture in America," Connie
had said. Rather than rattling around in the big old columned
mansion, however, Aunt Lillian rented it out, and lived instead
in a former porter's lodge at the rear. Driving down the driveway
to the rear of the mansion, Charlotte caught her breath at the
sight of the porter's lodge. It was the most perfect little house
she had ever seen: a single-story Greek temple in miniature,
encircled by a colonnade of Corinthian columns. The house

had an air of weathered antiquity that went with its owner: the paint was peeling and the property, as the name implied, was studded with huge old trees.

It was, quite literally, the house of Charlotte's dreams.

She had dreamed of it when her third marriage was falling apart. It had been one of those vivid dreams that the dreamer recognizes as being out of the ordinary, what Carl Jung had called an archetypal dream. She had been carrying it around with her for more than thirty years.

In the dream there were two churches: one was large, ornate, and overrun with women. The other was Aunt Lillian's house, a little white temple, simple and pure. She had to make a choice, but it was a clear one. She would choose the temple; it was so lovely. By contrast, the cathedral looked tasteless and vulgar. She started heading toward the temple, but then noticed that it was deserted. Why wasn't anyone there? Did all those women at the cathedral know something she didn't? She reconsidered. Yes, the cathedral was tasteless and vulgar, but its complex façade and baroque embellishments had a warmth and richness that the other temple lacked; it spoke of history and tradition and ritual. Was the little white temple too regular, too austere? She didn't think so, but everyone else seemed to. She was torn—charmed by the simplicity, but seduced by the ornament.

In her interpretation, the two churches stood for the state of being single and the state of marriage. In her dream, she had chosen the baroque cathedral.

She had tried to patch that marriage up, to no avail. He had been one of her leading men and was widely considered to be one of Hollywood's most charming. That he was also a drunkard and a womanizer she hadn't discovered until later. Her first marriage—to her hometown sweetheart—had fallen apart when she went to Hollywood; her second, to a New England blueblood, had been her most successful. She had had ten happy years with Will before he died of a heart attack in his forties. After her third husband, there had been a succession of lovers—Linc Crawford among them—before she had dared to enter that ornate cathedral for the fourth time, only a few years ago.

Her fourth husband, Jack Lundstrom, had built a small, family-owned mining company into one of the country's biggest conglomerates. She had always thought her best chances for marital success would lie with someone whose achievements matched hers, but in a different field, someone who wouldn't be threatened by being Mr. Charlotte Graham. When they'd met at a mutual friend's, they'd recognized themselves in one another, and been immediately attracted. Such is the power of narcissicism. She should have known better at her age.

They'd separated after two years. Now she suspected that he was about to ask her to come back. She had dreamed the dream again two nights ago. Actually, it had been in the early morning, the morning she had found Okichi-*mago*'s body. She wondered which church she would choose this time.

She parked the car behind an old Dodge in the driveway. As she got out of her car, she noticed that the huge old oak growing next to the driveway bore a plaque that said the tree was alive at the time of the signing of the Constitution. It described the tree as being fourteen feet around and the largest of its species in Rhode Island. Old Trees, she decided, was a fitting name for the residence of a woman who was nearly a hundred.

Past the oak, a mossy path led through a gap in a stone wall to the house. Charlotte followed the path to the front door, which was flanked by a pair of monumental Japanese temple urns. Above the door, pigeons nested in a transom window above the cornice. Their droppings littered the porch floor in front of the door. The door itself had a gigantic keyhole, which made Charlotte feel like Alice after sampling the liquid in the bottle labeled "Drink me."

The feeling of the house was one of lyrical decay, of a place that was lost in time, out of a mossy, tree-shaded dream. Newport was full of such places. A house such as this would be a treasure in Burbank, but here it was just another old crumbling edifice. The city had sometimes been compared to Troy, with its layer upon layer of history. In places like this, she felt as if she had broken through to one of the earliest layers.

Aunt Lillian met her at the door, her blue eyes shining. She had changed out of her kimono, and was again wearing a white kerchief on her head. She looked like a Normandy peasant. She showed Charlotte into the living room, which took up almost the entire first floor.

"I see why the house is called Old Trees," said Charlotte.

"Did you see the plaque on the bicentennial tree by the driveway?"

"Yes," said Charlotte.

"The National Arborists Association put it there in 1987," Aunt Lillian said. She gestured toward the back of the house. "I was just putting the kettle on for tea. Would you like to sit down?"

"May I help you?" asked Charlotte.

"If you'd like."

Charlotte followed her back to a tiny kitchen, which looked as if it hadn't changed since the turn of the century. A toaster oven sat on a counter next to an old gas refrigerator. The sink was made of soapstone. A steep, narrow staircase led up to the attic bedroom.

"Do you live here alone?" asked Charlotte as Aunt Lillian put the kettle on the old gas stove and set a Japanese lusterware teapot and two cracked cups on a battered old toleware tray.

"Yes," she replied. "I moved here when I was forty, into the big house. When my husband died, I moved over here. My son was grown and I didn't want to take care of that big place by myself. I never liked it anyway. Too pretentious. I prefer my little temple."

Charlotte was getting to the point in life where she was beginning to think of herself as old, but she could have been Aunt Lillian's granddaughter. If she had moved to Old Trees when she was forty, she must have lived here for fifty-six years—more than many lifespans.

"Where did you live before you moved here?"

"On the road. Tokyo for many years. That's where I met my husband. Peking. Canton, Seoul, Hanoi, Moscow, Reykjavik, Gothenburg, Havana, Trinidad, Lima: you name it. My husband wrote travel books. *On the Road in Mongolia, On the Road in Chile, On the Road in Mandalay, On the Road in the Balkans.*"

"I've read some of them," said Charlotte. "I enjoyed them very much. In fact, Edwin Harvey had been the most prominent travel writer of his generation."

"Just about everyone has. Everyone of a certain age, that is. No one under fifty ever heard of them. He wrote thirty-six. I wrote one myself," she added. "It was called *I Married a Gypsy*. I hated the title. But the movie *I Married a Millionaire* was a big hit, so everything had to be 'I Married a Whatever.' "

"I remember," said Charlotte. "One of my big early films was *I Married a Vampire*. I hated the title too."

They returned to the living room, where Aunt Lillian showed Charlotte to an armchair next to a table heaped with magazines: the Sierra Club bulletin, the *National Review* and *The Nation*, Japanese newspapers and magazines. A recent issue of *Japan Times* had a photo of Okichi-*mago* on the cover page.

Aunt Lillian clearly kept her mind active, and her choice of magazines indicated wide-ranging, if not downright conflicting, interests. Charlotte looked around the room. Scattered among the junk were some lovely things: a magnificent pink jade Buddha, a beautiful Chinese landscape painting.

"I see that you have some beautiful souvenirs of your travels."

"Not much really. Considering that this"—she waved a frail arm at the contents of the room—"represents a lifetime of traveling. I've given a lot away, of course. But I never really had all that much; we were always on the move. Never wanted much either. Didn't want to be encumbered by possessions. That *tansu* was the one piece of furniture I ever coveted." She pointed to a low Japanese chest made of a light-colored wood, with a branch of wisteria blossoms inlaid in multicolored woods across the front.

"It's very beautiful."

"Yes. It reminds me of sitting out on the veranda at Shimoda when I was a girl. I used to spend my summers there with Lavinia. The wisteria growing on the veranda there is the oldest specimen of Japanese wisteria in the country. Uncle Townsend grew it from a cutting he brought back from Japan. Paul's had his eye on that *tansu* for years. He wants it for Shimoda. I've practically had to chain it down to keep him from walking away with it. If there's anyone who loves beautiful things, it's Paul."

She was interrupted by the whistle of the teakettle.

"There's the teakettle," she said, rising. "He wants me to leave the *tansu* to him, but I'm not going to. No reason—just contrary, I guess. I figure its my contrariness that's kept me going for so long."

Charlotte started to get up, but Aunt Lillian laid a restraining hand on her knee. "Stay here, my dear. I wouldn't want to wear out one of my young visitors." Her blue eyes twinkled. "I'll be right back."

While she was gone, Charlotte surveyed the room, which was out of another century. Not the restored and sanitized century of Shimoda, but a faded, crumbling, and peeling century. The uneven plank floors were covered with an old braided rug; pots of African violets stood in little pools of sunshine on the windowsills. The room was shabby, but it had an aura of peace and refinement; Shawn would have called it *wabi*.

Aunt Lillian returned in a moment with the tea tray, setting it down between their chairs on a cracked leather ottoman which was stacked with books and magazines. Then she poured the tea, and passed a cup to Charlotte.

"I love your house," said Charlotte, as she stirred some honey into her tea with an old silver spoon, ornate and heavy, that looked as if it hadn't been polished in the last fifty years.

"I know it's decaying," said Aunt Lillian, as she munched on a piece of cinnamon toast. "But so am I. I figure we're a good match." She offered the cinnamon toast to Charlotte and then took another piece for herself. "I have a good appetite," she said. "I take it as a sign I'm not going to die soon. Pity," she added with a little smile. "I feel as if I'm about ready."

Charlotte smiled, and returned to the subject of the house. She'd had enough of death for the moment. "I had a dream about a house like yours once." She proceeded to tell Aunt Lillian about the dream.

"Well!" said Aunt Lillian when Charlotte had finished. She leaned back in her tattered chintz armchair, the glow on her face like light shining through a piece of old parchment. For a few minutes, she sat silently. Only the very old could be as still as she was, Charlotte reflected, as if all haste and striving were over and done with, and all that was left was waiting for death and meditating on the divine fate that had brought her to these ends.

Charlotte had had some reservations about recounting the dream to Aunt Lillian. She was afraid she wouldn't understand, but she had understood perfectly. Why shouldn't she? She had chosen the temple fifty-six years ago.

"Did you choose the temple?" asked Aunt Lillian.

Charlotte hadn't told her how it turned out. "No," she replied.

Aunt Lillian nodded knowingly. "I had a similar dream, years ago. A man I'd known and admired for many years had proposed marriage. I dreamed that I was on a rock in the ocean. The waves were crashing all around. My two married friends were on shore. I could have joined them, but I decided that I liked the excitement of being out there all alone on my rock. The rock was painted white, just like your temple."

"Did you ever have any regrets?"

"No, I didn't. Though it got pretty scary out there on my white rock sometimes, especially during typhoons." She looked up. "But I don't think it's about your temple that you came to see me, my dear."

"No, it's about Paul Harris."

"Oh, yes. What about him?"

"At the reception this afternoon, you told me that there was an error in my speech, that Paul hadn't just met Okichi-*mago* last year, that he had known her for many years. I wondered what you meant."

"Just what I said, my dear."

"When did he meet her, then?"

"I don't know exactly. It must have been twenty-five years ago."

"Twenty-five years ago!"

"Yes. He didn't just meet her, as you said in your speech; he created her." She went on to relate the story: "As you know, he's been collecting art in Japan for years. One year, he heard a story in a Kyoto geisha house about a little girl named Okichi who was supposedly a descendant of a child that was born to Okichi and Townsend Harris."

"How old was she then?"

"About six or seven. When he came back, he came to me about it. When I taught school in Tokyo, I did quite a bit of research on Uncle Townsend's stay in Shimoda; it's not far from Tokyo, you know. Paul asked me if I knew anything about a baby. I had heard rumors, but I was never able to confirm them. Most of the mixed-blood babies born to Japanese women were put to death: there was even a clandestine burying ground for them there, a cluster of little gravestones next to a stream in a remote valley. I assumed that if there had been a baby, it had been put to death too."

Charlotte listened in fascination.

"But I did know quite a bit about where he might look if he wanted to pursue it further. The Japanese are a nation of reporters. They keep records of everything. The Shimoda town office had a whole warehouse full of old diaries and daybooks. If there was a baby and if it had survived, there would be a record of it somewhere. On his next trip, Paul went to Shimoda and tried to track down the records. It became an obsession with him, documenting the authenticity of this rumor. Every time he went to Japan, he'd get a little farther."

"It turned out to be true, then?"

"Oh, yes. Okichi was supposed to have put the baby to death, but she gave it to a relative to raise instead. She probably wanted to keep it, but she was already a pariah; to admit to bearing a child of mixed blood would have meant even further ostracism. I always thought that her guilt at giving her baby away might have been one of the reasons she was so miserable in her later years. Paul found Okichi-*mago* living in the country with her grandmother, who was the granddaughter of Okichi's baby."

Charlotte took a minute to figure out the relationship.

"So Okichi-*mago* is Okichi's great-great-great-grand-daughter," she said finally.

"Yes. Three greats."

"What do you mean he created her?"

"Like Pygmalion created Galatea. From the day he found her, he managed every aspect of her life. She was his ivory image.

The grandmother died not long afterward, and he arranged for a guardian to bring her up. He supported her, he sent her to the best schools, he paid for her lessons—singing, samisen, flower arranging."

"The idea being, presumably, to turn her into a famous geisha?"

Aunt Lillian nodded. "The most famous geisha of her time. He studied the careers of the most famous geishas of the twentieth century and orchestrated her career accordingly; it was Paul who arranged for her to meet Tanaka, with the idea of his becoming her patron. He thought the patronage of a rich and famous businessman would enhance her career."

"It's just like Hollywood," said Charlotte, thinking of the many starlets who had been plucked out of obscurity and groomed for stardom by one movie mogul or another, including, to some degree, herself.

"Yes. Well, the geisha is to Japan what the Hollywood star is to America. Right down to being the subject of endless gossip."

"Was her romance with Shawn orchestrated too?"

"No, I don't think so," said Aunt Lillian, her eyes sparkling. "I think she did that on her own. Would you like more tea?"

Charlotte said yes, and Aunt Lillian poured her another cup.

"Why has Paul never married?"

"Because of his mother. He lived with her until he was nearly forty. She was a woman of exceptional grace and beauty. She had a lovely house, on Sutton Place in New York. Why should he have given up such a gracious life? I know what people say about such relationships, but there was nothing the least bit Freudian about it. If more men had mothers like Eleanor, fewer would ever marry. No one else could ever have measured up to her. Except, of course, Paul's own creation."

"Are you saying that he was in love with his creation?"

"Yes, but not in a romantic way. He was in love with her as he is with his restoration of the Temple of Great Repose. I was wrong when I compared him to the Pygmalion of Greek legend, who fell in love with his ivory sculpture. He was more like Henry Higgins in Shaw's *Pygmalion*. For Paul, transforming an impoverished Japanese orphan into a beautiful and famous geisha was less a labor of love than a scientific exercise or a technical challenge."

" 'I shall make a duchess of this draggletailed guttersnipe,' " said Charlotte, quoting from the Shaw play, which was based on the Pygmalion myth. She had played Eliza Doolittle in her younger days and the redoubtable Mrs. Higgins in a Broadway revival only last year.

"Actually, Okichi-*mago* was very much like Eliza Doolittle," said Aunt Lillian. "She didn't sell flowers, but at the time Paul found her she was selling little folk dolls that her grandmother made . . ."

"Aunt Lillian, Paul Harris wrote the speech that I delivered this afternoon. If he'd known Okichi-*mago* since her childhood, why was he perpetuating the idea that he had only met her last year?"

"He was creating a legend, my dear," she replied as she helped herself to another slice of cinnamon toast, and then offered the plate to Charlotte. "Does the Hollywood mogul who is creating a star reveal her taking diction lessons, having her eyebrows plucked, going on a reducing diet? No, he unveils her full-blown, like Minerva from the brow of Jupiter."

She was right. She remembered Paul talking about Okichi-*mago*'s mysterious benefactor. *He* had been the benefactor, the one who was pulling the strings of the marionette.

"She was his secret project," Aunt Lillian continued. "Paul is a very secretive man, despite his active public life. He kept his relationship with her locked away, like he does his spicy pictures."

Had Aunt Lillian seen his pictures? Charlotte wondered.

"Oh, yes," she said, answering Charlotte's unspoken question. "I've seen them. People tend to think of old ladies as being shocked by such things, but the truth is that if you've lived long enough, you're too old to be shocked by anything much, especially by something as silly as spicy pictures."

Charlotte smiled. "He showed them to me the other day."

"You should be very honored. He doesn't show them to everyone. I think they're quite amusing myself. I especially liked the one called 'The Phallic Contest,' " she said, her eyes twinkling. "I tend to think of it in the oddest places, like lawyers' offices and public meetings."

Charlotte threw back her head and laughed. The print was one of the earliest of the *shunga*. It showed a group of men with enormously enlarged penises sitting in a semicircle; it was a competition for who had the largest, the judges being the delighted women.

"I'd add producers' offices to the list."

For a minute, they giggled together at the joke.

"I've helped him keep his secret all these years, but I suppose it doesn't matter anymore now that she's committed suicide," Aunt Lillian continued, once they had stopped laughing. "I really don't know what prompted me to tell you about it at the reception." She shrugged. "Just my contrariness, I guess."

"She didn't commit suicide. At least, the police are quite sure she didn't commit suicide."

"I see." Aunt Lillian nodded her kerchiefed head. "That's why you're here. I wondered. I thought maybe I'd forgotten why you were here. My mind is getting to the point where it plays tricks on me sometimes. I have to be twice as sharp to keep up with it."

"Did you know Paul planned to make Okichi-*mago* his heir?"

"No, I didn't," she replied. "But it would make sense." Her blue eyes squinted in concentration.

"What is it?"

"That's why he called the family together for the geisha party! I wondered what he was up to. He hasn't gotten the family together in fifteen years. If Okichi-*mago* was his Eliza Doolittle, then the geisha party was her debut at the ambassador's garden party, the place where he would announce to the relatives that he was making her his heir."

Marianne had been right after all. He *was* going to blow them all up—figuratively, of course. By telling them he had made Okichi-*mago* his heir. "But he didn't make any such announcement," Charlotte said.

"No, he didn't. Maybe she turned him down. Maybe she was tired of having him manage every last detail of her life. I know I would have been, under the same circumstances. She was a modern young woman, after all."

" 'I'm a slave now, for all my fine clothes,' " said Charlotte.

"What?"

"It's a line from *Pygmalion*. Eliza's line."

It was a motive, a strong motive, Charlotte thought as she headed back to Briarcote. Yes, Tanaka could have killed Okichi-*mago*, but why commit murder over a severed contract? Yes, Marianne could have killed Okichi-*mago*, but as a way of eliminating a competing heir, it was a risky move. And, as Marianne herself had pointed out, with Okichi-*mago* dead, the chances that Paul would make Nadine's sons his heirs were all the greater. And yes, Nadine could have killed Okichi-*mago*. Of the three, she had the strongest motive, but it struck Charlotte as highly unlikely that this petite doll of a woman would have been able to muster the physical temerity to commit an act as violent as pushing Okichi-*mago* over the railing, despite what Lew had said. But Paul was a different matter: Paul had the means: the physical strength; he had the opportunity: at the time of the murder, he was in the house; and now he had a motive. He had spent twenty-five years grooming Okichi-*mago* to become his heir, and she had rejected his generous offer. Charlotte remembered her impression at the geisha party, that Okichi-*mago* had somehow failed to live up to Paul's expectations. Had he killed her because of it? As a result of her chat with Aunt Lillian, Charlotte had begun to develop a picture of Paul that was far from the urbane and charming sophisticate she had thought him to be: a homely man obsessed by beauty, a greedy man bent on possessing anything he thought beautiful, and perhaps a man driven by vengeance to smash his ivory image. Henry Higgins's bitter words sounded in her memory: "I tell you, I have created the thing out of the squashed cabbage leaves of Covent Garden; and now she pretends to play the fine lady with me." Like Henry Higgins, Paul may have been too successful. Okichi-*mago* was a Galatea who would not yield to his control. His ivory image had acquired a mind and a will of her own.

If she had turned him down, the person in whom she would have been most likely to confide was her little sister, Keiko.

· IO ·

KEIKO WAS STAYING with the other geishas at Edgecliff. Since Charlotte had to pass by there on her way back to Briarcote anyway, she decided to drop in. By now, it was going on eight. If Keiko was going to the fireworks, she had probably left already. But maybe she wasn't going. Japanese fireworks probably weren't the novelty to her that they were to most Americans.

She arrived at the red sandstone mansion a few minutes later. After parking under the *porte-cochère*, she walked up the stairs to the entrance. As she waited, she looked out at the grounds. Framed by an archway in the *porte-cochère* was a giant antique stone urn—it must have stood six feet tall— mounted on a copper stand. Beyond the urn was a lawn studded with enormous fern-leafed beeches, the bark of their pale gray trunks as gnarled and wrinkled as the leg of an old elephant. After a minute, the door was answered by a Japanese butler who escorted her through the Great Hall into the French morning room where she had talked with Keiko at the ball. The room must have doubled as a music room, she thought as she took a seat in a Louis XV-style armchair next to an ornate marble fireplace. The lunettes above the doors were ornamented with bas-relief sculptures of musical instruments. The whole room— paneling and all—looked as if it had been imported directly from a French chateau, and it probably was—that's the way the Newport barons had done things. Never mind that the French décor had nothing to do with the Gothic Great Hall. The designers of Newport's mansions had given little thought to architectural consistency. A Gothic mansion with a French breakfast room, a Moorish dining room, and a Chinese parlor wasn't unusual. All that mattered was that it be showy. Many people were enthralled by Newport's passion for poor taste, but Charlotte was more inclined to be offended by it. She had always had a mania for neatness: she liked her silverware lined up neatly in a drawer, her bankbook regularly balanced. She liked houses in which the style of one room matched the style of the next. She liked all the pieces to fit together.

The rhythmic clacking of *geta* on the marble floor of the Great Hall announced Keiko's presence. Though *geta* weren't usually worn indoors, a mansion such as Edgecliff, which was more like a hotel than a house, would be an exception; in this case, Keiko would have removed her *geta* at the entrance to her room. A few minutes later the butler escorted her into the room, where she bowed in greeting to Charlotte. Although she wasn't in her full finery—her hair wasn't formally dressed and she wasn't wearing white plaster makeup—she was still a model of elegance. It was part of the geisha's way of life to always look her best in public.

"I half expected you not to be here," said Charlotte. "I thought you might have gone to the fireworks."

"I'm packing," she explained. "We leave for Japan tomorrow. What can I do for you?" she asked with a demure nod of her head as she took a seat on the opposite side of the fireplace.

Charlotte explained about being asked to look into the circumstances of Okichi-*mago*'s death.

"Ah, yes," she said. "A detective was here this morning." Tears trickled from the corners of her narrow eyes. Pulling a tissue out of the bosom of her kimono, she wiped them away.

"Keiko, I have learned that Mr. Harris had plans to adopt Okichi-*mago* as his daughter and to make her his heir. If this is true, it would explain why someone might have wanted to kill her. Did she ever say anything about his plans to you?"

Her narrow eyes widened in surprise. "Yes, she did! But I didn't think Harris-*san*'s plans were related to her death." She looked up: "There are people who didn't want to see her become Harris-*san*'s heir?"

Charlotte nodded.

"I should have told the police," she said, with a self-reproachful shake of her carefully coiffed head. "But she told me not to tell anyone about it, and I didn't think it mattered."

"That's all right. I can tell them. What did she say?"

"It was just as you said. He spoke with her on the evening of the day we arrived, Wednesday. He told her that he wanted to adopt her and make her his heir. She told him that she would think about it."

"Do you know what her answer was?"

She nodded. "She told him no. It was a very difficult decision for her. She agonized over it. He had already changed his will and started the legal proceedings for the adoption."

"Do you know why she turned him down?"

"Yes. She discussed it with me. Being his heir would have entailed a lot of responsibilities: he wanted her to move here and take over the management of Shimoda. But she wanted to stay in Japan with Shawn. Also, she already felt badly about backing out of her agreement with Tanaka-*san* and she didn't want to incur another obligation that she wasn't able to fulfill. Besides, she didn't know him that well; she only met him last year."

Apparently Okichi-*mago* had never told Keiko that her relationship with Paul was of long standing. "Do you know when she gave him her answer?"

"Yes. It was on Thursday evening, just before the geisha party. I wondered if that's why she was crying when she sang 'Raven at Dawn.' Because she felt as if she'd let everyone down."

Charlotte's heart was pounding as she got back into her car. "Just before the geisha party," Keiko had said. In her mind, she went over the pieces of the puzzle again, fitting them together to form a picture. She started with the first piece: the mother whose beauty and graciousness no other woman could match. Faced with the impossibility of ever finding a woman to equal her, Paul creates one of his own. Then, after spending the best part of a lifetime and countless dollars sculpting his ivory image, he concocts a grand plan to unveil his creation. He convinces the Black Ships Festival Committee to add Okichi Day to the program, and to invite Okichi-*mago* to be mistress of ceremonies. Then he plans a geisha party to introduce his creation to the family and to announce that he is making her his heir. He has already started legal proceedings. Then she tells him she's not interested. He can't believe it. The monstrousness of her selfishness, her ingratitude. One of Mrs. Higgins's lines from *Pygmalion* popped into her head: "You certainly are a pretty pair of babies," she tells her son Henry and his friend, "playing with your live doll." Paul had also been playing with a live doll, a doll that refused to be manipulated. She returned to her mental picture puzzle. His moment of triumph, the geisha party, turns to ash. It's a terrible experience: he resents his guests' presence; they wonder why they're there. After the geisha party, he finds Okichi-*mago* waiting for Shawn under the rendezvous tree. Overcome with rage, he pushes her over the railing. She remembered what Miller had said about the hardest murderers to catch being those who kill in the heat of the moment. She also remembered the brutality of the later *shunga* Paul had liked so much. Did his taste for them reveal a predilection for violence? After the murder, he realizes what he has done. He decides to make the murder look like a suicide. Although any one of the suspects would have known about the Okichi legend, it was Paul who was the most familiar with it, and to whom the idea of camouflaging the murder as a suicide complete with Okichi-*mago*'s comb and mirror would have been most likely to occur. He also had access to the house and could easily have removed the items from their cases. The reason Miako hadn't barked wasn't because he wasn't a barker, but because the intruder was his master. Damn! She had *liked* Paul. She had even liked the notion of his having a secret life; it made his upstanding public persona more human.

She had to tell Lew, she thought as she drove down the driveway. At the ornate wrought-iron entrance gates, she stopped the car. Instead of going back to Briarcote, she turned right, and headed back to the shopping center across the street from the casino. After locating a pay phone, she called Briarcote to tell Connie and Spalding she wouldn't be home for dinner. Their cook, Mimi, wouldn't mind: she had been with them for many years and had an easygoing attitude toward sudden changes in plans. Then she called Lew.

A little girl answered the phone. "This is Tiffany," she said.

"May I speak with your daddy, please," asked Charlotte.

"This is Charlotte," she said once Lew had answered. "I have to talk to you. I think I've figured out who killed Okichi-*mago*." Suddenly she realized that she was starving. Except for tea and cinnamon toast at Aunt Lillian's, she hadn't eaten since her light lunch at noon. "Do you want to have dinner?"

Lew consulted for a moment with Toni. "We were planning to leave for the fireworks in a few minutes. But I can have a quick drink with you beforehand and meet Toni and the kids there. I'll meet you in twenty minutes at the Clarke Cooke House. It's on Bannister's Wharf. Do you know where that is?"

Charlotte did: it was one of several old wharves on the waterfront whose original eighteenth-century buildings had been converted or rebuilt into bars, restaurants, and boutiques.

She arrived at the wharf a few minutes later and killed the extra time by window-shopping. She felt an enormous sense of relief. The interlocking pieces of the puzzle all fit together; the world was in order once again. She was reminded of the collection of old "Mystery-Jig" puzzles that she and her second husband had once found tucked away in the attic of his family's rambling old summer home on Long Island Sound. They had had enormous fun with them. "Read Enclosed Short Mystery Novelette, and Solve the Crime Yourself, Then Check Your Solution with This Three-Hundred-Piece Jigsaw Puzzle," the box cover had said. She had checked her solution of Okichi-*mago*'s murder against the puzzle, and it had fit. Except for one piece—the piece that was labeled "Paul's grief." Paul had seemed genuinely shocked at the news of Okichi-*mago*'s death, a shock whose magnitude seemed out of keeping with his being the murderer. A flicker of doubt flared up at the back of Charlotte's mind, but she snuffed it out. He could have been acting. She, of all people, should know how easily emotions could be feigned. But Paul wasn't an actor, another part of her brain told her. The flicker of doubt flared again. But even people who weren't actors were capable of dissimulation, she reassured herself.

In the course of her ruminations, she had wandered over to the adjoining wharf, where she paused to admire an old sailboat that was docked next to a row of shops. Though she didn't know anything about sailing, even she could see that the boat was a beauty: the golden-hued wood decks glowed, the polished brass of the hardware gleamed, the lines were sleek and elegant. The name painted in gold letters on her bow was *Bastet*, Palm Beach.

"She's a beauty, isn't she?" said a voice from behind.

Charlotte turned around; it was Lew. "Oh, hi. She sure is."

"A classic Alden schooner, 1924. Past winner of the Newport-to-Bermuda race. She used to be Billy's boat."

"Billy Montgomery?" asked Charlotte. She remembered his talking with Nadine about his classic yacht at the geisha party.

Lew nodded. "He found her down in Tortola one winter. Like a lot of Newport people, he's migratory: the islands in the winter, Newport in the summer. She'd crashed onto a reef; she'd almost sunk. He spent two winters fixing her up: recaulking the hull, stripping the decks down to the original wood, replacing the rotted sails."

"Paul Harris told me he lost her in a divorce settlement."

Lew nodded. "She was put up for auction. She was worth half a million or more, but the city of Baltimore bought her for three hundred thousand. They used her for some Outward Bound-type program for inner city kids. The proceeds from the sale were divided between Billy and his ex-wife, but there wasn't much left by the time the divorce lawyers took their share."

"Couldn't he have bought her back at the auction?"

Lew shook his head. "He didn't have the money. What family money he'd once had he pissed away—pardon the expression— a long time ago. I shouldn't say he pissed it away. He spent a lot on restoring *Bastet*. But when you don't have any income, it goes pretty fast, especially when . . ."

"When what?" prompted Charlotte.

"I'm trying to think of how to say this without sounding cruel. My grandmother from down South would have described him as somebody who doesn't have a lot of hay in his barn."

Charlotte laughed. "My grandmother from New York City would have said his elevator doesn't go all the way to the top."

"There you are, the country mouse and the city mouse. He's never had to have much hay in his barn. Everything's always been handed to him on a silver platter. Billy's an innocent; he just wants everybody to like him. He's the guy who picks up the tab for a round of drinks, he's the guy who invests in a buddy's half-assed business scheme."

"He's the guy whose sister buys out his inheritance for a fraction of its value." She explained what Paul had told her.

"Exactly," said Lew. "He planned to go into the charter business. He got his captain's license and everything. It would have been the perfect job for him: he loves sailing, he loves to party. But when he lost *Bastet*, that idea was out the window. Newport is full of people like him: people who come from a moneyed background, but don't have the cash to support that lifestyle anymore, and don't have wits or ambition enough to earn a real living . . ."

"It sounds like you know him pretty well."

"We're old school chums. St. George's."

Charlotte raised an eyebrow. St. George's School was an exclusive Episcopalian prep school in neighboring Middletown—not the kind of school someone like Lew would be likely to attend.

"I know," he said, smiling. "I'm not your usual St. George's type." He explained that he had gone there on a church scholarship for altar boys. He nodded at Trinity Church, the elegant old Episcopal church overlooking the harbor. "My family's been members of Trinity for generations. Anyway," he continued, "I'm not worried about Billy. People like Billy lead charmed lives. They're like cats; they always manage to land on their feet. I always thought *Bastet* was a fitting name for a boat owned by Billy."

"What does it mean?"

"Bastet was the Egyptian cat goddess: a fertility goddess, I think. Billy always said that the boat had her own mind, like a cat, that he never felt as if he really owned her. After she was sold, he told me that he liked to think of her as having wandered off for a while. 'She'll be back,' he predicted. 'Cats always return to the keeper who takes the best care of them.' From what I understand, she was mistreated by the city of Baltimore, which couldn't afford to keep her up. She's since been sold again."

"She looks like she's in pretty good shape now."

Lew nodded in agreement.

"What's she doing here?" asked Charlotte.

"I would guess she's up here for the Classic Yacht Regatta later this summer. But I could be wrong." He smiled speculatively. "Maybe she's come back to her favorite keeper."

A few minutes later they were sitting in the restaurant, which was located in an imposing eighteenth-century mansion that had been moved in the seventies from the historic section of town to the wharf. Originally a ship captain's house, it was a warren of small dining rooms with low ceilings and uneven plank floors. The rooms were decorated with antique maps and prints of sailing ships. The dining area to which they were shown was on a third-floor deck with a fine view of the harbor through latticework screens. In the harbor, a forest of masts bobbed against the pale pink of the evening sky; boats had sailed in from far and wide for the fireworks display. A warm breeze blew in through the screens, and the candle on the table flickered behind its hurricane glass. Charlotte felt as if she were in an old plantation house in the Caribbean rather than on a busy tourist wharf in New England.

"Fine job," said Charlotte as she sat down on a green faux bamboo chair: the color scheme was green and salmon pink. "How did you manage to get a table on such short notice?" The restaurants on the waterfront were mobbed with people who wanted to watch the fireworks with a drink in their hands.

"I know the maître d'," he explained. "This place isn't my usual habitat. It's a hangout for the summer colonists." He nodded at the bar, where a small group of tanned and handsome young men were talking about the rescue of a sailor who'd been swept overboard in a race. "But I thought you'd like it."

"I do," said Charlotte. "Actually I think I've been here before, but it was a long time ago." To avoid being recognized, she sat with her back to the dining room. She didn't want to be interrupted by autograph hounds. She looked around her. "Quite a place for a ship captain's house."

"It was a lucrative business," said Lew. "The triangle trade. Slaves were brought from Africa to the Caribbean to work the sugar cane plantations, sugar and molasses were shipped from the Caribbean to Newport and processed into rum, and rum was shipped to Europe. That's how people like me ended up here."

A waiter took their drink orders—a Manhattan for Charlotte and a beer for Lew. "Okay, what have you got?" asked Lew once the waiter had left.

Charlotte went on to explain what she had found out: about Paul's long acquaintance with Okichi-*mago*, about his decision to make her his heir, and about the rage he must have felt when she turned him down. To her, he seemed to be the only suspect with even a halfway credible motive. "I think it's in the can, as we used to say in Hollywood."

"Sounds like it," said Lew. He stroked his mustache pensively. "I don't think there's any urgency—he's not likely to take off for parts unknown—but I'll speak to the chief tonight and let him know what you've found out."

But even as she spoke, Charlotte wondered. She knew that a film was never in the can when you thought it was. There were always scenes to reshoot and loose ends to tie up. Depending on audience reaction to the sneak previews, there could even be a new ending. Or a couple of new endings. Sometimes it never got in the can, period.

"What have the police found out?" she asked.

"Nothing. There were no prints on the comb, the mirror, or the cup. Whoever put them next to the brazier either wore gloves or wiped the prints. Lots of prints at the temple and at the main house, but we don't know who they belong to yet. Everyone who was there that night will have to be fingerprinted. We're working on that; you'll probably get a call tomorrow."

"Did they talk with the housekeeper?"

"Yes. She didn't have anything to report. Except for one thing. She said the burglar alarm was turned on when she arrived in the morning. The police went over the entire house with her, looking for anything unusual. There were no signs of forced entry. Which also points to Paul Harris. Ironically, it's Harris who's making all the arrangements about the body."

"Even in death, he's still running her life," said Charlotte. "What arrangements is he making?"

"Everyone in Japan is cremated. Not enough room to bury them, I gather. Rather than shipping the body back to Japan to be cremated, he's arranged for it to be done here and for the ashes to be sent back to Japan. There's going to be a Shinto funeral ceremony in a few weeks; it's going to be held at the Temple of Great Repose in Shimoda."

Ironic was right, thought Charlotte. Having the ceremony at the Temple of the Great Repose would enhance the legend; never mind that he'd killed her in a replica of that temple.

The waiter returned to take Charlotte's dinner order. The menu was classic French. She ordered *côtellettes d'agneau grillées*, a. k. a. grilled lamb chops. The lamb, game, and vegetables were raised on the restaurant's own farm, the menu said.

"A good choice," said a voice from behind.

It was Billy Montgomery. Tanned and handsome, he was wearing a V-necked, cable-knit tennis sweater and a light blue shirt in which he looked like he should be at the helm of his lovely old boat.

"Hey, Lew! How ya doin', man?" he said as he pounded Lew on the back. "Nice to see you, Miss Graham." He extended his hand to Charlotte and then turned back to Lew. "I like those spectacles," he said, referring to Lew's wire-rimmed glasses. "Very distinguished."

"Thanks," said Lew. "Have to keep up the image."

"I didn't know you two knew one another. What brings you here tonight?"

"Miss Graham's been helping the police with the investigation into Okichi-*mago*'s death," Lew explained. "She's been filling me in on what she's found out. She's been talking with the guests at the geisha party."

"You didn't talk with me," Billy protested.

"I didn't get to you yet," she said. "Did you see anything unusual?"

"Nope," he replied. "Went right home. Didn't see anyone. Actually, I didn't go right home. I went to the Marriott. I was meeting a young lady there. I didn't see anyone at Shimoda, but I did see someone at the Marriott."

"Who was that?" asked Charlotte.

He smiled a mischievous smile. Although he and Marianne looked nothing alike—he was blond and blue-eyed, while she was dark and brown-eyes—they shared the same devilish grin. "Cousin Paul," he replied.

"You saw Paul Harris at the Marriott?"

"Yes, I saw Paul Harris at the Marriott." He nodded knowingly. "I thought so. He told you he was at home in bed, right? Didn't want Nadine to find out about his little peccadillo."

"Tell us more."

"From beginning to end?"

Charlotte nodded.

"Well, I was sailing a Finnish Swan in the Volvo Newport Regatta that day. The regular crew was a man short. Anyway, our boat came in first and the owner offered to treat the crew to a lobster dinner at the Marriott. I couldn't go because of cousin Paul's geisha party. But I agreed to meet this nice young lady I met during the race there after the party."

"And?" Charlotte prompted.

"And, there we were having a drink in the lounge. The lounge at the Marriott is in the middle of this big open space." He waved his arms. "You know, with the rooms all around."

"An atrium," said Lew.

"Yeah, that's what they call it, an atrium. Anyway, we were sitting in the lounge in the atrium and I see cousin Paul walk into the lobby and get into the glass elevator. He takes the glass elevator up to the fourth or fifth floor. Then he walks down the corridor and knocks on the door of one of the rooms, and a woman lets him in. If you want to conduct an affair in secret, I don't recommend the Marriott as the place to do it."

"Are you sure it was him?"

"Sure I'm sure. Would I mistake my own cousin?"

"Did he see you?"

"I doubt it. He seemed in a big hurry to see his lady friend. He was carrying a bottle in a box; it looked like champagne."

"What time was that?"

"Oh, a little after twelve." He snapped his fingers in mock dismay. "Oh darn, now I've gone and gotten cousin Paul into trouble."

"On the contrary, I think it's more likely that you've gotten him out of trouble," said Charlotte.

"Thanks, Billy," said Lew. "I see *Bastet* is in town. I told Miss Graham that maybe she was returning to her former keeper."

"You know," said Billy, the corners of his lips turning up in a smile, "you may be right." He turned to Charlotte: "If you ever want any more information, you know where to find me." He nodded at the small bar off the dining room where the cluster of tanned young men were talking.

Charlotte was relieved at Billy's news: Paul was off the hook. Her sense of order was restored; someone she liked was no longer a murder suspect.

"Paul's relationship with Nadine has been on the skids for a while," Lew explained once Billy was out of earshot. "Nadine told Toni that she thought he was having an affair with a young woman from his firm. Would he have had time to kill Okichi-*mago* and get to the Marriott by midnight?"

"I don't think so," said Charlotte. "Not if he dropped Shawn off at The Waves first. Especially not if he stopped to buy a bottle of champagne." She sighed. "I guess it's not in the can, after all."

After her dinner, Charlotte had gone straight to bed and slept for a solid twelve hours. She had awakened with a dream fresh in her mind. It was *the* dream. Once again, she had to choose between the white temple and the baroque cathedral. But she had awakened before she could make the choice. Over breakfast in the dining room—the small one that sat six, not the big one that sat twenty-four—Charlotte filled Connie and Spalding in on what had happened: her suspicion of Paul, and his alibi. For Spalding, her story only confirmed his opinion that the whole

Harris family was oversexed. "At least we're not repressed, dear," was Connie's teasing retort. Charlotte felt badly that she had not seen more of her gracious host and hostess, but they had been busy too. Keeping the Black Ships Festival on an even keel after Okichi-*mago*'s death hadn't been an easy job. After breakfast, Charlotte attended church with Spalding and Connie at Trinity, where Lew had served as altar boy. It was a lovely old colonial church, whose gleaming white spire was the focal point of the waterfront. Trinity was famed for its architecture, which was based on Sir Christopher Wren's English churches, and its age: built in 1726, it was one of the oldest Episcopal churches in the country. Among the other worshipers were Lew and Toni, and their three handsome children: two boys and an adorable little girl. Charlotte tried to concentrate on the sermon, which the priest delivered from Trinity's famous wineglass pulpit, but all she could think about was the murder. Billy's revelation that he had seen Paul Harris at the Marriott meant that she had to start all over. If it were true, it explained Paul's grief: the one piece of the puzzle that hadn't fit. She should have known. When a piece didn't fit, it was usually a sign that the solution wasn't right. To Paul, losing Okichi-*mago* had been like losing a daughter. She thought back to her conversation with Spalding about *giri*. Maybe Paul had thought, like Keiko, that Okichi-*mago* had been upset at the geisha party because she had turned down his generous offer. Maybe he had even thought she committed suicide to atone for wronging her benefactor. If so, it would explain why he had been so relieved to hear that her death wasn't a suicide.

Paul's presence at the Marriott that night also explained some other things: why he had said he was at home in bed, for instance. He hadn't wanted to admit to his affair in front of Nadine. She remembered his glancing at Nadine when she had asked him where he'd been at the time of the murder; she had thought then that it was because he was with Nadine. It also explained why he hadn't turned on the burglar alarm: if Nadine had still been there when he left, he didn't want to tip her off that he wasn't planning to come back after dropping Shawn off. And it also explained why the burglar alarm was turned on when the housekeeper had arrived in the morning; he had turned it on when he returned later that night. There was another little piece of the puzzle it explained too: why he hadn't heard Miako bark. He had said it was because Miako wasn't a barker, but Miako had barked readily enough on the morning Charlotte had discovered Okichi-*mago*'s body. The real reason was that Paul wasn't there. But although Paul's presence at the Marriott explained a lot, it also left Charlotte with the same pathetic list of suspects that she'd started out with: Marianne, Lester, Nadine, Tanaka. She would have to talk with Tanaka. She also wanted to talk with Billy again. Both Paul and Lew had told her Billy wasn't a player in the Shimoda inheritance sweepstakes, but she wanted to see for herself.

After church, Charlotte headed for the beach. She was tired after all her running around and she needed time to sort out her thoughts. Connie would join her later for lunch. Spalding was lunching at the country club prior to the final event on the Black Ships Festival program: the Black Ships Festival Golf Tournament. It was a new addition to the program, a sop to the Japanese mania for golf. She arrived at Bailey's at about noon. Bailey's Beach Club, or the Spouting Rock Beach Association as it was formally known, was said to be the most exclusive beach club in the country ("Bailey's beach or bust" had been the slogan of many of the century's earlier social-climbing millionaires), but no one could have guessed it. Typical of ultra-exclusive clubs, Bailey's was devoid of pretension: a crescent of simple wooden beachfront cabanas and a two-story stucco clubhouse, painted gray with lemon trim. Members at Bailey's liked to complain that the swimming there was the worst in Newport, as if belonging to Bailey's was a burden that they were forced to put up with, and in fact, the water did seem to have more than the usual amounts of seaweed, algae, and battered plastic, but the setting couldn't have been more lovely. Unlike Newport's public beaches, which were long, straight swaths of sand, Bailey's was a little jewel, a sandy white crescent nestled among the rocks. Perched on the ledges surrounding the beach were the cottages of Newport's summer colonists. Among these was Briarcote, whose slate roof was just visible above the banks of wild roses lining the Cliff Walk.

To Charlotte, Briarcote's proximity to Bailey's was one of its main attractions. She loved this little beach, especially in the late afternoon after most of the beach-goers had gone home. On a hot and sunny Sunday afternoon, as this was, the beach was crowded, especially at the east end. By law, the east end of the beach was reserved for the public. Popularly known as Reject Beach, the public section of Bailey's was a favorite with the college students who flocked to Newport every summer to work in its bars and restaurants. The reject end of the beach was now packed, but most of the crowd would be gone by three or four. She also liked Bailey's because no one bothered her here. The members of Newport society who made up Bailey's membership weren't impressed by movie stars, or at least, not by movie stars who weren't tycoons in their own right, which Charlotte wasn't. Connie liked to complain that her years of achievement on the screen counted for nothing in Newport's social circles; it was Spalding's old money and Cliff Walk property that carried the weight. "Marilyn Monroe could come back from the dead and no one at Bailey's would even bat an eye," she said with more than a hint of affront in her voice. But Connie was overstating her case. Newport had never been the kind of conservative hideaway where people of great breeding and respectability lived quiet lives of the utmost refinement, though there were a few of those, like Spalding. Which was not to say that Newport's social lions didn't like to *think* it was such a place. Indeed, it often seemed to Charlotte that the newer the money, the greater the snobbery. She was always amused at how quickly those who acquired fortunes concocted the pedigrees to go with them. Though it had its share of failings, Los Angeles, where she had lived on and off for the last fifty years, at least had no social pretensions: in Los Angeles, as a fellow actress noted for her acerbity had once remarked, society was anyone who'd gone to high school.

After a dip in the ocean, which was chilly but delightful, Charlotte stretched out in a chaise longue on the porch of the cabana, and ordered a glass of iced tea from one of the waiters who circulated among the members and their guests. If membership at Bailey's earned one a permanent niche in Newport's social pantheon, having a beachfront cabana at

Bailey's elevated one to its empyrean heights. Though they were nothing to write home about—a simple wooden structure with two small dressing rooms, a shower, a toilet, and a porch—Bailey's beachfront cabanas were as eagerly sought after as an invitation to the royal enclosure at Ascot. Spalding had once commented that he sometimes felt as if the vultures were circling: cabanas only became available when the old-timers passed away. Social climbers were known to have called the club to inquire about the availability of a cabana before the funeral. Charlotte felt quite privileged sunning herself on the porch of the Smiths' cabana, since—God forbid—a good number of the Bailey's members were relegated to *inside* cabanas. In contrast to the simplicity of the cabanas themselves, most of them were beautifully decorated. The walls of the Smiths' cabana were hand-painted with a design of pink and blue flowers intertwined with blue ribbons, which matched the design of the fabric on the cushions of the beach chairs. Even the beach towels bore the same design, Charlotte noticed as she got up to get herself some suntan lotion. After greasing up, she lay back down in the chaise, a big hat shielding her face. As she basked in the sun, she idly watched the sailboats on the water, the nannies chasing down their charges, the dogs from Reject Beach playing Frisbee with their owners, and felt her mind growing blessedly empty. After a few minutes, she closed her eyes and felt herself drifting off.

She was awakened by a voice in her ear, a voice with a Cockney accent. "There's someone here who says he'd like to speak with you. He says it's urgent. Shall I show him in?"

She opened her eyes: it was the club manager. Clubs like this always had British staff. An infatuation with the Mother Country was part of the picture. Never mind that it was a Cockney accent, as long as it was British. "Did he give his name?"

"Yes," the manager replied. "A Mr. Lewis Farrell."

"Yes, please," she replied.

In a minute, Lew, accompanied by the manager, emerged from the corridor leading to the clubhouse. She could see from his expression that something was wrong. "What is it?" she asked.

"It's Shawn. He's been murdered. Chief Kilkenny called me a few minutes ago. I stopped off at Briarcote, and the maid told me you were here. It happened at The Waves. Do you want to head over there?"

"Of course," said Charlotte, half in shock. She quickly threw a beach dress over her bathing suit, and headed out with Lew.

"When did it happen?" she asked as they passed through the lobby.

"Sometime late this morning. Lani discovered the body when he got back just a short while ago."

"How was he killed?"

"Knifed. I don't know any more than that."

Charlotte was puzzled. How could anyone have knifed someone as strong as Shawn? An aikido expert, a champion sumo wrestler. He was probably one of the strongest men in the world.

· II ·

IN A FEW minutes, they had arrived at The Waves, whose entrance courtyard was filled with police cars, gumballs flashing. As with Okichi-*mago*'s death, the crime area had been cordoned off with yellow plastic tape. After talking with Lew, a policeman let them pass into the inner courtyard. The murder had taken place at the condo where Charlotte had met with Shawn just the day before. Or more precisely, as they found out once they were inside, on the terrace of the condo. After being admonished by a guard not to touch anything, they passed through the paneled living room and out to the terrace. It was swarming with police; crime scene investigators armed with cameras, calipers, and plastic bags were busy photographing and measuring everything in sight. At first, Charlotte couldn't see the body; her view was blocked. But when she did get a glimpse of it, she knew why the killer had succeeded in killing Shawn. He sat cross-legged on a pillow at the center of the canvas practice ring, facing the ocean. Only his back was visible, a huge red blotch staining the indigo-on-white pattern of his kimono. His head hung forward over his crossed legs. The pillow, originally a cream color, was also stained with blood, as was the canvas mat. The killer must have sneaked up on him from behind and stabbed him while he was meditating.

Following Lew, she moved closer. As they came around to the side of the corpse, she got a look at Shawn's face and she felt her stomach contract into a tight knot. Okichi-*mago*'s death hadn't seemed quite real. The kimono, the makeup, the hairstyle, had all made her look like a doll. Apart from her feet, there weren't even any signs of injury. But this was a disturbingly real corpse.

"Jesus," said Lew, turning his head away.

Charlotte thought again of her conversation with Shawn. "If you die every day in your mind," he had said, "you won't fear death." Maybe it was just the awkward angle at which his cheek pressed against his crossed leg—it was supposedly a myth that corpses bore any expression at all—but it certainly looked like fear on his waxen yellow face.

Miller crouched over the body, notebook in hand. As before, he was dressed in starched khakis and a button-down blue-and-white striped shirt with a cheery red bow tie. "Another interesting case," he said. "Guess this is my lucky week."

Lew grimaced. "Doesn't it get depressing, dealing with dead bodies all the time, Doc?" he asked.

"Sometimes boring. Unattended deaths. Drug overdoses. The same old thing. But never depressing. It's the live bodies that I find depressing. I'm much too soft to take care of the living. With the dead, I don't care about them and they don't care about me. I don't even recognize them. That happened with old Bill Kramer; drowned last year. I'd known him for thirty years, but it wasn't until I looked at his toe tag that I realized who the body belonged to." He looked down at Shawn's body. "Stabbed through the heart. Looks like a professional job to me, Lew."

"A professional job? But he wasn't a Mafioso or a drug dealer. At least, it seems highly unlikely."

The medical examiner shrugged. "I'm just telling you what I think. The thrust would have to have been made with considerable force to get through the muscle. Also, it would have to have been aimed just right. Which is why I think it was a professional job." He continued: "You know, this isn't the first murder at The Waves. There was a murder here in the thirties. Guy blew his wife's head clean off with a Springfield .30/06. Interesting case . . ."

"Excuse me, Doc," said Lew. He explained to Charlotte: "If I don't interrupt him now, he'll go on all day. Instead of mansions and historic landmarks, Doc has this whole town mapped out in terms of death: a murder in this mansion, a suicide in that apartment house . . ."

Miller grinned his goofy grin.

Lew turned back to the doctor: "How long has he been dead, Doc?"

"Not too long," Miller replied. He slid a hand under Shawn's kimono. "He's still warm. Not even much postmortem lividity yet," indicating the purplish hue that had started to discolor the skin on the undersides of Shawn's legs. "A couple of hours at the most."

"What about the weapon?" asked Charlotte, who had noticed several policemen combing the rocks below.

"An ordinary hunting knife would be my guess. With a long blade, at least six inches. Sharp point. One edge. But I doubt we'll find it. Our murderer probably tossed it into the drink. I figure he either came through the living room or up the stairs from the Cliff Walk."

"Any witnesses?" asked Lew.

"The detective-captain can tell you better than I can."

Sullivan had joined them by the corpse.

"None that we've located so far," Sullivan said. "His roommate was out. He's the one who discovered the body. The other sumos were over in the other condo." He looked down at the body with a baffled expression. "I can't figure out why he was in this position."

"He was meditating," Charlotte told him. "He told me that he often meditated out here. Meditation is part of a sumo wrestler's daily workout," she explained in response to his perplexed expression.

He nodded. "Psyching himself up," he said.

"In a way," said Charlotte. That wasn't it, but she wasn't going to bother explaining to a former jock whose yardstick of understanding was probably limited to the pre-game pep talk.

Now that the initial shock had passed, Charlotte was struck by something peculiar about the body. The crown of Shawn's head had been shaved, and his thick, dark brown hair hung loosely down. She thought of his topknot, and then realized what had happened. "His topknot has been cut off," she announced.

"Topknot?" said Sullivan.

"Sumo wrestlers wear their hair in a topknot. It's the symbol of the sumo wrestler's way of life. Somebody's cut off his topknot."

"Is that significant?" he asked.

"Maybe," she replied. Who would have wanted to cut off Shawn's topknot? she wondered as she explained about the topknot to Sullivan. Shawn's rival, Takafuji? Someone who didn't want to see him become a *yokozuna*? Or someone who wanted to make the murder look like it was related to sumo when it was really related to something else.

Like Okichi-*mago*'s murder.

Charlotte sat at the kitchen table at Briarcote and watched Mimi work, chopping onions, toasting bread, opening a can of tunafish. She was making a sandwich for Charlotte, who had missed her lunch with Connie at Bailey's. A few minutes later, she served Charlotte on a chipped plate in the small dining room. As she ate, she stared at the collection of china that lined the wall opposite her and reviewed recent events in her mind, trying to make sense of it all. She didn't know what to think. Not only had she made no progress with Okichi-*mago*'s murder, there was now another murder to solve. The perfect lovers, Okichi-*mago* and Shawn, both dead. She thought of the puppet play. Neither death had been a suicide, but the outcome was the same. Unable to become husband and wife in this life, they would be united in the next, reborn on the same lotus before Buddha's throne.

The removal of Shawn's topknot pointed to professional jealousy as the motive, but Charlotte's intuition still told her that his death was linked to Okichi-*mago*'s. If the murderer *was* the same, he had given up on the niceties. No more elaborate stagings: Shawn's murder had been down and dirty. In her thoughts, she kept coming back to Tanaka. Shawn said he had seen someone who he thought was Tanaka on the Cliff Walk on the night of Okichi-*mago*'s murder. Tanaka had reason to kill Okichi-*mago* and he had reason to kill Shawn: not only had Shawn stolen his geisha, he was probably going to defeat Takafuji in the next sumo tournament. Tanaka's presence on the Cliff Walk wasn't much to go on, but it was something. And something was better than nothing. Murder would seem to be out of character for a man of Tanaka's stature. But then . . .

She thought of something that Spalding had once said about the Japanese—an observation based on his years as deputy chief of mission in Tokyo. "The Japanese are motivated by three things: pride, nationalism, and downright irrationality. In other words, you never know when they'll go ape." Maybe Tanaka had gone ape.

After lunch, she set out for Edgecliff. Again, she parked the car under the *porte-cochère* next to the giant urn. Again, the Japanese butler escorted her through the Great Hall into the morning room. As she waited, Charlotte scanned a Japanese English-language magazine that was lying on a table. Tanaka was pictured on the cover. The caption was "Leader of the Japanese neo-nationalists?" If there was anyone who wouldn't want to see an American attain *yokozuna* status, it would be a Japanese neo-nationalist. Within a few minutes the butler returned with Hayashi, who bowed in greeting and then announced that Tanaka-*san* was in, and that he would be happy to see her. Charlotte was pleasantly surprised: she had thought he might be playing golf in the Black Ships Festival tournament. She followed Hayashi up the red-carpeted marble staircase to a second-floor landing decorated with a ten-foot-high stained glass window depicting the Crusaders conquering Jerusalem. From there, they climbed a few more stairs to the arcaded gallery overlooking the Great Hall. Tanaka's office was located at the end of a wood-paneled corridor, at the rear of the mansion. A brass plaque mounted on the wall bore the name of the Yoshino Electronics Corporation, and an engraving of the corporate logo of a cherry branch in flower. After inviting her to take a seat in a sparsely furnished anteroom, Hayashi disappeared into the adjoining office. He emerged a few seconds later and invited her to follow him into the inner office.

The office was surprisingly Spartan for one of the world's richest men, but then, Tanaka was known for living modestly. Like many other successful Japanese executives, his origins were humble. He had started work at age nine as a messenger boy in an electronics factory. As a young man, he had supposedly pawned his wife's antique kimono (Charlotte was reminded of Okichi -*mago's* seashell kimono) to raise the capital to realize his dream of founding a company to manufacture an improved wall switch. His company had gone on to become one of the world's biggest suppliers of electrical products. Although the Newport office was just a remote outpost of his empire, Charlotte suspected that his offices in New York and Tokyo were similarly austere. The American executive's taste for luxury was disdained by the Japanese executive, who considered it one reason for America's economic decline. The Japanese had little respect for an economic culture that rewarded ineffective executives with enormous salaries and fancy perks. If a Japanese executive didn't deliver, he took a cut in pay. Even successful executives like Tanaka considered luxurious lifestyles an affront to their workers. The furnishings of his office were ordinary: a sleek black lacquered desk, a low couch, and a few chrome-and-leather chairs. What was interesting about it was the decorations: it was a virtual shrine to Takafuji. A huge photograph on one wall showed Tanaka and some other businessmen clustering around Takafuji, who was seated in front of a silver punch bowl into which they were pouring bottles of sake. An enlargement of Takafuji's *tegata*, the handprints signed with a sumo wrestler's name, which were sold or given away as souvenirs, occupied another wall. On a side table was a photo of Tanaka and Takafuji playing golf. Charlotte hadn't realized Tanaka's depth of commitment to Takafuji; she had thought of his sponsorship more in terms of his sending off an annual check.

Coming from behind the black desk, which overlooked the Cliff Walk and the flint-gray Atlantic, Tanaka stepped forward to shake her hand. "I'm very pleased to see you again, Miss Graham. I am a great fan of yours." In keeping with the retreat status of the Newport office and the fact that this was a Sunday, he was wearing a gray sweatsuit instead of a business suit.

"Thank you," she said, returning his handshake. Despite his slight build—his white head only came up to her shoulder—he had a strong grip and an eager, self-assured smile. As she sat down on the couch, she could see waves breaking on the offshore ledges; it was from these waves that The Breakers took its name.

"What can I do for you today?" he asked as he returned to his seat. As at the opening ceremonies, he spoke excellent

English. He was known for his skill with the language and for the crafty ease with which he dealt with Americans.

Charlotte told him about Shawn's death, but he'd already heard. From whom? she wondered. Then she explained that she'd been asked to look into the recent murders by a member of city government.

"Two murders in one week," he said, shaking his snow-white head. "It is a terrible thing, for both our countries. The United States is a violent country: something like this would never have happened in Japan."

Charlotte agreed with him that it was a violent country, but she wasn't about to join in his America-bashing. "I see that you're a sumo fan," she said, nodding at the pictures on the wall.

"Yes," said Tanaka. "My company sponsors Takafuji."

"What does being a sponsor entail?" she asked.

"The sumo stable is very expensive to operate. Most *rikishi* have sponsors who help pay their expenses." He nodded at the photograph of Takafuji at the silver punch bowl. "That picture was taken at a party on the occasion of Takafuji's promotion to the rank of junior champion two years ago." He turned back to Charlotte. "I noticed you at the sumo match. Did you enjoy it?"

"Very much," she replied.

"I am glad. We were very disappointed when Takafuji lost. As Mr. Smith no doubt told you, Takafuji was hoping to break Akanohana's winning streak. There is no doubt that Akanohana is—or rather, was—a great *rikishi*. His death will be a great loss to the sport, but the Japanese are very nationalistic; we hate to see a foreigner excel at our national sport."

Hate it enough to commit murder? was her unspoken question.

"Of course, Akanohana's tragic death means that we no longer have that worry," he added with an ironic little smile.

"I wanted to ask you some questions about the evening of the geisha party," said Charlotte.

Tanaka nodded.

"As you know, your card was found in the brazier. Someone appeared to be trying to make it look as if Okichi-*mago* committed suicide because she felt she had gone back on her word in severing her relationship with you."

"Yes. It wasn't very clever of them. I don't think Okichi-*mago* had many regrets about severing our relationship."

"What about your regrets?"

"I had regrets, but not regrets enough to kill her."

Charlotte nodded. "I spoke with Shawn yesterday. He told me he returned to the temple after the party to meet Okichi-*mago*." She waited for his reaction, but there was none. "He said he saw you on the Cliff Walk. I'd like to know why you were there and whether you saw anything unusual."

"I've already gone over the answers to those questions with Detective-Captain Sullivan from the Newport Police Department," he said. His voice carried a hint of irritation.

Charlotte took it that he was annoyed at having his time wasted; his tone of voice seemed to imply that Americans were so disorganized that they had to do everything twice. "I understand," she replied. "But I'd appreciate it if you would repeat for me what you told them."

"Gladly," he replied with a little nod of his head. "After the party, my aide, Mr. Hayashi, and I returned here to Edgecliff. But I was restless; I was thinking about an impending business deal. I decided to take a walk on the Cliff Walk. I often take walks late at night."

"Did you go back out right away?"

"I changed into more comfortable shoes first: I had been wearing *geta*. But that only took a few minutes. I got back out to the Cliff Walk at about eleven forty-five. I walked down to The Breakers and back. I was only gone about twenty minutes, maybe twenty-five."

"Did you see anything unusual?"

"Not see, heard. Two things. One: I heard the dog next door barking: Miako. He kept it up for a good ten minutes or more. I wouldn't have noticed, except that he doesn't usually bark at night."

"What time was that?"

"Just before midnight."

"And the second?"

"I heard someone on the point. The person was drinking;

I heard the pop of a beer can being opened as I went by. Since I didn't hear any voices, I concluded that the person was alone."

"The point?" said Charlotte.

Tanaka beckoned her to the window.

The lawn stretched out to the cliff's edge, interrupted only by the balustrade that paralleled the cliff's edge, and beyond the balustrade, the macadam strip of the Cliff Walk.

Tanaka pointed to a rocky peninsula to the right of the lawn, just past the head of the pebbly channel that Charlotte had followed down the cliff on the morning she'd found Okichi-mago's body. The point and the temple marked the two ends of the crescent beach.

"Teenagers," said Tanaka. "They like to sit out there and drink beer at night. It's a dangerous pastime. Several have fallen off. If you could find out who it was, he might be able to help you."

The phone rang and Hayashi answered it. "It's for you, Miss Graham."

It was Lew. "I hope you don't mind my calling you there. The maid at Briarcote told me where I could find you. We've got a suspect in Shawn's death. Sullivan's bringing him down to the station now. Want to join us?"

Charlotte said she would and he gave her directions.

After thanking Tanaka for his help, she excused herself and left.

She arrived at the Newport Police Station a few minutes later. It was located in a modern business district just past the Old Colony House, a magnificent two-story colonial brick building dating from the early eighteenth century, which had been the seat of government for the colony of Rhode Island. One of the many portraits of George Washington by Newport's native son, the painter Gilbert Stuart, hung inside. Like the equally historic buildings around it, it comprised one layer in the many-layered city that was Newport. If the Old Colony House represented one of the bottommost layers, the police station was at the very top: an impersonal institutional building, as devoid of character as a warehouse. A dispatcher showed her into Sullivan's office.

Lew was there, as well as another policeman.

"Did Tanaka tell you anything?" asked Lew.

"Only about the kid or kids on the point."

"Yeah," said Sullivan. "He told us about that too. We've questioned all the kids we could dig up who were in the vicinity of the Cliff Walk that night, but we haven't found any who'll admit to being on the point around midnight."

"What's happening?" asked Charlotte.

"One of the sumo wrestlers in Takafuji's stable—they're staying at the Treadway—saw a box with a topknot in it among his belongings," said Lew. "He called Lani about it and Lani called us. One of the men is bringing them both in. Lani's coming along to translate. They should be here any minute."

Charlotte thought of what Spalding had said about Takafuji roughing up one of his attendants and kicking a member of his fan club. Anyone with his reputation for meanness would seem to be capable of murder.

"Do you know anything about this guy, Lew?" asked Sullivan. He pronounced the name slowly: "Ta-ka-fu-ji."

"No, but Miss Graham does," said Lew.

"Only what I learned about him from Spalding Smith during the sumo tournament."

"That's more than I know," said Sullivan.

"He was Shawn's rival," Charlotte replied. "They've been on parallel paths during most of their sumo careers, but recently Shawn jumped ahead. Shawn won his last official tournament—he won the Newport tournament too, but that wasn't an official tournament. If he'd been alive to win the next official tournament, he would have been promoted to grand champion, the highest rank in sumo."

"Were they friendly rivals or unfriendly?"

"Unfriendly, I gather. Takafuji didn't like the fact that an American beat him at the national sport." She proceeded to relate some of the incidents Spalding had told her about. "There's something else, too." She continued: "When I visited Shawn, I noticed a topknot sitting on a table. When I asked him about it, he told me that he got one in the mail before every tournament."

"You've lost me," said Sullivan.

"It was a form of malicious mischief, like sending a retirement card to a boss you hate before he's ready to retire, only much more vicious than that, of course. Shawn said he suspected Takafuji of being the sender."

Sullivan nodded.

A second later, the door opened and a policeman entered with Lani and Takafuji. Lani was wearing a voluminous kimono, Takafuji gray sweat pants and a blinding yellow "I love Newport" T-shirt. Takafuji reeked of the sweet-smelling pommade that was used to hold his heavily oiled topknot in place.

Sullivan greeted them and invited them to take a seat in a pair of folding chairs. Next to them, the burly detective-captain looked like a midget.

As the sumo wrestlers settled into their seats—the chairs seemingly incapable of supporting their enormous weight—Sullivan lifted a long, trunklike lacquered wicker box decorated with Japanese characters onto his desk. He used handkerchiefs to avoid getting his fingerprints on the wicker.

"The sumo wrestlers keep their stuff in these wicker trunks," he explained. "This is Takafuji's." He opened the lid and removed a small cardboard box, which he set on his desk. Then he lifted the cover.

Inside lay a dark, glistening topknot. The end that had been closest to the scalp was loose and the tips of the hairs were coated with blood. At the sight of it, tears began to roll down the fleshy, pockmarked cheeks of the sweet-faced Hawaiian. He wiped them away with a fist the size of a small ham.

According to Spalding, Lani was prone to such emotional displays. Although it wasn't in accordance with the sumo creed, this emotionalism was one aspect of his personality that had endeared him to the Japanese.

"Ask him how it got there," Sullivan commanded.

Takafuji sat patiently in his chair, the fabric of his T-shirt straining under the pressure of his breasts.

Lani translated the question for Takafuji, who replied with a long answer in Japanese, accompanied by many hand gestures.

"He says he doesn't know," Lani replied. "His attendant found it in his room while Takafuji was eating his *chanko-nabe*."

"*Chanko-nabe*?"

Lani explained that it was a hearty fish and vegetable stew that sumo wrestlers eat at their midday meal; on that day, it had been taken communal style in one of the motel's function rooms.

"Was there anyone else staying in Takafuji's room?"

Lani translated the question.

Takafuji shook his head. If being questioned as a possible murder suspect upset him, he didn't show it. His face betrayed no emotion except maybe meanness. Beneath the straight black line of his eyebrows, his high cheekbones reduced his eyes to slits, and his thin, narrow mouth was turned down at the corners.

"Ask him where he was at the time of Hendrickson's murder," said Sullivan. "We estimate that he was killed around eleven."

Again, Lani translated. "He says he was playing Space Invaders from ten until noon," Lani replied after Takafuji had answered. "He says he likes to play Space Invaders. It helps him to condition his fighting spirit," he added with an uncharacteristic note of sarcasm in his soft, kindly voice.

So much for the sumo mystique, thought Charlotte. Shawn meditated on death; Takafuji played Space Invaders.

"Where?" asked Sullivan.

"He doesn't know the name of the place. It's across America's Cup Avenue from the Treadway, on that cobblestone street that runs parallel to it. He was there when it opened at ten."

"Ryan Family Amusements," said Sullivan. He looked up the number in the phone book and dialed. "This is Detective-Captain Sullivan from the Newport police," he said. "Did you have a sumo wrestler in there earlier this morning?" He listened for the reply, and then nodded. "What time did he leave?"

One thing about a three hundred and eighteen pound sumo wrestler was that he was easy to pick out in a crowd, especially a crowd of American teenagers playing video games.

"Thanks," said Sullivan as he hung up the phone. "They say he was there all morning." He turned to his assistant. "Have the guy at Ryan ID him. Then dust his room for fingerprints. Check with the staff: the desk clerks, the chambermaids. Find out if they saw anyone hanging around the room."

Takafuji asked a question.

"He wants to know if he's in the clear," said Lani.

"Yup," said Sullivan, giving him the thumbs-up sign.

The giant wrestler leaned back with a grunt of smug satisfaction.

"But he's not off the hook yet," Sullivan added. He mentioned Shawn's receiving the topknot in the mail, and asked Lani to ask Takafuji if he knew anything about it.

Lani asked the question, and Takafuji shook his head. "He says he doesn't know anything about it," Lani said.

"Ask him why he thinks someone planted the topknot in his trunk"—he waved an arm at the wicker box—"or whatever you call that thing."

Lani translated the question and Takafuji's reply: "He says it must have been because he's Akanohana's rival. He thinks someone wanted to make it look as if he committed the murder."

Sullivan nodded. "Tell him that we'll have to keep his trunk here to dust it for fingerprints. Tell him that we regret any inconvenience this may cause him and that we thank him for his cooperation."

Lani translated for Takafuji, who nodded in agreement.

"When are you scheduled to go back to Japan?" asked Sullivan.

"Tonight," Lani replied.

"I'm sorry to say that you'll have to stay around a little longer."

For a few minutes, they discussed arrangements, and then they all left.

"That was a bust," said Lew as he and Charlotte walked to the parking lot. "I'm sorry I dragged you all the way down here for nothing."

"It wasn't for nothing." She checked her watch; it was five

o'clock and she was starved. "Do you want to get something to eat?"

"I'm due home for dinner at six. But I'll grab a beer with you. Do you want to go to The Ark? They have an oyster bar until seven."

"I love oysters," said Charlotte.

"Good. I'll meet you there." He gave her directions.

Charlotte picked up the thread of their conversation where she had dropped it. They were sitting at the brass-and-mahogany bar at The Ark, a favorite hangout of the Newport sailing crowd: "All the oysters you can eat until seven for a quarter each." A quartet in the corner played classic jazz.

"It wasn't a bust," she said as she dipped another oyster in cocktail sauce, and then swallowed it whole. "I think Shawn may have been killed because of Takafuji, if not by him."

"What do you mean?"

She described her meeting with Tanaka and explained about Yoshino Electronics' sponsorship of Takafuji.

"Let me see if I've got this right," said Lew. "Tanaka might have had Shawn killed to advance the career of his protégé."

"Or his right-hand man might have had Shawn killed," she said. She told him about Hayashi's "Stop Akanohana" sign.

But despite what she said, she had doubts. She still suspected that Shawn's death had something to do with Okichi-*mago*'s; there was simply too much correlation between them.

"But then, why plant the topknot in Takafuji's trunk?"

"You're right," said Charlotte. She took another sip of wine and put her mind to work, her famous black eyebrows knitted in concentration. "We know Shawn was there on the night of Okichi-*mago*'s murder," she said. "What if he saw something that someone didn't want him to see?"

"Why wouldn't he have said anything to you?"

"Maybe he didn't know that he saw it."

A bartender cleared away the empty glasses. "Can I get you a refill?" he asked. Then he looked up. "Hey, it's Lew Farrell," he said. He reached a hand over the bar. "How're ya doin', old man?"

"Good, good," Lew replied. "And yourself?"

"Hangin' in there, I guess," he said. "Business is slow this year. I fill in here when I get the chance. Make some extra bucks. What can I get you?"

"Another glass of wine for Miss Graham and another beer for me."

"Coming right up," said the bartender, disappearing around the other side of the oval bar.

"Do you know everybody in town?" asked Charlotte.

"Just about," Lew replied, with a broad smile. He was a man who clearly enjoyed his role in local politics.

The bartender returned in a minute with their drinks.

"Hey, I see *Bastet's* in town," said Lew. Lew explained to Charlotte that he and the bartender, whose name was Pete, had often sailed on the *Bastet* with Billy.

"Yeah," Pete replied as he dried some glasses and then hung them upside down in the rack that was suspended over the bar. "She's up here for the classic yacht regatta. But I hear she's staying."

"What do you mean?"

"She's up for sale, and Billy says he's buying her back. Says he's going to charter her out of Newport in the summer, Tortola in the winter. But you know and I know that what he says he'll do and what he does aren't always the same thing. He just left here a few minutes ago. 'A cat always returns to its favorite keeper,' he said. But I've been hearing that line for years."

"I know what you mean. What's he planning to use for money?" asked Lew. "His good looks?"

"Hey, he's gotten pretty far with his good looks," said the bartender, with a knowing grin and a wiggle of his eyebrows.

Charlotte assumed he was referring to rich women.

"An inheritance from a rich uncle in California, he *says*." The bartender raised his hands. "Hey, it's none of my business, but if he has enough dough to buy a seven-hundred-and-fifty-thousand-dollar boat, I wish to hell he'd pay me back the six hundred and fifty bucks I loaned him last month to help him buy a used car." With that, he left to attend to some other customers.

"Lew, I have an idea," said Charlotte once the bartender was out of earshot. She looked around at the crowded pub. "Is it safe to talk in here?"

"Not unless you want something to be all over town in five minutes."

"Then let's go."

They finished their drinks and left. Outside, they stood by Lew's car, which was parked next to The Ark in a spot that appeared to be legal. Charlotte was impressed. Finding a parking spot in downtown Newport at the height of the season was close to impossible. After cruising around for fifteen minutes, she had finally had to pay seven dollars to park in a lot.

"You even know all the parking spaces," she teased.

"In this town, knowing where the parking spaces are is an essential survival skill. Well, what is it?"

"If Billy was due to inherit that much money from a rich uncle in California, I think I would have heard about it from Connie."

"Then where do you think he got it?"

"I thought you said Billy was an innocent," she teased.

"I did. But even I can be wrong."

"I can think of a couple of possibilities," she replied in answer to Lew's question. "A)—which is the most unlikely one: somebody paid Billy to kill Shawn and make it look like Takafuji did it."

Lew shook his head. "Billy couldn't plan his next five minutes, much less a murder. To say nothing of the fact that he doesn't have the guts for it. Scratch that idea. What's B?"

"B) Billy was witness to a murder—either Okichi-*mago*'s or Shawn's—and is blackmailing the murderer. The only trouble with that theory is that, if it were true, I'd expect him to be more discreet about his newfound money."

Lew shook his head. "Not Billy. Billy is constitutionally incapable of keeping his mouth shut. But the inheritance story is a good cover-up. People are coming into big inheritances all the time in this town."

A motorcycle raced around the corner, the noise of its engine temporarily ruling out the possibility of conversation.

"I'm willing to hazard a guess that the blackmail victim is Tanaka," Charlotte continued once the motorcycle had passed. "He's got the bucks, and he's the only likely suspect we have left. Paul also has the bucks, but he was somewhere else at the time. Did the police check that out, by the way?"

"Yeah. Billy was right; he was at the Marriott. A desk clerk who knows him by sight remembered seeing him come in, and he admitted to being there after the police put some pressure on him." He switched back to the subject of Billy: "But how do we find out if Billy's really the blackmailer?"

"First we have to find out if he's telling the truth. From what you say, he has a pretty high bullshit index."

"This is true," said Lew.

"One of us could pose as a yacht buyer."

"One of us would have to be you," said Lew. "If the color of my skin alone doesn't make me suspect as a potential yacht buyer, anyone in town is going to know that I can't afford to buy a boat for that kind of money."

"But you know all about boats," Charlotte protested. "I don't know the first thing about them."

"I'll fill you in."

Charlotte had nearly forgotten. The Black Ships Festival closing ceremonies were to be held at seven at Perry's tomb in the Island Cemetery and she was supposed to be there. After saying goodbye to Lew, she drove out to the cemetery, which was fittingly located on Farewell Street.

Perry's tomb was a huge marble sarcophagus at the rear of the cemetery. Like the area around his statue in Touro Park, the area around the tomb had been demarcated by colorful red and white banners bearing the Black Ships logo. A semicircle of officials had assembled inside the banners.

Charlotte took her place at the back of the gathering behind some members of the press. As an official representative, she was supposed to put in an appearance, but at least she didn't have to say anything.

Spalding nodded at her from the other side of the semicircle.

The ceremony was brief. Under the circumstances, everyone

was eager to get it over with. The usual remarks about Japanese-American friendship were followed by a few prayers, and that was it.

As the cluster of officials was breaking up, Just-call-me-Ken came up to her and handed her a small box elegantly wrapped with handmade Japanese paper. "Some pictures from the geisha party," he said. "A souvenir of the festival."

"How nice," said Charlotte, genuinely pleased. She barely had time to thank him before he was off distributing similar boxes to the other official representatives, from both the United States and Japan.

As she was leaving, Charlotte caught sight of a familiar white kerchief in the crowd. She caught up with the kerchief out by the lane that wound through the cemetery. "Aunt Lillian?" she said.

Aunt Lillian turned around, her blue eyes sparkling.

"Oh, it's Charlotte. How are you, my dear?"

"Very well, thanks," she replied. "Aunt Lillian, does Billy Montgomery have any uncles or great-uncles who might have died and left him some money?" Charlotte knew there were no relatives on the Montgomery side, but she didn't know about the Harris side. Perhaps Billy was referring to a great-uncle.

Aunt Lillian thought about it for a minute. "No, my dear. He has only one uncle, Charles Harris, and he's very much alive."

Charlotte remembered now that Connie had a stepbrother who had taken the Harris name. "What about great-uncles?"

"No. Oodles of great-aunts and second cousins and the like. But none of us have any money to speak of. The only Harrises who have any money anymore are Connie and Paul. And Marianne, of course."

"Thank you," said Charlotte.

Her inquisitive blue eyes shined. "Is that rascal Billy telling tales again?"

"Maybe," Charlotte answered. "I don't know yet."

· 12 ·

AFTER BREAKFAST THE next morning, Charlotte set out for town. She was going to see a man about a boat. But first she wanted to go back to the temple. She wanted to review everything that had happened—on the spot. She knew from experience that there was nothing like being there to jump-start the thought processes. She parked a few blocks south of Shimoda and walked out to the Cliff Walk. She wanted to approach the house as she had on the morning she had found the body, but she didn't have time to walk the whole length of the Cliff Walk. Unlike that morning, which had been overcast, this morning was bright and sunny. On days like this, Newport reminded her of someplace other than New England, some-place other than America, in fact. It was a property of the light: despite the bright sun, it was a soft, hazy, golden light, a light that was dulled by the centuries. Though it was only just after ten, The Breakers was already crawling with tourists. Some peered through the tall wrought-iron fence lining the cliff; others gazed out over the balustrade of the second-story loggia. After The Breakers came a couple of private homes, and then Edgecliff. Just past the little channel that she had followed down the cliff that morning was a promontory, the "point" where Tanaka had heard someone opening a pop-top can. As she drew even with it, she noticed a little trail in the underbrush and followed it out to the end, where there was a little clearing, a place for drinking beer or making love. It was beautiful, but also scary: fifty feet below, the waves beat against the base of the cliff. For a moment, she looked out to sea. It was said that you could see the Gay Head cliffs of Martha's Vineyard

from here on a clear day, but she couldn't make them out.
Then she turned in the other direction. At the other end of
the shingle beach was the temple, perched on its little knoll.
As she gazed out, she found herself looking directly at the
spot where Okichi-*mago* had been pushed over the railing. If
the person who had been sitting here that night had also been
looking in this direction, he would have been eyewitness to a
murder.

She hadn't made the connection before between Tanaka's
hearing someone on the point and Okichi-*mago*'s murder, but
now she did. Had that person been Billy? she wondered. And
if it was, had he then blackmailed the murderer?

She hadn't even needed to go as far as the temple for a
jump-start, she thought as she turned back. It was a strong
possibility: Billy drank beer; Billy was familiar with the area.
Like Marianne, he'd probably spent his summers here as a child.
Perhaps the point had been a favorite spot that he returned to
whenever he had the chance. The moon had been full that night,
or nearly so. He could easily have seen what was happening
at the temple. This time Charlotte's New England horse sense
told her that she was on the right track. But what about his car?
If he'd stayed on, wouldn't Shawn have seen his car? Then she
remembered Lew saying that he lived in a caretaker's cottage on
the grounds of Bois Doré. Bois Doré was the mansion where
the coal baron had hung the gold fruits from the trees. It was
only a block away; he could easily have walked. There was
also the problem of time: would he have had time to witness
the murder, walk home and pick up his car, and still be at
the Marriott in time to see Paul arrive a little after twelve?
She took a minute to figure it out. The answer was yes, but
just. She took a deep breath. She had come up with a couple
of answers, but she was still faced with finding the answers
to the big questions, namely who had murdered Okichi-*mago*
and Shawn.

It turned out to be a woman that she had to see about a boat.
Her name was Misty, a fitting name for a boat broker. Lew had
directed her to Northrup & Johnson, a boat broker with offices
in a converted nineteenth-century sail loft on Bowen's Wharf,

the tourist wharf where *Bastet* had been docked. Northrup & Johnson specialized in "large power and sailing yachts for the discriminating yachtsman," with offices on the East and West Coasts, Cannes, and Marbella. Charlotte would hardly have called herself a discriminating yachtsman, but Lew had tutored her enough on the phone that she wasn't going to make a total fool out of herself. Besides, he assured her, rich people like herself didn't need to know about boats. They hired people to take care of their boats for them.

Charlotte wasn't all that rich, but that was a fact that was lost on people in the world outside of Hollywood. Certainly she wasn't rich enough to be able to plunk down close to a million dollars on a boat, to say nothing of the vast sums it must take to keep it up. While waiting for Misty, she had leafed through the *Newport Port Book*, a guide to local marine services: fuel, sails, carpentry, galley equipment, crane services, crew placement, electronic equipment, engine services, fire equipment, marine insurance, rigging. The ways in which such a boat could eat up money were endless. Fifty years in front of the cameras had allowed her to accumulate a sizable nest egg; she also had her New York townhouse in Turtle Bay, her vacation house in Maine, and her condo in Los Angeles (she hated Los Angeles, but it was convenient to have a place to stay there). But much of the money she had earned over the years had been squandered by her mother, whom she'd always supported, and who had felt entitled to live in high style after the years she had slaved to support Charlotte and her sister. If Charlotte had sometimes been accused of thinking like a man, it was because she had lived her life as a man with a family to support—an extravagant one. She didn't begrudge her mother the spoils of Hollywood, but she had always been offended by her extravagance. By nature, Charlotte was temperate, a trait that she must have inherited from her tightfisted Scottish father, who had never contributed a cent toward his family's support despite his successful law practice. The only contribution he'd ever made was to pay for her tuition at a posh girls' finishing school. Although Charlotte appreciated her education now, it had seemed like a cruel joke at the time because she hadn't had money enough to keep up with the other girls. Then there was her sister, to say nothing of all the other relatives who had been hanging around for the last fifty years with their hands out.

But Misty didn't know that. Misty thought she was a rich Hollywood star.

"Is there any particular boat you're interested in?" she asked.

"Yes," Charlotte replied. "I'm very interested in *Bastet*."

"She's a sweetheart, isn't she?" After calling up *Bastet* on her computer screen, Misty proceeded to reel off her vital statistics: "A seventy-three-foot Alden schooner, built in 1924. Four thousand nine hundred feet of sail, a GMC one thirty horsepower diesel engine, carvel planked long leaf yellow pine, bronze fastened on double-sawn oak frames, lead keel, teak deck on oak beams, restored teak and holly cabin sole, Honduras mahogany interior, Sitka spruce spars, new stainless standing rigging, a full complement of Ratsey-Laphorn sails . . ."

"What's the asking price?" interrupted Charlotte.

"Seven hundred and fifty thousand," Misty replied as she pushed a button on her keyboard to print out the data. "She's fully equipped for world cruising," she continued, still reading from the screen. "Included are charts for the entire world, flags for many foreign countries, a complete inventory of spare parts, as well as china, glasses, cookware, linens, and blankets."

As Misty spoke, Charlotte's imagination carried her off to exotic ports: Bora Bora, the Molucca Islands, Madagascar. In her mind, she pictured herself drinking daiquiris on the fantail against a palm-fringed shore.

"Would you like to see her? The owner's not here at the moment. We can go aboard if you'd like."

Charlotte said she would.

After ripping off the data printout, and grabbing some keys, Misty led her out to where the boat was docked.

Even with Lew's tutoring, Charlotte couldn't relate to the vital statistics, but she could relate to the interior. From the moment she descended the companionway into *Bastet*'s main salon, she was in love.

"She's been beautifully restored," Misty said as she walked around the main salon, pulling up the leaves of the folding mahogany table and opening the doors to the little cupboards that were tucked away here and there. "She can accommodate up to fourteen on short trips, with five or six a comfortable number for long trips. Plus four crew members."

Charlotte had been on yachts before, but they had been Hollywood yachts, encrusted with chrome and mirrors, designed to impress. This was a yacht meant for private enjoyment: the cozy mahogany-paneled main salon was fitted with brass oil lamps, a Persian rug, and leaded glass cabinets. There was even a little fireplace surrounded by delft tiles decorated with blue sailing ships.

"What do you think?" Misty asked.

"I want to build a fire, pour myself a glass of sherry, and stretch out on the settee with a book," replied Charlotte.

"I know." She nodded her pert blond head. "You don't see yachts like this very often anymore. Come and see the head."

Following her down a corridor, Charlotte peered into the head. Even the bathroom was beautiful, with an exquisitely crafted mahogany sink and cabinet and a teak toilet seat.

As a child, Charlotte had always dreamed of having a playhouse or a tree house of her very own. The *Bastet* was like that. Everything you needed tucked away into alcoves or displayed behind leaded glass cabinets, all overlaid with the rich red glow of antique mahogany. It was a perfect little floating world. She could see why Billy might resort to blackmail to get it back.

"There's been a lot of interest in this boat," said Misty as they climbed back up the companionway. "We've had one buyer interested for some time, but no offer yet. Then a second buyer came along just this morning and put down a deposit. The second buyer is someone who owned the boat two owners ago, so I think the deal will go through, but you never know."

Charlotte wondered how much of a deposit Billy had put down. "How much of a down payment is required?"

"Ten percent," said Misty. "For example, if you were to offer the asking price, the deposit would be seventy-five thousand dollars. The deposit is held in an escrow account. Usually the seller comes back with a counteroffer."

"You mentioned that another buyer had already made a down payment. Does that mean that it's too late for me to make an offer?"

"Not at all. We continually submit offers until the seller signs a purchase and sale agreement. If your offer is more attractive to the seller than the earlier offer, it's not too late at all."

"I'm prepared to offer cash," said Charlotte.

"The other buyer is also prepared to offer cash," said Misty. "However, I'm sure that if you make your offer attractive enough, the seller will consider it seriously."

"If the seller were to accept my offer, how long would it take to close? I'd be interested in closing as soon as possible," Charlotte added.

"A cash deal?"

Charlotte nodded.

"Well, the buyer usually has a marine survey done, which takes about a week. The boat has to be hauled out of the water. But sometimes the buyer waives the marine survey. In that case, the deal could be concluded in a very short time— say, a week or so."

Back at the office, Charlotte told Misty she would think it over and get back to her.

So! thought Charlotte as she left, Billy hadn't been lying. He *was* buying *Bastet* back. And he had already put down a deposit, which meant that he had already received some of the blackmail money. Misty hadn't revealed how much Billy had offered, but Charlotte suspected he had offered the full asking price. After pining after his boat all these years, he wasn't going to risk being beaten out by another buyer. Also, Misty had used the full asking price in her example of what the deposit would be. If she had just accepted a deposit from Billy, the figure would still be fresh in her mind. What's more, he had offered cash, which meant that he expected to receive the rest of the money by the closing date. Charlotte suspected that he would want the boat as soon as possible. From what she knew of him, delayed gratification wasn't his forte. Misty had said that some buyers waived the marine survey. Again, Charlotte wondered if Misty had said that because her experience with Billy was fresh in her mind. As she drove back to Briarcote, she tried to put herself in Billy's place. If he had witnessed the murder on Thursday night, the idea had probably occurred to him immediately that this was his chance to buy back *Bastet*. He would probably have contacted the murderer on Friday. By telephone, most likely. He could also have sent a note, but it would have taken longer and it might have been traceable. He makes the phone call, disguising his voice. Demands the money. Probably in installments. Seven hundred and fifty thousand dollars was a lot to ask for all at once, no matter how rich the blackmail victim was. He probably wouldn't have gone into the delivery arrangements on the phone; he would have wanted to keep the phone call short for fear of revealing himself in some way. Further instructions to follow. Then what? Another phone call, a note? She had the feeling she was closing in on the solution. It was a sense she got. She also got it on the set when everything was going well; she could tell in advance that the picture was going to work. The only trouble was, she didn't know where to go from here. She needed a script. She didn't even know how long she was staying, she thought as she pulled into the driveway at Briarcote. Except for the Sayonara Party that Spalding and Connie were throwing for the Black Ships Festival Committee on Wednesday evening, the festival was over. She should go back to New York. But she couldn't, not yet.

No one was home at Briarcote. Charlotte was glad of it. She wanted a minute to put her feet up and relax. After helping herself to a glass of lemonade, she did exactly that. Put her feet up on the old coffee table in the library. She hadn't even looked at a newspaper in a week, she thought as she noticed the Sunday newspapers neatly stacked on one side of the table. Newspaper! Maybe Billy had communicated with the murderer through the newspaper. It was certainly worth checking. She started with Saturday. If he had put an ad in on Friday, it probably wouldn't have run until Sunday, but she would check Saturday anyway. She scanned the column headings in the classified section of the *Newport Daily News*: "Situations Wanted," "Child Care," "Notices & Personals"—that's where it would be. She read down the "Notices & Personals" column: "Is your drinking a problem? If you want help call Alcoholics Anonymous." "Pregnant, upset? Call for counseling." "Single? Try video dating." Nothing. The *Newport Daily News* wasn't published on Sunday, so she checked the "Personal Notices" column in the classified section of the *Providence Sunday Journal* next. It was the same story: AA, pregnancy, singles, bill problems, reward for information leading to, answers to your Bible questions. And, at the very end, a five-line notice: "Re: events of the night of July 27–28. 1. Sunday, midnight: the observation deck at Sachuest Point; 2. Tuesday, midnight: The Bells; 3. Thursday, midnight: the bridge at Purgatory."

The night of July 27–28 was the night Okichi-*mago* had been killed. The rest sounded like drop-off points. It certainly looked like blackmail.

She got up and walked over to the phone on Spalding's desk. She looked up the number for the city solicitor's office and dialed. A secretary answered. Charlotte asked for Lew and then waited anxiously for him to pick up.

In a minute, he was on the line.

"Lew, I think I've got something," she said, her voice quavering with excitement. "Do you know a place called Purgatory?"

He replied that he did; it was a chasm in the rocks that formed a steep cliff at the west end of Second Beach.

"Is there a bridge there?" she asked.

"Yes. An observation bridge that spans the head of the chasm."

"What about a place called The Bells?"

"It's an abandoned carriage house at Brenton Point."

"One more. What about Sachuest Point?"

"A wildlife sanctuary in Middletown, near Second Beach."

"Is there an observation deck there?"

"Yes, for the bird watchers. Now it's my turn to ask questions," he said. "What's this all about?"

"I think those are the places for the money drops. Have you got the classified section of the *Providence Sunday Journal* there?"

"I think so. I'll look." He returned in a minute. "Okay, I've got it."

"It's on the first page," Charlotte said. "Number 109. 'Personal Notices.' At the bottom of the column." She waited while he looked.

"I see what you mean," he said finally. "They're all isolated spots."

"I just came from the boat broker. Billy put a ten percent deposit on *Bastet* this morning. The asking price is seven hundred and fifty thousand. He's going to pay the rest in cash. If this notice is what I think it is, he's due to pick up the second installment from Okichi-*mago*'s murderer tonight at The Bells. I think we should plan on crashing the party. What do you think?" She could just imagine the gleeful smile on Lew's long, narrow face.

"I think that's a very good idea."

They were driving along Ocean Drive, the winding eight-mile drive along the wild, rocky southern coast of the island. It was one of Charlotte's favorite drives in the world: jagged rocks, sheltered sea coves, and sweet, sandy beaches on one side; lily-covered inland ponds, wild roses and honeysuckle, and marshes filled with tall, waving grasses on the other, all swirling in the soft, shimmery gold mist—part fog, part sea air—that was the distinctive feature of the local atmosphere. On the ocean side of the road, there were occasional glimpses of gabled stone mansions on rocky outcroppings, or rolling lawns and colorful flower beds hidden behind neatly clipped privet hedges or elegant stone walls. Out on the sparkling sea, large and small sailboats plied their way in and out of the east passage to Narragansett Bay. Past the cottages and beaches, the area opened up into Brenton Point State Park, a ninety-acre nature preserve at the tip of the island, which had once been a private estate. The park was a favorite destination of day-trippers; families from nearby Providence and Fall River were picnicking on the grass, fishing from the rocks, flying kites, and playing soccer.

Charlotte and Lew were there to check out The Bells, the burned-out shell of a once-elegant old carriage house that took its name from its bell tower. The ruined carriage house was all that was left of the old estate, which had long ago been demolished. Though it was located only a hundred feet or so from the park administration building, they would never have found it had Lew not known where it was. The entire area was overgrown with scrub brush: a dense thicket of wild roses, tangled vines, and stunted trees. They reached it via a narrow, winding path that had been mowed through the undergrowth.

"It must have been beautiful," said Charlotte as the ruined carriage house came into view. Despite the grass growing on the steeply pitched slate roof and the gaping black holes where the windows had been, one still had a sense of what it once had been like: the lovely old stonework, the tall, stately brick chimneys, the walled entrance courtyard.

"Not since I can remember," said Lew. "I used to come here as a kid. Make a campfire, drink beer, yell at the moon: all the things that kids do to raise cain." He smiled. "I haven't been here in probably twenty-five years. Last time I can remember was a Newport Folk Festival in the sixties. The kids from out of town used to camp out here." He looked around. "It hasn't changed much."

From the courtyard, they entered through one of the carriage bays. Inside, it was a different story: despite the box stalls for the horses, it looked more like an abandoned subway tunnel than a carriage house: the floor was heaped with broken glass and rubble. Beer cans and bottles were piled up in the corners, and graffiti covered the walls. A sign warned trespassers to keep out.

"So," said Charlotte, her voice echoing in the big, empty space, "where's our boy going to wait for his mark? That is, if he gets here first. He might decide to wait until the murderer leaves before picking up the money."

"I would guess upstairs," Lew replied. He led her over to a staircase in a corner, which led to a second-story loft.

Charlotte followed him up the stairs.

"He could see everything from here," said Lew as they reached the top. He pointed to one of the dormer windows: "Out to the courtyard"—then he pointed to one of the holes in the floor—"as well as down to the first floor. Plus, he couldn't be seen here himself. He would want to remain anonymous. He wouldn't want to take the risk that the murderer would kill him."

Kill him! Bells went off in Charlotte's head. "Lew! Remember when we were speculating that Shawn might have been murdered because he saw something he didn't know he'd seen. What if what he saw was the murderer? The murderer also sees Shawn, but doesn't think that Shawn has seen him. Then he gets a demand for money from an anonymous blackmailer."

Lew picked up the thread of her thoughts. "The murderer concludes that Shawn is the blackmailer and kills him—or has him killed—to avoid having to pay the blackmail money as well as to keep Shawn from going to the authorities with what he knows, or what the murderer thinks he knows."

As she gazed out at the courtyard, Charlotte examined the theory for flaws and chips, turning it over in her mind as if it were a piece of porcelain that she wanted to buy. But it was perfect: no flaws, no chips, no faded spots.

"It's a good theory," said Lew. "A very good theory."

But as Charlotte turned it over in her mind again, she turned up not just a flaw, but a gigantic crack. "Damn, it doesn't work," she said.

"Why not?"

"If the murderer thought he'd done away with the black-mailer—namely Shawn—then why did he show up with the first installment of the money at Purgatory last night. Which he must have done, otherwise how would Billy have gotten the money to make the deposit on the boat this morning?"

Lew stroked his mustache, thinking.

"Unless . . ." Charlotte continued.

"Unless what?"

"Unless Billy also concluded that the murderer had mistaken Shawn for him. If Billy had been sitting on the point, he would have seen Shawn looking for Okichi-*mago*. He might have figured out that he was the intended victim of Shawn's murder and called the murderer up after Shawn's death with a friendly little reminder that he had better keep his appointment . . ."

"In which case, the murderer must have been very surprised. He thinks he's killed the blackmailer and he finds out that he's killed the wrong man."

"In which case, Billy had better watch out. If the murderer killed Shawn because he thought Shawn was blackmailing him, what's to keep him from killing Billy? We didn't have any trouble figuring out where Billy got the money for the down payment. With Billy's big mouth, it shouldn't be hard for the murderer to figure it out either."

"Especially if the murderer hangs around any bars. I think we'd better talk to Sullivan—fast," said Lew.

"I think that's a good idea," Charlotte concurred.

After they had finished checking out The Bells, Lew dropped Charlotte off at Briarcote and then went on to the police station to talk with Sullivan. Now all Charlotte had to do was wait. But waiting was hard work. After a few minutes of pacing nervously, she started ransacking her pocketbook for a cigarette. She only smoked occasionally, but when she felt the urge, it was intense. She found not only a packet of cigarettes, but something else as well: the gift package that Just-call-me-Ken had given her at the closing ceremonies. It was exquisitely wrapped, with sharp, crisp edges. She remembered receiving similarly wrapped packages in Japan, where gift-wrapping was a time-honored art. Red and white cords held a fresh piece of white paper in place over the face of the box, on which both her name and Mori's were written in an elegant hand. Inside were seven or eight photographs of Charlotte at the geisha party: being introduced by Paul, talking with Shawn, pouring sake for Keiko. It was a lovely idea for a present. She stubbed out her cigarette. The photographs had given her an idea. If it didn't pay off, at least it would help kill time until this evening. She would visit Mori and ask to see his other photographs. He had been taking pictures throughout the geisha party. In thinking about the murders, she kept coming back to the party. Had something happened there that had prompted someone to kill Okichi-*mago?* Maybe the pictures would tell. After calling first, she set out down Bellevue Avenue again. Much as she loved this beautiful street, it became tiresome when you had to travel it several times a day. It had taken her only a day and a half to figure out the shortcuts that allowed her to avoid much of the Bellevue Avenue traffic—an achievement that had astonished Connie. "There are people who've lived here all their lives who haven't figured out how to avoid Bellevue Avenue," she said. Charlotte's rejoinder was that that they must not have ever lived in New York.

Mori was staying at the other end of Bellevue at the Viking Hotel, named after the stone tower in the nearby park which was supposedly built by the Vikings. She parked in front of the art museum and walked down to the hotel. Just-call-me-Ken was waiting for her at one of the umbrella-shaded tables in the patio café next to the hotel. His briefcase lay on the table. As she approached, he rose and bowed deeply.

Charlotte greeted him and thanked him again for his gift.

"It is my pleasure," he said. "It is a custom we have in Japan: to give a small gift as a memento of a special event that you have shared with friends. We call such small gifts *o-miyage*."

Charlotte repeated the word. "It's a lovely custom," she said.

"I have the other photographs here, if you would like to see them," said Mori, laying a hand on his briefcase. "Photography is my special hobby."

"I'd like to see them very much," said Charlotte.

Taking a seat, he opened his briefcase and removed a stack of photographs, which he handed over to Charlotte.

As Mori looked on, Charlotte took a seat and started sifting through the pictures: Tanaka sitting on his knees, singing the *kouta;* Marianne clinging to Shawn's shoulder; the kitten-faced Keiko beating the drum; Dede flirting with Justin (she was a girl after her mother's own heart); and Okichi-*mago* of the turquoise-flecked green eyes, a cluster of red camellias behind her ear, a green sake cup in her hand. She was wearing the sea-shell kimono; Charlotte shuddered as she remembered the way the gold and silver threads had shimmered under the water. She continued sifting through the pictures. Then she found it. She had almost passed it by before realizing that this was the picture that told the whole story. Not only why Okichi-*mago* had been murdered, but who had murdered her. Her hand shook as she held it up to look at it more closely.

"You like that picture?" asked Mori with a pleased smile.

"Yes," she replied. "May I have a copy?"

"Of course. Take that one; I can make another. I sent these out to be printed, but at home, I do all my own printing. I can make copies of all of them for you if you'd like."

"Thank you very much, but I'd just like this one. This could be a very important picture," she added. "It might help to explain Okichi-*mago*'s death. Is the negative stored in a safe place?"

Mori removed a thick three-ring binder from his briefcase and showed her how he had catalogued the slides of the Black Ships Festival according to event in plastic see-through sleeves.

Charlotte expressed admiration for his system.

"When I return to Boston, I will store them in a fireproof filing cabinet," he assured her. He handed her his business card. "If you want more prints, just let me know."

"Thank you very much," she replied.

Charlotte and Lew met Sullivan and his assistant, a young policeman named Brogan, in the parking lot at Brenton Point State Park at ten. They had wanted to get to The Bells in plenty of time to avoid running into Billy. Sullivan asked them to join him and Brogan in their unmarked van, and for a few minutes, they discussed their plans. Sullivan and Brogan would wait inside the building; Charlotte and Lew would wait in the underbrush along the path. A backup team would be waiting in the parking lot in three other unmarked cars in case additional help was needed, and to monitor the arrivals and departures of the blackmailer and his victim. All the cars were parked at the end of the long parking lot that lined Ocean Drive, far enough away from The Bells not to arouse suspicion. On a weekend, there would have been plenty of other people around—lovers, stargazers, fishermen—but tonight there were only a few other cars. Charlotte and Lew were there strictly on sufferance. Sullivan and Brogan would be doing the dirty work; Charlotte and Lew would be the witnesses. Sullivan could hardly have kept them away—it was because of Charlotte that they were there in the first place—but he had given them a strict lecture about not getting involved. If there was any shooting, they were to lie low and stay low. He didn't want a dead film star on his hands, or a dead city solicitor either.

"And keep quiet," he further instructed them.

After radioing back to the station, he reached for the door handle. "Now we're off to meet our mystery murderer," he said.

"He's not a mystery murderer," said Charlotte. It was her first chance to get a word in edgewise.

"What do you mean, he's not a mystery murderer?" said Sullivan as he opened the door and then shut it again.

"I know who the murderer is, and why he killed Okichi-*mago*."

Sullivan turned around, his gray eyebrows flying up in surprise.

Charlotte removed the photograph from her pocketbook and passed it across the back of the seat to Sullivan. As she did, Lew craned his neck to see.

Sullivan switched on the interior lights and studied the photo. "What the hell is this?" he barked.

"This is a picture that was taken by Ken Mori at the Temple of Great Repose on the night of the geisha party."

The picture showed two women standing side by side at the railing looking out to sea; it was taken from the rear. "One is Okichi-*mago* and the other is Marianne Montgomery. Can you tell which is which?"

"Nope. They look the same to me."

"That's exactly my point," said Charlotte. She remembered thinking that night how much they looked alike. Both women were the same height and shape. Both wore navy blue kimonos embroidered in gold with a small pattern, both wore the high black-lacquered pompadour that geisha wear on special occasions, and both were wore white *tabi* socks and black-lacquered *geta*.

"Let me see that," said Lew, reaching over the seat.

Sullivan passed it back.

"They look like twins," said Lew.

"It was a case of mistaken identity," said Charlotte. "Okichi-*mago* was killed by Lester, who thought she was Marianne." She proceeded to explain. "Marianne has a long history of sexual promiscuity, or rather, had—until she met Lester. That was five or six years ago. She's been pretty good since then, but there have been occasional lapses."

"Lapses," snorted Sullivan.

"She's particularly prone to lapses after a big success; it's as if success gets her hormones flowing. Anyway, when she met

Shawn at the opening ceremonies of the Black Ships Festival, she had just unveiled a new collection to rave reviews. It was clear from the body language she was sending Shawn's way that she was on the verge of another lapse."

"Sounds like a drunk going on a bender," said Sullivan as Lew passed the picture back to him.

"That's a pretty accurate analogy, in fact. At the geisha party that night, she flirted outrageously with Shawn. Shawn was committed to Okichi-*mago*, but Marianne was ignoring that. At the party, Shawn sang a song about meeting his lover at the rendezvous tree. As the party was breaking up, Lester and Marianne had a fight, and Marianne told him she would walk home."

"What was the fight about?" asked Sullivan.

"He called her a nasty name. Correction: every nasty name in the book. After that, Lester drove Spalding and Connie and me back to Briarcote and then returned to Shimoda."

"To kill Marianne?"

"I don't think he was planning to kill her then. Maybe he felt bad about leaving her stranded there, or maybe he just wanted to see what she was up to. In any case, he passed Shawn on the way. Paul had given Shawn a ride back to The Waves after the party, but Shawn was returning for the rendezvous with Okichi-*mago* under the pine tree."

"Lester sees Shawn and thinks he's going back to meet Marianne?"

"Exactly. Lester must have known about the romance between Shawn and Okichi-*mago*, but it didn't make any difference: in his eyes, Shawn was going back to meet Marianne. Maybe he made the connection with the song or maybe the song went over his head—it doesn't really matter. Meanwhile, Marianne had decided to walk home on the Cliff Walk."

"In this get-up?" said Sullivan, waving the photograph.

"She took it off and walked home in her under-kimono."

Sullivan shook his head, but he didn't doubt her. He'd seen far stranger behavior from the summer colonists.

Charlotte went on to describe what had happened: "When Lester arrives back at the temple, he comes upon a woman standing at the railing, waiting for her lover. He thinks the woman is Marianne; it's dark, and from the back they look alike. The sight of her confirms his suspicion that she has stayed behind to meet Shawn. Her flirtation with Shawn is the straw that breaks the camel's back. He's seen this happen before. He's accepted her apologies and believed her pledges that it wouldn't happen again. Now it *is* happening again. Overcome by a jealous rage, he pushes her over the railing."

She remembered Paul's story about Lester trying to smash his car. At the time, she thought he was exaggerating, but now she suspected he was telling the truth.

"I told you there was nothing that guy wouldn't do," said Lew.

Charlotte nodded and continued with her story: "But as the face of his victim spins around, Lester realizes that the woman he has killed isn't Marianne, but Okichi-*mago*." Charlotte remembered the staring, slanted eyes of the dummy; she could imagine Lester's horror when he saw Okichi-*mago*'s face. "At first, he's shocked by what he's done. But when he considers his dilemma, he realizes that he's actually in a better position with Okichi-*mago* as his victim than he would be had he succeeded in killing Marianne. He's familiar with the Okichi legend as a result of living at Shimoda. He knows that she died by jumping off a cliff, and he knows that she died exactly a hundred years ago. He decides to make the death look like a suicide."

"What about Shawn?" asked Lew.

"Shawn's on his way, and Lester knows it," said Charlotte. "He's pretty sure Shawn didn't see him on the road—pedestrians don't usually notice the drivers of the cars that pass them by, especially late at night. But his car is a problem. After moving his car out of sight behind the carriage house—he must have moved it because Shawn didn't say anything about seeing it—he conceals himself behind the shrubbery and waits for Shawn. Shawn arrives a few minutes later, walks out to the temple, looks around for Okichi-*mago*, and, not finding her, leaves. Lester is betting that he won't peer over the railing at the rocks below, and he doesn't."

Sullivan stared out over the dashboard, his thick pink fingers tapping a nervous tattoo on the wheel.

"Now Lester's work begins. Fate is working with him: Paul has gone out, as he discovered when he moved his car around to the back of the carriage house. The dog hears him, but since there's no one home to hear the dog [except Tanaka, she thought], it doesn't matter. Lester enters the house. Though he has a key, he doesn't need to use it. Expecting Paul to return momentarily, Nadine left the door unlocked when she went home. Then he removes the comb and mirror and the sake cup from their cases, taking care not to leave any fingerprints. As a Federal felon, he knows his prints are on file and if by chance his scheme doesn't work, he doesn't want to be identified as the murderer."

"The extra sake cup," said Lew.

"The extra sake cup," she repeated.

"But if Lester saw Okichi-*mago*'s face," said Lew, "why didn't he see the extra sake cup in her hand?"

"I don't know," said Charlotte. "Maybe he didn't look at her outstretched hand. Or maybe he saw it, but it didn't register. He was under considerable stress." She continued: "Then he carries the comb, the mirror, and the sake cup out to the temple and plants them by the brazier. He also burns Tanaka's business card, just as Okichi burned Harris-*san*'s calling card in the legend."

"Or in the movie," said Lew.

Charlotte smiled.

"I always said that these movies put ideas in people's heads," said Sullivan, who had stopped tapping and started taking notes. "How'd he get Tanaka's business card?"

"Tanaka had been handing out his business cards to the other guests earlier in the evening," she replied. "The Japanese are always handing out business cards."

Sullivan nodded.

"As for Billy," Charlotte continued, "while Lester is pushing Okichi-*mago* over the railing, Billy is sitting on the point, drinking beer. Maybe he's dreaming of being able to buy back his yacht, *Bastet*, which he lost in a divorce settlement. Anyway, when he witnesses the murder, he realizes that this is his chance: Lester can easily afford to fork over enough money for Billy to buy his boat back in exchange for Billy's keeping his mouth shut. Billy calls Lester the next day, disguising his voice. He asks Lester to start getting the money together, with the first installment to be paid Sunday night. He tells him to look in the 'Personal Notices' column of the *Providence Sunday Journal* for further instructions. The *Journal* gives the locations of the drop-offs: the first at the bridge at Purgatory, the second at The Bells."

"Which is what brings us here tonight," said Lew.

"Meanwhile Lester is trying to figure out who the blackmailer is. He thinks back to that night. Maybe Shawn recognized him on the road or recognized the car. He concludes that it is Shawn who is the blackmailer."

"Another case of mistaken identity," says Lew.

"Lester starts making arrangements of his own. He's served eighteen months; he doesn't want to be put behind bars again. He's not taking any chances that the blackmailer will keep his end of the bargain. He calls some of his former jail-house acquaintances and arranges to have Shawn killed. It doesn't hurt that Shawn had also been the object of Marianne's affections."

"He would have had no problem finding a small-time hood to carry out the job in this state," said Sullivan.

"He wouldn't have done it himself?" asked Lew.

"I don't think so," said Charlotte. "He strikes me as the kind of guy who delegates responsibility." Suddenly she remembered the man with the field glasses who had watched Shawn and her that morning. She wondered if he was the contract killer. She mentioned the incident to Sullivan, who made a notation. Then she continued: "Lester had attended the sumo match and knew about the hostility toward Shawn. He instructs the killer to make it look as if a rival sumo wrestler was the murderer by cutting off Shawn's topknot."

"First this guy mistakes Okichi-*mago* for Marianne, then he mistakes Shawn Hendrickson for Billy Montgomery. I'd say he has a real problem figuring out who's who," said Lew.

"Or else he's just an unlucky guy," said Charlotte.

"An unlucky guy who's going to be even more unlucky in a few minutes," said Sullivan. He checked his watch. "We'd better get going before they start the party without us."

· 13 ·

CHARLOTTE WAS HIDDEN in the underbrush at the side of the grassy path that led to the walled courtyard of The Bells. Lew was hidden about ten feet away, also at the side of the path. Both had an excellent view of the path and of the courtyard itself. The moon, which had been full only a few days before, shed a lot of light, and it was still clear, though puffs of fog had begun to blow in off the ocean. Sullivan had theorized that the murderer would leave the money either in the courtyard or on the first floor. He was hiding in one of the second-floor dormers, far enough away from the stairs that Billy wouldn't see him if he decided to wait for the murderer on the second floor himself. Brogan was on the roof. Now all they had to do was be patient. In the darkness, Charlotte became conscious of all kinds of scratching, rustling, and drumming noises that she wouldn't otherwise have noticed. She tried to remember from long-ago science classes which animals were nocturnal: raccoons, mice, skunks, bats, nightcrawlers? Every once in a while, there were other sounds: the plangent call of a whippoorwill, the eerie trill of an owl, and a ratchety noise that sounded like an old clock being wound up, a tree frog perhaps? There was also the honk of the Brenton foghorn and the clanging of a bell buoy, like an empty can being kicked along the street. The damp air was fragrant with a mixture of smells: the salty tang of the sea, the sweet, humusy smell of damp earth, the intoxicating sweetness of honeysuckle flowers in bloom, and the sharp, unpleasant odor of overgrown privet.

As she waited, her thoughts drifted off to Jack Lundstrom, her fourth husband. Contrary to her expectations, he had never shown up. She couldn't accuse Connie and Spalding of being co-conspirators in an effort to get them back together, after all. She wasn't sure whether she was happy or sad about it. She was very fond of Jack—he was always good company, and there were often times when she was lonely—but she wasn't sure she was ready to become a wife again. After trying it four times, she figured that it was about time for her to throw in the towel on wifedom. Then again, as the poet said, hope springs eternal in the human breast; maybe it would work if she gave it another try. Her thoughts were interrupted by another sound, distinct from the scratching and rustling. It was the sound of footsteps on the grass. They were the furtive footsteps of a heavy-footed man who was trying not to make noise. She hunkered down into her nest in the underbrush. The man passed a minute later. From her hiding place, she could only see his lower half. But that was enough: he was wearing reptile skin cowboy boots. It wasn't Billy who had arrived first, but Lester. Over his shoulder, he carried an airline flight bag that bulged at the seams. Crouching down a little further, she saw him enter the courtyard, pause for a minute, and drop the flight bag. Then he turned around and left as stealthily as he had come. When he reached the parking lot, Sullivan's men would take him into custody. Meanwhile the flight bag sat in a pool of moonlight in the middle of the courtyard. If Billy had demanded seven hundred and fifty thousand dollars, the bag would contain a third of that. But Charlotte suspected that he had asked for a million. It was a nice, even figure: seven hundred and fifty thousand for the boat, plus another two hundred and fifty thousand for operating expenses. In which case, the flight bag would contain three hundred and thirty-three thousand. Not a bad haul at all.

Her legs were getting stiff, but she didn't dare move for fear of making too much noise. She was amazed that Lester hadn't heard her: in the silence, her breathing sounded as loud as a steam engine. After ten or fifteen minutes, the sound of a twig snapping alerted her that someone else was coming. This time the steps were softer and faster—the rippling steps of light, nervous, hurrying feet. She crouched down again to get a better view. After a few seconds, another pair of legs

appeared. When she saw them, she realized that she had been
wrong about Billy: he was an innocent after all, just as Lew
had said. But she had been right about someone witnessing the
murder, and blackmailing Lester as a result. That someone had
tiny feet shod in expensive red suede moccasins embroidered
with the crest of a well-known designer. She was holding a
pearl-handled derringer in her dainty, white, immaculately
manicured hand, which was adorned with a diamond and pearl
ring. Although she couldn't see her face, Charlotte was sure
who it was. The diminutive, elegantly shod feet and beringed
finger could only belong to one person: Nadine.

For a moment, Charlotte was nonplused; Nadine's appearance on the scene was not what she had expected. The
last piece of the Mystery-Jig puzzle didn't jibe with the solution
she had so carefully worked out. In her mind, she reexamined
the pieces to see where she had gone wrong. Nadine had said
she stayed behind until the caterers left while Paul gave Shawn
a ride home. But what she really stayed behind for was to see
if Paul came back. Maybe he had said something that aroused
her suspicion or maybe she had found out somehow that his
other lover was in town. Either way, she suspected that he had
an assignation, and she was going to hang around to check it
out. As Charlotte watched her approach the courtyard, she
worked out the new solution. When Paul doesn't come back,
Nadine realizes that not only is he not going to marry her,
he's probably going to dump her. No sooner has she come to
this realization than Lester shows up. She sees him go out to
the temple, come back and move the car, and conceal himself
from Shawn. Then she sees him carrying Okichi's things out
to the temple. Maybe she discovers Okichi-*mago's* body after
he leaves, or maybe she doesn't put two and two together until
she hears about the suicide, but in either case she quickly sees
that Lester is the answer to her problems. If Paul dumps her,
she'll lose her source of financial support. The sale of the lot
on Bellevue Avenue—Charlotte thought of the beeches with
a pang in heart—would tide her over for a while, but what
about after that? But by blackmailing Lester, she can live
for the rest of her life in the style to which she's become
accustomed. As Spalding had said, people will go to almost

any lengths to hang onto their houses on Bellevue Avenue. She knows Lester is willing to pay through the nose to avoid going back to jail. And her newfound riches aren't likely to arouse suspicion in a town in which large inheritances are an everyday occurrence. As for the person on the point, it had probably been a teenager, just as Tanaka had said. But that still left Charlotte with the question of where Billy had gotten the money to buy the boat.

All this took but a minute or two for her to think through. By now, the woman had reached the courtyard. Her face still wasn't visible—she was wearing a scarf that shielded her profile—but when she leaned over to pick up the flight bag, Charlotte could see that it was Nadine. As she turned to leave, Sullivan appeared in one of the dormer windows on the second story with his service revolver drawn. "Police," he shouted. "Drop your gun!" Brogan was covering him from the roof with a shotgun.

At Sullivan's command, Nadine took off with the speed of a gazelle. Before he could even get a shot off, she had fled the courtyard, and was headed down the path toward the parking lot.

As Nadine approached her hiding place, Charlotte raised herself from her crouching position. In one second, Mrs. Vanderbilt's famous words ran through her mind: "Just pray to God, my dear. *She* will help you." Then, as Nadine came running down the path, she deftly stuck her right leg out in front of her. Nadine took a header, and her gun went flying.

Emerging from her hiding pace, Charlotte quickly retrieved the gun, and stood over her quarry, the gun aimed at her head.

In a second, Lew was at her side.

"Good work," he said.

"I haven't used that trick since fourth grade."

"Uncle Brewster," Connie was saying.

"Who's Uncle Brewster?" asked Charlotte. "Aunt Lillian told me that Billy didn't have any uncles, much less any rich ones."

"He's actually not an uncle. Don't ask me what he is. He's the grandson of my great-uncle. Lillian probably didn't tell you about Uncle Brewster because she'd forgotten about him, as we all had. He's the original hippie. I shouldn't even call him a hippie, because he came way before the hippies. He went out to California in the fifties. I guess you'd have to call him a beatnik."

"How did Billy meet up with him?"

"Billy went out to live in Haight-Ashbury in the sixties and looked him up. Brewster was in his early forties then, but he seemed ancient to the young hippies like Billy. They looked up to him as the grand old man of the counterculture. Of course, we all knew he had a lot of money, but we never thought about it because he didn't live like a rich man—more like a bum, in fact."

"*Wabi*," muttered Charlotte to herself.

"What?" asked Connie.,

"Never mind," said Charlotte with a dismissive wave of her hand.

"I guess he thought of Billy as a man after his own heart," Connie continued. "They've kept in touch all these years. One thing he could be sure of: Billy wasn't going to use the money to buy a pretentious stockbroker Tudor in Old Greenwich and become a member of the establishment; I think that was his main concern."

"No," Charlotte agreed, "I guess he could count on that." She remembered what Lew had said about people like Billy leading charmed lives. As Lew had predicted, he had again landed on his feet, like a cat. "But how did he come up with the money so fast?" she asked.

"I imagine he borrowed it. It's not difficult to borrow against a big inheritance. Spalding did it when his mother died."

Connie and Charlotte were standing on the terrace at Briarcote. The Sayonara party was just getting underway. Charlotte could sense that Connie and Spalding—but especially Spalding—would be glad to get it over with. Two murders weren't what he had bargained for when he had taken on the presidency of the Black Ships Festival Committee.

It was a beautiful evening. The evening light had tinted the sea a still, luminous green, which was flecked with turquoise: the color of Okichi-*mago's* sake cup, and of her eyes. On the horizon, the sea made a line that was as sharp as a knife against the pale blue bowl of the sky, which was marred only by a few wispy clouds high in the heavens.

Charlotte would miss the floating world that was Newport.

A number of guests had already arrived, among them Paul Harris. Charlotte noticed him talking earnestly with Dede. She had abandoned her streetwalker look for an outrageously short Japanese-style tunic. It was the perfect outfit for someone with her lovely figure and long legs. Charlotte was surprised to see them talking together: she hadn't thought Paul would ever speak to Dede again after the indentations her spike heels had made in his tatami mats.

Connie noticed Charlotte's glance and raised her crossed fingers.

"Are you responsible?" asked Charlotte, nodding at the twosome.

"I hope so," said Connie.

"What did you do?"

"I told Paul that Dede was planning to major in historic preservation at college next year," said Connie. "She's very interested in it. It's a natural subject for her: she's very artistic and she's fascinated by historic houses. I guess she picked that interest up from spending her summers here in Newport. The whole town is one big historic restoration."

"Do you think she's going to replace Okichi-*mago* as his protégée?" asked Charlotte speculatively.

"Maybe," Connie replied, her blue eyes shining with hope. "He's the kind of man who needs a protégée. Somebody to mold. And God knows, Dede needs a father figure. Spalding's been a good grandfather to her, but she's never had a father figure. If he did take her on, it would be the best thing that's ever happened to the family. Marianne and Paul could cease their bickering."

"And Paul could die without an heir and feel as if Shimoda were being left in good hands," said Charlotte.

Connie's attention was diverted by the new arrivals, among them Lew and his wife and children. As a member of the local committee to promote tourism, he was an *ex officio* member of the Black Ships Committee as well.

As Connie chatted with Toni, Lew joined Charlotte at the bar. "I just thought I'd let you know," he said, a wide smile on his face, "Sullivan picked up the contract killer this afternoon."

"He did!" said Charlotte exclaimed. "How did he track him down so fast?"

"Parking ticket," said Lew. "When he was scoping out The Waves, he parked his car at the end of Ledge Road, which is a no-parking zone. The police ran a check of parking ticket recipients against the files and came up with his name, or rather one of his names—he has about a dozen aliases. Routine inquiry and a stroke of luck—it's what does the trick in police investigations every time."

Charlotte remembered seeing the police scooter ticketing the parked cars on Ledge Road on the morning she had visited Shawn. "What did he look like?" she asked. "Did you see him?" She was thinking of the wandering tourist she and Shawn had seen on the Cliff Walk, the man wearing the baseball cap and yellow windbreaker who had studied them through his field glasses.

"Yeah. I was there when they brought him in. A thin guy with long, scraggly hair, a baseball cap, and very weird eyes: hard and shiny. They kind of rolled around in his head like loose marbles."

Charlotte hadn't seen his eyes, but the rest of the description fit the man she had seen on the Cliff Walk perfectly. She remembered him looking down at a piece of paper. She had thought at the time that it was a map, but it had probably been a photograph of his mark.

"A free-lance criminal: anything you want for a price. Burglary, safecracking, dope-peddling, murder. A witness identified him, someone who lives in one of the second-floor condos at The Waves. Saw the whole thing, but was afraid at first to come forward. They also found some bloodstains in his car that they expect will match Shawn's blood."

So, Lester had bought himself a killing, just as she had suspected. She thought back to Miller's tips on how to get away with a murder: either do it yourself on the spur of the moment or hire somebody else to do it for you. Lester had tried it both ways.

"Something else too," said Lew as the bartender handed him a beer for himself and a wine spritzer for Toni.

"What?"

"Remember the topknot you saw at Shawn's condo? The one that someone had sent to Shawn to harass him?"

Charlotte nodded.

"It was Hayashi," said Lew. "After what you said about him holding up the sign at the sumo match, Sullivan decided to bring him in for questioning. When they started grilling him about Shawn, he got scared and admitted to sending the topknot. He said he did it because he didn't want to see a foreigner become a *yokozuna*; it was an insult to Japanese national pride."

It was also jealousy, she thought, remembering how he had mooned over Okichi-*mago* at the geisha party and later insulted her by calling her *Tojin* Okichi. "Did you see the paper today?" she asked.

"Didn't get a chance," Lew replied. "What did I miss?"

"Yoshino Electronics just bought Paragon Studios. The idea is to merge the technical and artistic sides of the business. Tanaka and Hayashi may not like Americans, but they're going to have to get used to us if they're going to be running the country's biggest entertainment company," said Charlotte. It was one thing to buy office buildings and factories, but it was quite another to take over a business that struck so close to the heart of the American spirit.

"I guess we're going to have to get used to them as well," said Lew. "Was Paragon your studio?"

"Mine and most of the top stars in the business," she said. "Which means the Japanese now own all my old movies." It was the pending deal with Paragon that Tanaka must have been thinking about when he took his midnight stroll on the Cliff Walk on the night of Okichi-*mago*'s murder.

Toni had joined them, and Lew handed her her drink. The children had taken off for the cove at the foot of the lawn. The sight of them reminded Charlotte of Nadine's sons. Their fate was the only unpleasant note in the final outcome. She had no qualms about Nadine going to jail, but she hated to see her boys suffer on account of it.

"What's going to happen to Nadine's kids?" she asked

Lew. "Are they going to be ostracized because of what their mother did?"

"I'll defer that question to my lovely wife," said Lew.

"I doubt it," said Toni. "People aren't ostracized by society anymore because a relative has committed a crime. Not by Newport society, anyway. If that were the case, there wouldn't *be* a Newport society. In fact, in some circles, having a relative who's committed a crime, or, for that matter, even having committed a crime yourself, carries a certain cachet."

"At the worst, her crime will be looked on as a social climbing accident," Lew added. "Injuries sustained in a fall off the ladder."

"But who's going to take care of them?"

"Probably their aunt and uncle," Toni responded. "The brother of Nadine's former husband and his wife. They live here in Newport. They've practically raised Justin and Charlie anyway. When Nadine stayed with Paul, they always stayed there. Their sons are about the same age." Her warm brown eyes smiled. "They'll be all right. They're good, solid kids."

Charlotte was relieved.

As they talked, Charlotte caught sight of Marianne on the other side of the crowded terrace. She had battened herself to the side of a handsome young naval officer. Her nostrils were quivering, and her eyes had taken on a trancelike glaze. Hadn't she learned? thought Charlotte. The last time she'd gone off the wagon she'd nearly gotten herself killed.

Lew's glance followed Charlotte's. "I can just envision the next Marianne Montgomery collection," he commented with a devilish grin. "The return of pea jackets and bell bottoms."

"She could call it 'Anchors Aweigh'," said Charlotte.

Lew burst into laughter.

As he joined them, Spalding figured out from the direction of their glances what they were laughing about, and adopted the expression of pained forbearance that he assumed with regard to anything that had to do with Marianne's sexual eccentricities. Charlotte suspected, however, that he was fascinated by the ease with which his stepdaughter acquired and shed men.

"We were just observing that Marianne doesn't seem too

upset about Lester's arrest," said Charlotte.

"She's not upset about the arrest, but she's pretty damned upset about him trying to kill her. Actually, I think that's what this is all about," he added, nodding at the couple. "A combination of nervousness and the need for male companionship. I can't say that I'm all that displeased about Lester's being out of the picture," he added. "But I'm worried about what's coming next."

Charlotte looked over at the handsome naval officer. "A naval officer isn't a typical choice for Marianne," she oberved. "Maybe the incident with Lester has inaugurated a shift toward a more conservative choice of lovers."

"I certainly hope so," said Spalding, with a weary shake of his white head. After a pause, he pulled a newspaper out from under his arm and opened it up to show it to Charlotte and Lew. "I thought you would be interested in seeing this," he said.

It was a Japanese newspaper. An aerial photograph on the front page showed the Temple of Great Repose in Shimoda, the temple where Okichi had lived with Townsend Harris and which was to be the site of Okichi-*mago*'s funeral service. The courtyard in front was packed with people; others waited in long queues outside the gates.

"What are all those people doing there?" asked Charlotte.

"Pilgrims," said Spalding. "Okichi-*mago* and Shawn are the front-page story in every newspaper in Japan. They're calling it the greatest love story of the century." He turned to the second page, which showed photographs of Okichi-*mago* and Shawn, both individually and together. "Lovers are flocking to the temple from all over the country to pay homage to them."

"It's like *The Love Suicides at Sonezaki*," said Charlotte. "Immortality in this world and the next."

"Exactly," said Spalding. "They've been beatified."

They were joined by Just-call-me-Ken, whose eyes shined behind his sporty aviator glasses.

"I see that you've seen the newspaper," he said. "I got a call from Kanazashi-*san* in Shimoda this morning. He says his hotel is full of pilgrims who have come to visit the temple. He wants to organize a tour for the Japanese to visit the temple in Newport. I'm going to work with him on it. Our goal is to make the Newport festival as big as the Shimoda festival."

"If the story of Okichi and Townsend Harris could become a legend, I suppose the story of Okichi-*mago* and Shawn could become an even bigger legend," said Lew. "Maybe Yoshino Electronics will make a movie of it," he added.

"I'm too old to play the part this time," Charlotte said as she looked again at the newspaper. A close-up showed a young couple laying a bouquet of red camellias on the gallery of the temple.

As she looked up, she caught a glimpse of a tall, distinguished-looking man out of the corner of her eye. He was talking with Paul Harris. It was Jack Lundstrom, her fourth husband. Like Paul, he was an art collector. As a successful businessman, he had plenty of money to spend on art, and he had amassed a valuable collection of modern paintings. Charlotte guessed they were talking about the influence of the *ukiyo-e* artists on the modernists.

Turning her head, she caught Connie's eye, and fixed her with the accusing stare that had often withered her leading men.

Connie's blue eyes sparkled as she made her way across the terrace. "Isn't it nice that Jack could make it to the party," she said as she reached Charlotte's side. "He just happened to be in town, and I invited him to come. I knew he'd enjoy meeting Paul."

"He just *happened* to be in town?" said Charlotte sarcastically.

Connie smiled. "He's going to be staying with us tonight," she said. "I knew you wouldn't mind. You two are such good friends."

Charlotte took a sip of her drink and thought again of her dream. She had thought that when she saw Jack, she would know which to choose: the temple or the cathedral. But she was just as confused as ever. More so, because his intentions, which had been vague before, were now clear. He wouldn't have come to Newport if he weren't seeking a reconciliation. The thought of the dream reminded her of Aunt Lillian, who had spent fifty-six years out in the ocean on her white rock. "Where's Aunt Lillian?" she asked.

"She just called," said Connie. "She said she wasn't feeling up to coming. She's been working on her will. She says she has to be ready when the time comes. But she's been saying that for the last twenty-five years. She asked me to give you a message. I didn't really understand it, but she wanted me to pass it along exactly as she said it. Maybe you'll understand. Sometimes I think her mind isn't what it used to be."

"What's the message?" asked Charlotte.

"She wanted me to tell you that she's leaving you the Japanese wisteria chest. She said to be sure to tell you that it's for your temple, the temple of your dreams."